GW00859477

1

Garden

Of

Sparkling

Delight

Deborah Varen

FOR NADIA

Forward

Tis, a vulnerable young Brazilian girl, finds herself speeding through the night towards the lights of a big city. Her companion is a man who has promised her parents that he will find their daughter work as a maid. What awaits her there is something different however, and her life becomes increasingly fraught with danger both mental and physical.

Interwoven into this tragic and violent storyline is the account of a young doctor whose life and love affair in the south of England are in stark contrast to the dangerous, sexually abusive situation in which Tis finds herself. Yet their stories and that of their families become closely linked.

Cameos of some of the book characters can be found in my blog –

debvaren.blogspot.co.uk

CONTENTS

Contents

Chapter 1

The little girl watched, fascinated, as the tiny ant tried to climb to the top of the small heap of dust trickling in through the crack in the flimsy wooden wall. Each time it got to the summit, more dust cascaded down on top of it, tumbling it down to the bottom of the pile where it had to struggle all over again to ascend the side of the ever increasing miniature mountain. Suddenly the small child reached out her finger and scooped the insect into the palm of her hand.

'You may be small, but I don't see why you should have to die,' she whispered to the ant. 'Here, you can hide under my bed until this storm dies down.' But the wind continued to blow, rattling every warped timber in the shack's fragile structure like a terrier worrying an old rag. All round the room little heaps of dust were accumulating and the air was laden with gritty particles which got into every conceivable crevice. The door creaked opened and a tired looking woman, the child's mother, Ana, appeared in the doorway. She had to raise her voice in order to be heard above the howling of the gale.

'You all right Tis? Get into bed and try and forget this storm. I expect it will soon blow itself out.'

'All right Mamãe,' replied the girl, and crept under the bleak assortment of old blankets that were on her bed. Burrowing down into their pungent depths, she attempted to shut out the noise of the wind, but the vibrating of the shack and the rattling of the doors and windows was harder to ignore. 'I wonder what happened to my ant?'

she thought, 'I hope he's found a crack to hide in.' The very thought of the draughty space under the bed however, made her feel how comforting it was to be curled up in the warmth and safety of her blanket nest and she soon became drowsy and fell asleep.

Usually, in this part of Brazil, prolonged storms were rare, but this one persisted for most of the night, so that by morning dust had drifted into every nook and cranny in the living room where Tis slept. Towards dawn however, the anger of the wind became an uneasy mutter and the insubstantial little home stopped shaking. Soon the white storm clouds which streaked the sky turned to gold as the sun ventured up from behind the rim of the world to lighten a new day.

When daylight had fully come, the arduous task of cleaning up after the gale began. In most of the shacks in the tiny community women appeared with brooms and began chasing the dust back where it belonged. Swish, swish went the brooms as the inhabitants called to each other across the dirt street. The noise woke Tis, who crept out from under her bedclothes, and ran a hand through her hair, which felt gritty and stiff. Her mouth was dry and her whole body seemed to itch under its layer of grime. Suddenly, remembering the ant, she bent down to look under the bed but there was nothing but the ubiquitous dust to be seen. Not surprisingly the ant had vanished as if it had never existed. At that moment her mother came in through the street door banging the last remnants of dirt off her broom.

'Did you sleep all right Tis?' she asked.

'Yes' replied Tis, 'but I feel itchy all over.'

'The dust's got in everywhere,' replied Ana frowning. 'I could do without this,' she added wearily rubbing her hand across her forehead. 'I feel so tired these days. I don't know why. Go with Yara and get some water,' she ordered, straightening her back. 'We shall need extra today.'

'Is there anything to eat Mamãe?' asked Tis plaintively.

'Oh Tis, I wish there were but there isn't,' replied her mother, looking distractedly at her nine year old daughter who was far too thin for her age. Indeed, she looked as scrawny as the stray dogs that haunted the village street, their spare flesh stretched too tightly over their bony skeletons. Saying nothing more, Tis turned and went out into the street.

Wearily she climbed up the rickety steps of the shack next door and called out for her best friend.

'Yara, come and help.'

'Just coming,' answered a voice from inside. The door opened and Yara came bouncing down the steps. Her cheerful face looked grave for a moment as she glanced at her friend and saw how tired she seemed.

'You all right, Tis? I guess the noise kept you awake didn't it? I've never known it to blow for so long. Does your mum want water?' she queried, 'mine does too,' she added. 'Come on. Let's go.'

Together the two girls took a large bucket the 100 metres to the village's only tap, filled it, and carried it carefully back to Tis's house. This was not easy as Yara was older and taller than her friend but they had done this so many times before that they had worked out a way of holding the bucket between them so that the water didn't spill. Returning to the tap they fetched a second one for Yara's mother.

'Let's both have a drink Tis,' said Yara. 'Then we can go and find firewood. Hopefully the wind will have blown some dead branches down.' Tis scooped out a brimming mug full for Yara, idly watching the overflow run down its side to make a random spatter on the dusty floor. 'How does she stay so cheerful,' she asked herself, 'when I feel so dirty and miserable?' The two collected a couple of old ropes to help them drag the wood home, and set out.

Firewood was hard to find near the shacks as it had all been collected years ago, so a long wandering search lay ahead of the two girls. The country through which they walked was hot and dry. The drifting dust had smoothed out the contours of the landscape with a caressing hand, so the surface resembled the flesh of a fat old man, all gentle curves and insubstantial trembling hollows. On they trudged, two small figures in a vast landscape of bushes, rocks and trees. Overhead the sun shone out of a serene blue sky, where an opportunistic vulture kept watch in case there was anything to be scavenged.

'I do wish the rain would come,' said Tis as they trudged along. 'The heat's curling me up.'

'Oh Tis! You do say funny things,' replied Yara. 'Let's just go up to the top of this next ridge and then we'll go home. See, that's where the coast road is and we can watch the traffic go by for a few minutes. We've got enough wood anyway. Look, we'll leave what we've got down here and fetch it on the way back.'

The vegetation grew a lot more closely on the sides of the ridge, so it was not until they were almost at the top that they realised that there was a car drawn up on the wide verge. Not wanting to be seen, they crept up the last few feet and peered cautiously round the trunk of a tall coconut palm. An unexpected scene met their eyes. There, by the side of the road just a few metres away, was a black shiny saloon car with its bonnet up and peering inside the engine was the driver dressed in a smart uniform and peaked cap. Beside him stood another man who was large and fleshy, with a questing stomach that seemed eager to get to places before him. He had tried to confine it in a neat white safari suit but it had been a vain exercise and the offending belly was bulging over the top of his trousers in an effort to escape. The big man looked cross, and stood scowling at the driver who was clearly doing his best to mend the car. Inside the car were two more people. One was a lady who seemed to be made of pale gold, as her hair, skin and even her dress seemed to shine. Next to her sat a boy of about twelve years of age, reading a book with desperate intensity. He had obviously got to a very exciting part and didn't want to miss a word, despite the fact that his family were apparently marooned in the middle of nowhere. He sat hunched up and very still, with a frown of deep concentration on his face.

As they watched, the man called to the woman who immediately got out of the car and took a large bag and a blanket out of the boot. She spread the blanket on the ground and began to unpack the most delicious food the two watchers had ever seen. To children fed exclusively on rice and beans, the endless succession of sandwiches, bottles of brightly coloured liquid, cakes, chicken legs and salad looked like an exotic and incomprehensible feast. The man came and gingerly lowered himself onto the ground, and the woman called the boy, who regretfully put his book down and joined them. All three began eating, but the boy ate slowly, and had a thoughtful, faraway look on his face as if he was still living the exciting events of the story in his book. Suddenly his face cleared as he came back to the present moment, and at that point he caught sight of Tis looking at him from behind the palm tree and their eyes met. For a moment or two he appeared to hesitate as if not sure what he was looking at, but then he realised that there was a real face in the shadows; a little heart shaped face with large brown eyes and an expression of wistful longing. He muttered something quietly to his mother, who looked up, then picked up two chocolate bars wrapped in bright purple wrappings which she held out to the two girls. Yara stepped boldly out from behind their palm tree, irresistibly drawn towards the lure of the food, but Tis shrank back into the surrounding foliage trying to make herself invisible. Slowly, Yara approached until she was within reach, held out her hand, grasped the bars and then turned round and fled quickly back to the tree. As they disappeared over the edge of the ridge in a puff of dust, the boy remarked wonderingly to the lady,

'Were they real?'

'Why, yes, they were, and they were very hungry, poor little things,' she replied thoughtfully.

Tis and Yara slithered down the steep side of the ridge and then sat under a bush to look at their treasure.

'I'm going to take mine home to share with mum,' declared Tis.

'Me too,' agreed Yara 'but not before I've had a bit.' Carefully, she unwrapped the very end of the bar and took a tiny bite off one corner. 'Heaven,' she murmured with eyes closed, and then sat for a full minute savouring the unfamiliar taste of the chocolate melting in her mouth. 'I wonder what the boy said to his mother, Tis,' she pondered 'do you know?'

'Yes, I think so,' replied her friend smiling. 'Fortunately they were speaking English or I wouldn't have understood. I think he said, "were they real," but I didn't understand what the woman replied. She spoke too quickly and we were too far away by then.'

Yara snorted in disgust.

'How stupid! Of course we're real. We're just hungry that's all. You're so lucky your mum teaches you how to speak English Tis,' she added wistfully. 'I wish my mum was as clever as yours. Perhaps I could go and get a job as a maid in Beleza like your mum did.'

'Don't say that Yara,' said Tis anxiously. 'What would I do if you went away? You're my best friend.' Yara looked at her thoughtfully.

'Tell me, what's it like in Beleza?' she asked. 'Your mum must have told you all about working as a maid there. Did she like it?'

'I think she did,' replied Tis. 'It was hard work

though as it wasn't only two English people she looked after. She had to take care of their small boy as well, and he was naughty.'

'What was the nicest thing she did?' queried Yara. Tis thought for a moment.

'She told me once about Christmas in the house,' she replied dreamily. 'It sounded lovely. I remember her saying that she and the lady cooked all sorts of strange food, and made a large white iced cake with a red ribbon round it. The table too was decorated, with a red and silver cloth and lovely glasses. There was a beautiful gold decoration in the middle that had four lighted candles, and three gold angels, which went round and round when the candles were lit. Mum said she'd never seen anything so beautiful. Her mistress gave her our pressure cooker as a present then,' she added 'so she must have liked her.'

'That was kind,' commented Yara, trying to visualise what the Christmas meal table must have looked like. 'I would love to go and do that too. Anything would be better than living here. We don't even go to school,' she added in disgust. 'What chance have we got? I want to do something exciting,' she exclaimed, banging her fist down onto the dusty ground, a look of dissatisfaction passing fleetingly across her normally cheerful face.

When they reached home with the firewood, Tis found her mother sitting at a table, in the centre of which was a glittering heap of beads. The table had been dragged to the open door so that the maximum amount of light would fall on it, and she was busily threading the beads onto thin nylon string to make necklaces and bracelets. Ana spent many hours each day doing this in order to earn a little money for the family. As she sorted through the beads, searching for the right colours for the pattern she was making, they sparkled in the sunlight in rainbow shades of blood red, ultramarine, gold and green, sending a kaleidoscope of colours dancing on the walls of the drab room. Once she had assembled the beads in the right order there was a click, click, click sound as each one was threaded meticulously onto the string and dropped down to nestle next to its fellow.

'Come and help,' she commanded, glancing up. So after a quick drink of water, Tis sat on a stool and began to thread. As they worked, she told her about her meeting with the people in the broken down car, but she didn't say anything about the chocolate.

'That's going to be a surprise,' she murmured, mentally hugging herself in happy anticipation. Slowly, as the day waned, the pile of bracelets and necklaces grew, and the pile of beads diminished. Bead after shining bead was captured and marshalled into glowing patterns on the nylon thread. Not for the first time, Tis speculated who would wear these beautiful pieces of jewellery, and where they would be when they wore them.

'Perhaps one of my bracelets will be worn by a rich girl as she walks by the sea, whatever that looks like,' she mused. Tis had never actually seen the sea. It was too far away to walk to, but she had spoken to people who had been there, and it sounded like the most wonderful place in the world.

It was as they threaded beads that Ana would teach Tis how to speak the English she had learnt from her mistress in the city. It helped to while away the time.

Today however, they talked of other things as they assembled bracelet after bracelet, necklace after necklace.

'Mamãe,' enquired Tis, 'did you enjoy working in someone else's house?'

'Well, yes,' answered her mother doubtfully. 'I suppose so. It was hard work and not much rest. I did have a nice room to myself though which was lovely, and plenty of food. It was difficult to give it up and come here to marry your Dad, but I love him like you do Tis, and that makes everything good doesn't it? I do miss him when he's not here,' she added unhappily.

'I wish he would come home too,' agreed Tis sadly. 'When is he going to get a break from the sugar plantation? It must be six weeks since he came home last. I hate it when he's not here.'

'So do I,' sighed her mother. They worked on in silence for a little while, too tired to talk, until the pile of bracelets and necklaces was complete. By now the daylight had begun to fade and it was time for their daily meal. Usually mother and daughter would prepare this together, but Ana noticed Tis was wilting like a little flower that is drooping through lack of water, so she said,

'I'll get the food Tis. You go and sit on your bed and rest.'

'May I look at the book Mamãe?' questioned Tis.

'Yes,' replied Ana, and reaching up to a high shelf over the door, took down one of her most treasured possessions. It was a child's book that her mistress had given to her whilst packing up to go back to England.

Carefully, Tis took the book and slowly turned over the pages looking at the brightly coloured illustrations of a little blue engine with a grey smiley face. She was too tired to attempt to read the words, but she gazed at each picture with great concentration trying to imagine she was part of each scene.

'It helps me forget how hungry I am,' she murmured to herself as she looked intently at a tiny figure of an odd looking man in a tall black hat.

By now, the shadows in the room were beginning to lengthen as the light was fading fast. Ana collected some of the firewood Tis had brought home, and using the precious pressure cooker, cooked their meal of beans and rice on the stove, flavouring it carefully with garlic and salt. When it was ready, she brought the heavy pan over to the table where Tis was already waiting, and carefully spooned a measured amount onto each of their plates. Tis gazed with anticipation at the plain food in front of her. All day long she had looked forward to this moment when the perpetual toothache of her hunger would at last be satisfied. After the last grain of rice had been carefully hunted down and eaten, she jumped up from the table and went over to her bed where she had hidden the chocolate. Returning quickly she placed it in front of her mother, a big smile on her face.

'What's this Tis?' questioned Ana.

'The lady gave it to me.' Tis explained smiling. 'I brought it back to share with you.'

'That was kind of her,' commented Ana, 'and kind of you too Tis,' and gently taking the bar she broke it in two giving half back to her daughter. Tis took a small bite and savoured the delicious moment when the chocolate dissolved on her tongue and ran down the back of her throat.

'Shall I eat the rest all at once?' she asked herself. 'Or shall I take tiny bites, like Yara?' This was a hard question to answer. 'I'm going to eat it all at once,' she decided, and crammed the remaining chocolate into her mouth. As she ate her own piece, Ana remarked, smiling,

'M'mm, that was good. It reminds me of Beleza. There were always plenty of sweets there.'

That night as she lay curled up in her bed, trying to recapture the glorious taste of the chocolate, Tis thought that it had been a good day after all despite the storm.

Miles away, in a hotel by the sea, a young boy lay between cool, cotton sheets listening to the incessant murmur of the air conditioning. As he drifted off to sleep he remembered the brown heart-shaped, elfin face surrounded by a halo of green leaves and wondered dreamily if he would ever see it again.

Chapter 2

A couple of days later, Tis was woken by the sound of a heavy vehicle, laboriously making its way down the village street. It was hard work for the truck, as the street was pockmarked with holes, and the engine had to labour in first gear to make any progress. Tis jumped out of bed and ran to see what was happening. As she arrived at the door, the truck stopped, the passenger door opened, and out climbed a tall, broad shouldered, slightly stooping figure. With a surge of delight she realised that it was her father.

'Papai!' she shouted, running down the steps to meet him. Hearing the commotion Ana came out to investigate, and husband, wife and daughter hugged each other joyfully.

'I hitched a ride with cousin Manolo,' said Carlos. 'He's on his way to the coast. He's going to call for me tonight,' he added. 'I had to come and see you both; I miss you so much. But I'm here for the whole day,' he announced cheerfully, his face smiling down at them.

'The coast,' Tis thought. That means the sea. Suddenly a wonderful thought leapt into her head. 'Papai,' she said. 'Ask cousin Manolo to take me with him. I want to see the sea. It must be beautiful. Please Papai, please,' and she looked up at her father beseechingly.

'I don't know whether he will take you, little one. Let's go and ask him,' laughed Carlos. Together father and daughter walked round to the driver's cab where cousin Manolo was still sitting.

'My little daughter wants to see the sea. Will you take her with you?' asked Carlos. A large, dark, hairy face looked down at Tis making her feel a bit afraid, but in the middle of all the whiskers was a pair of kindly eyes.

'I guess so,' said Manolo. 'I'll just stretch my legs and have a drink of water. Then we must be off.'

A few minutes later Tis found herself perched high in the cab of the lorry, legs dangling, and holding on tightly to the seat, as the vehicle bounced and rattled over the rough track. Once on the highway the kilometres flew by and in a couple of hours the lorry reached a grove of trees, where it came to a juddering halt. Manolo, who had been silent during the journey, turned to Tis and said,

'I'll drop you here Tis, and come and collect you again at the same place this evening. I should keep away from the big hotel building where the foreigners stay. Don't keep me waiting, ok?' He came round to the passenger side of the lorry and lifted her down placing her gently on the ground.

As Tis gazed around she noticed that the trees were coconut palms just like the ones near her home, and looking down she saw that there was clean white sand beneath her feet. Glancing to her right she could see through a break in the vegetation, the high wall of a large, new building, which must be the hotel Manolo had warned her about. Near this was a shabby hut, which appeared from the shutter set into the front wall, to do duty as a shop from time to time, but at the moment the shutter was down and there was nobody about. Tis stood still for a minute, tingling with both excitement and apprehension in her unfamiliar surroundings.

'But where is the sea?' she said out loud, looking questioningly in all directions, 'and where am I allowed to go?' She then noticed a narrow path, which seemed to lead away from the hotel, and deciding it was probably safe, followed it. As she walked along the track, which threaded its way through the slender trunks of the coconut palms, Tis became aware of a strange odour she'd never smelt before. What could it be? She wrinkled her nose and breathed in deeply. It smelt good. Breasting a small rise in the ground a wonderful sight met her gaze: the sea, at last! With eyes wide open and every nerve in her body tense, Tis stopped in complete astonishment, as she stared at the scene before her. She had never imagined that anything could be so wonderful. There was the sea, blue and sparkling. Little waves teased the silvery white sand, and sunlight glittered on the dancing water. To her right, the smart, new hotel had its frontage on the edge of the beach. White umbrellas and wooden sun loungers were arranged in an orderly row at the foot of a long terrace. However, it was not the hotel that held Tis's attention, but the brightly painted wooden boats drawn up on the beach. Near one of these a young lad was industriously cleaning a fishing net. As if in a dream, Tis walked slowly across the warm sand and squatted down beside him.

'Where does it end?' she enquired.

'What end?' said the fisher boy looking at her curiously.

'The sea,' replied Tis.

'Oh, it goes on forever,' said the boy, in the offhand manner of one who has lived by the sea all his life. Looking down, Tis noticed that the net was dotted with little bits of weed, broken shells and other strange, unrecognisable objects.

'Shall I help?' she enquired.

'If you like,' said the boy, and the two of them began to check the net, hole by hole, picking out the rubbish. As the last fold was lifted, Tis saw something that made her catch her breath. There, nestling in the net, half hidden by the sand was a large, pink and brown shell.

'What's that?' she exclaimed.

'Oh, it's only a shell,' said the boy who by now was feeling quite superior to this little girl from the Interior, 'do you want it?'

'Oh yes, yes!' said Tis in a voice intense with yearning, and picking it carefully out of the net, she cradled it in her hands. It was a beautiful shell, perfect and gently curled, with an intricate pattern of brown and pink swirling lines on its outer edges. At its opening, the pink shaded gently into brown and there was a row of points that looked as if they were standing guard on the hidden space inside. Entranced, Tis ran her finger along the shell's side, brushing off the sand.

'If you hold it to your ear,' said the boy, 'you can hear the sea.' Tis did as she was told, and listened spellbound to the low sighing sound, which seemed to come from deep within its heart.

'Can I really have it?' she enquired, concerned lest he change his mind.

'Yes,' said the fisher boy magnanimously. He had been intending to take it to the shop in the grove to sell to the tourists who stayed in the hotel, since it was a particularly fine shell, and they would have paid a good deal for it, but to his surprise he found that he felt sorry for this small girl with the large intense eyes and ragged clothes.

Tis sat back in the sand gazing at the sea and the empty beach while she wriggled her toes in the warm white sand.

'Please,' she said hardly daring to ask, 'can I go into the sea?'

'Well of course you can,' he said jumping up laughing. 'The sea belongs to everyone. I thought everybody knew that.' This made Tis feel very ignorant and she hung her head in shame.

'Come with me,' the fisher boy cried springing to his feet. He caught her hand and ran as fast as he could go into the tiny waves at the water's edge. The spray rose round them like shining stars which fell back down again in sparkling droplets. The water was warm and the beach gently shelving, so they splashed out into the bay until the sea reached their knees. Then he pulled her down into the shallow water and she sat laughing and amazed, with the sea swirling all around her. Tis, who had never even sat in a bath full of water, let alone a whole ocean, was entranced at the feel of the sea on her body, and the salty taste in her mouth. Shaking the water out of her eyes, the little girl looked at the young fisher boy sitting beside her. Her face was radiant.

'Heaven,' she breathed.

'It may be heaven for you,' exclaimed the lad

jumping up, 'but if I don't get home soon to help my dad, I shall get into trouble. Oh, if you want a drink, there's a bottle of water in the boat,' he added, and surrounded by a halo of multicoloured spray, he bounded back to the shore.

Tis lay back on her elbows for a long while in the shallow water just looking, feeling and listening, while the sea gently moved her to its own secret rhythms. She was trying to fix every detail of the scene and every feeling in her body in her memory forever. After a while she got up and splashed dreamily back to the shore. She noticed that one or two of the loungers now had people lying on them in the shade made by the white umbrellas, and seeing a patch of shadow by the fisher boy's boat she drank thirstily from his water bottle, then curled up on the soft, warm sand. Soon the rhythmic splashing of the wavelets on the shore and the plaintive call of the gulls, as they tracked to and fro across the blue arc of the sky, lulled her to sleep.

Had Tis looked at the people on the loungers, instead of helping the fisher boy, she would have seen to her astonishment that one was occupied by the same boy who had so avidly read his book in the broken down car. He was obviously reading another exciting story since he was concentrating intently while rubbing his head in a preoccupied, agitated manner. Presently, the portly man, and well-dressed woman who had been with him on that occasion, came down the steps from the terrace.

'Your Uncle Rhys has to go back to Beleza on business, Aidan,' said the woman, 'so he wants us to have lunch at once. Put your book down now please.'

'Let me just finish this paragraph mum,' pleaded the boy looking up abstractedly.

'Hurry then,' replied his mother and together she and Rhys turned and went back towards the terrace.

'That boy spends too much time reading, Emily,' said Rhys in an irritated voice, as they walked up the steps together. 'He needs to do more, live more, get around a bit. He should be swimming and playing beach games, not sitting down all the time.' Emily bit her lip and said nothing. This was a constant theme with her brother-in-law and it irritated her.

'I'd love to contradict you,' she thought. 'But then Aidan would miss out on these holidays you pay for. When he reaches eighteen,' she added crossly to herself, as she sat down at the table, 'he'll be able to go where he likes, as he'll have his trust fund. Then you can go abroad on your own, because I shan't be coming with you!' Sometimes indeed, she wondered just why it was that Rhys took them with him at all. It certainly wasn't because he found her company congenial. He made that clear in many subtle ways. 'Why do I detest this man so?' she asked herself. 'His personality grates on mine, and he's insensitive I know, but I can't quite put my finger on what really makes me dislike him. I only know,' she thought sadly, 'that when I'm with him, I feel constantly irritable and defensive. If only he would stop criticising Aidan, that would help a bit. Thank goodness he's going away again for a couple of days. Not that he'll tell us what he's done when he comes back. He never does.' As if reading her thoughts, Rhys remarked conversationally,

'You only come on my business trips for Aidan's

sake, don't you Emily?' and for a moment he looked as if he really sympathised with her. Any nascent feeling of liking for her brother-in-law died immediately however, for as soon as the words were out of his mouth, he leered at a girl in a bikini who passed close to their table on her way to the beach, and then ordered a gargantuan lunch that would have fed a poor man for a week. 'Only here once,' he remarked cheerfully, 'Got to make the most of it.' Just then she glanced up and saw Aidan ambling up the terrace steps. He put his book down on an empty table behind his chair and sat down, gazing dreamily about him, still lost in the story he'd just been reading.

Eventually, when the last lick of his dessert had gone, Rhys belched and got up to go.

'I may not be back until the day after tomorrow Emily,' he said, 'so don't worry about me. But I don't think you do anyway,' he added unkindly. Speechless with exasperation, Emily watched him as he walked back into the hotel, and was amazed to see him scoop up Aidan's book from the empty table and surreptitiously stuff it into the pocket of his jacket. She half rose to stop him but then sat down again thoughtfully.

'I suppose he may have a point,' she conceded to herself. 'Aidan ought to do something other than read all day. He might just as well go on holiday in a library!' A few minutes later Rhys appeared in the car park beside the terrace and she noticed with surprise that he didn't have his lap top with him, only a suitcase. She was still wondering how he could conduct his business without it when he got into his hired car and drove away. When she had finished her coffee, Emily began to feel tired, so she got up from the table where Aidan was still eating a large bowl of ice cream saying, 'I'm going to my room to lie down for a while Aidan,' and went into the hotel.

After failing to find his book where he thought he had left it, Aidan wandered out to the row of loungers to look for it, but it soon became obvious that it had mysteriously vanished. At a loss for something to do, he changed into his swimming trunks and moodily splashed to and fro in the shallow water of the bay for a while. He then sat down under one of the umbrellas and gazed discontentedly at the view. Frankly he was getting bored with it. He could see the same wide curving beach, the same blue sparkling water, and the same little boats that he'd looked at yesterday. But what was that beside the nearest boat? It appeared to be a body lying very still. He got up to investigate, and soon found himself looking down at the sleeping form of a small girl, who was lying curled up under the lee of the boat. He noticed that she seemed to be clutching a shell in her hand. However, what caught his attention most was the child's elfin face. Up swept lashes, gently caressed salt streaked cheeks, and one dark brown tendril of hair rested on her forehead like a curled leaf. She looked tiny and insignificant: a piece of flotsam washed up on the beach waiting to be taken out again by the next high tide. Aidan also noticed that the sun, which had now moved its position, was shining full onto the little body and he remembered all those things his mother had told him about sunstroke and sunburn.

'Well, I can at least cover her face,' he thought kindly, and took his handkerchief out of the pocket of his shorts. For a second or two he hesitated as this had been especially embroidered for his father by his grandmother. It had his initials AV, Andrew Vickers, in one corner and twining round them his grandma had worked two little fishes. She had embroidered about thirty of these and Aidan used them every day as they gave him a precious feeling of connectedness to the father he could hardly remember. Try as he might he couldn't even bring his face to mind, but when he put his hand into his pocket and felt the handkerchief it was almost as if he was there with him. 'What shall I do dad?' he mused. 'Shall I cover her face or shall I keep it? What would you do?' and he turned the handkerchief over and over in his hands in indecision. Gradually he began to feel sure that his father would have covered the child even if it meant losing something precious, so bending down he softly laid the hankie over her face to shield it from the sun. Then, as an afterthought, he quietly scooped handfuls of sand from the beach trickling it gently down onto the bare legs until they too were completely covered.

Several hours later, Tis awoke. At first she couldn't understand where she was or why her face and legs were covered up. Reaching up, she removed the handkerchief, sleepily stuffing it into the pocket of her old shirt. Then she cautiously raised her head over the gunwale of the fishing boat. An amazing sight met her startled gaze. There was the sun, sinking into the deep blue water of the bay, and from its base stretched a golden path, right across the sea to the water's edge. Still half asleep she stumbled down the beach. Swirling thoughts tumbled round in her head, then, one caught her attention and wouldn't let go.

'I shall walk on that golden path,' she thought 'I can go on and on to where it meets the sun!' Flinging her arms out wide she stepped, mesmerised, into the water. Then she heard something that stopped her. It was the sound of a heavy lorry toiling along a sandy road. Uncle Manolo! He had come to get her. Behind her, home, mother, father, Yara and all she knew and loved, but before her a wonderful golden path. Her arms fell limply to her sides. Her shoulders drooped, and a disappointed child stumbled up the beach to the waiting lorry.

Sitting on the terrace, Aidan watched the little figure walk down the beach from the shelter of the boat, and stand at the water's edge gazing out into the bay. He saw her arms raised, but he didn't hear the lorry, and watching from the terrace, an image was burned into his brain that he would remember as long as he lived; the black silhouette of a small girl whose arms fell to her side, bent her head and walked slowly up the beach into the dark trees.

Chapter 3

Aidan was bored. Three years had passed, and in fact he should have been too busy to be bored since he was sitting in a classroom listening to his GCSE Botany teacher droning on about creeping buttercups. Botany however, was not his favourite subject, Zoology was, and he already felt he knew every single characteristic of that particular plant, and couldn't see how they would help him to be a better doctor anyway.

'I don't imagine doctors write many prescriptions for buttercups,' he said to himself sarcastically. He was jerked out of his reverie however, when the teacher began explaining that on the field trip the next day they would each need to have a partner. Ordinarily this would not present a problem to Aidan, as he had a good friend called Jake, with whom he worked on a regular basis. But Jake had bronchitis and hadn't been answering his texts all morning. There was just a chance that he'd be better by tomorrow, although, when Aidan had phoned Jake the previous evening his mother had answered the telephone and informed him that Jake was grumpy, feverish, and coughing most of the time.

'It's like trying to live with a consumptive cactus,' she had said with a good deal of exasperation tingeing her normally cheerful voice. 'Do come round tomorrow Aidan. You could play some computer games together and that might make him a bit easier to live with. Anyway,' she added, 'I expect you'll be bringing the course notes. Jake can't afford to miss them if he's going to pass his GCSE's'. The chances of Jake getting back in time Aidan feared were therefore rather remote, and if he didn't come, then he knew he would have to pair up with one of the girls from the neighbouring girls' comprehensive with whom they were sharing the field trip.

'She'll be the one nobody wants to be with,' he thought crossly. 'Skinny, scragged back hair, glasses and zits!' He moodily chewed the end of his biro thinking, not for the first time, what a very thin man his botany teacher was. 'He looks rather like an animated spring onion,' he said to himself, and smiling wryly at his own wit, he critically inspected the teeth marks on the end of his pen.

The next day, although bright, was cold and windy, and Emily fussed round Aidan, insisting that he take his anorak, and deluging him with motherly advice.

'I'm not a child,' he thought in exasperation. 'I shall soon be sixteen and she still treats me like a four year old. But then,' he conceded, 'I suppose I'm all she's got.'

The coach, when it arrived from the girls' school, was only half full and there were still plenty of empty seats after the boys had boarded, so Aidan was able to sit by himself. The route passed through some lovely scenery, but he missed most of it as he had his nose in the latest thriller on his e-book reader. He also missed the opportunity to take a long look at the only girl who like himself was sitting on her own. Their destination was Cardogan's Head on the South coast, home to the classic cliff plants the students had to study as part of their field trip. On arrival in the car park at the foot of the Head, they all piled out of the coach into a biting East wind that made them shiver and do up their coats. Several of the bolder girls tried to shelter behind the boys, and there was much giggling and milling about. Aidan was glad his mother had insisted he take his anorak as he alighted from the warmth of the coach and felt the cold air swirl round him. He shivered and forgave her for fussing. A few minutes later, after the teachers had sorted out the chaos, the 'Spring Onion' came bustling up to him accompanied by the spare girl.

'This is Kirsty,' he said, 'she hasn't got a partner, so you two will work together.' Aidan regretfully tore himself away from his story, and looking up saw a plump girl wrapped up in a navy anorak with the hood shading a face that was turning pink with either cold or shyness.

'Oh great!' he said to himself. 'The blushing school dumpling, just my luck,' and he stuffed a consoling peppermint into his mouth, churlishly omitting to offer one to his new acquaintance.

The two of them then began the long trudge up the narrow winding path to the top of the promontory. As they came up the last steep slope and onto the short grass of the Head, a spectacular view met their gaze. There in front was the Isle of Wight and the rough waters of the Solent, and behind them a large tidal basin where the river Sette ran out into the sea. Achingly blue sky merged with green, wave-ruffled water, and the wind wrapped them round in a cold embrace that all but carried their breath away.

Kirsty and Aidan, who had been given a large grid by the 'Spring Onion' to help them in their assignment, wandered aimlessly along looking for a good place to start. Neither had yet said a word to the other and the silence was beginning to be embarrassing.

'Oh drat,' said Aidan to himself, 'this is hopeless.' However, out loud he said, 'Let's go by this gorse bush. It'll give us some shelter,' and so saying he plumped down on the grass and fitted the grid over a likely looking patch. Kirsty stood beside him, clipboard in hand and pen poised.

Aidan was aware that behind the gorse bush they were out of the wind and that the sun was quite warm. He could feel its heat on the back of his neck and wished that he could take his coat off. Looking intently at the area he had staked out, he desperately tried to recall what he should be searching for, but his mind was a complete blank as he hadn't been paying much attention when the 'Spring Onion' had briefed them. As he stared desperately at the grid he became aware of a lovely smell. It was sweet and aromatic, with overtones of earth and grass. Then he noticed a patch of small purple flowers in one of the sections and realised that he could at least identify these particular plants as his teacher had mentioned several times that they were prolific on the Head. Aidan also remembered being amused by its name. He looked closer, blowing a long peppermint breath over the flowers to the great astonishment of a passing ant that paused under a leaf, trying to identify the strange odour.

'This must be Wild Thyme,' he said to himself. Feeling pleased, he looked up at the girl as she stood beside him and found himself staring into a pretty, intelligent face. Bright blue eyes regarded him speculatively and her head, now devoid of the enveloping hood, was covered with a thick mop of auburn curls that seemed to glow in the intense sunshine. All thoughts of Wild Thyme deserted him completely and he found himself gazing at her as if she had undergone some sort of

Cinderella transformation.

'What have you found?' queried Kirsty after what seemed a very long pause.

'Wild Thyme,' muttered Aidan, and then in a fit of honesty and desperation he added, 'but I'm not much good at this. Why don't you do the looking and I do the writing?'

'Ok then,' replied Kirsty. So they changed places and soon Aidan was having a hard job keeping up with the stream of information that Kirsty told him to write down.

Long afterwards, Aidan was hard pressed to recall what they had talked about as they finished their project and ate their sandwiches in the lee of the gorse bush. Equally elusive was the subject of their conversation as they shared the same coach seat on the way back home. All he knew was that he felt at home and comfortable in her company. She was a good listener, and he was quite disappointed when the coach pulled into his school car park and he had to get off.

'Well, that was fun,' he said to himself, 'but I don't suppose I shall ever see her again.' Later on that night as he stretched out in bed, the thought occurred to him that he hadn't told Kirsty his name. 'The wretched "Spring Onion" didn't introduce us properly,' he remarked crossly. 'I know her name but she doesn't know mine.' He then spent a drowsy five minutes trying to work out why it mattered. 'I don't suppose it does matter much,' he murmured eventually and turning over soon fell fast asleep to dream of Wild Thyme, auburn hair and falling in a prickly gorse bush.

Chapter 4

All was quiet in Tis's village. The moon painted the little settlement in a silvery glow, giving it a temporary beauty that was lacking in the all too revealing brightness of day. Little light shone from most of the shacks as weary workers gratefully enjoyed a few hours of respite from the daily grind of survival. But there was also a vulnerability about this seemingly peaceful scene, a helplessness much relished by the stranger who moved quietly in the darkest shadows, peering in at the illuminated, un-curtained windows. He saw a great deal which delighted him. Yes, there were several young girls here, and one or two of them would be attractive if they had more flesh on their bodies. He smiled to himself and thought of the money they would bring him and all it could buy. Then he tiptoed away and laid his plans.

A few months after Tis's trip to the sea, mother and daughter were seated at the table talking by the light of a single candle. The beads had been put to one side and lay heaped in little sparkling mounds of blue, vermilion and gold.

'How long is it before the baby comes?' asked Tis for the hundredth time that month.

'Oh Tis, I'm not sure,' replied her mother, 'but I don't think it can be long now, I'm so huge,' and she rubbed her stomach wearily. Tis hugged herself, as she thought how lovely it was going to be to have a baby in the house.

'I do so wish he'd hurry up,' she said.

'You keep saying "he",' replied her mother, 'but we won't know for sure whether it's going to be a boy or a girl until the baby comes. Don't be disappointed if it's a girl.' Tis, who was quite sure the baby was going to be a boy, smiled a little secret smile and went to bed where she burrowed down under her old blankets and soon fell asleep. In the early hours of the morning, the house came alive again to the sound of footsteps and quiet voices. A little later a thin wailing pierced the silence and then ceased, but still Tis slept on.

Morning came, and the moon's fierce brother, the sun, shone. He had no sentimental desire to make the village appear romantic as the moon had done, and it was revealed in all its stark deprivation. Tis slept late as her mother failed to call her as she usually did. When she eventually woke, she sat up and rubbed her eyes noticing how high the sun was.

'What's happening? Why hasn't Mamãe woken me?' she thought. In alarm, she jumped out of bed and hurried into Ana's room where, to her utter astonishment, she found her mother was fast asleep. Opening her mouth to call to her, the words died on her lips as her eye fell on a tiny baby nestling in a large cardboard box. Tis gazed down at the small face and thought she had never seen anything so beautiful. The baby, who was sleeping in a very determined manner, had one little hand resting on the cotton wrap that swaddled him, and Tis gazed at it enchanted. As she peered closer, she saw with delight, the fringe of delicate pink nails that adorned the miniature finger ends. Reaching out, she gently touched the tiny hand and to her great joy the baby opened its eyes and seemed to look at her. Then the delicate blue veined lids fluttered closed again. Gradually she became aware that she was being watched, and turning her head she saw that her mother had woken up.

'Lovely isn't he?' said Ana in a soft, tired voice.

'He's beautiful,' breathed Tis. 'My baby brother, at last. Can I hold him?' At that moment the baby stirred and opened his eyes again. He moved his head and Tis, not waiting for her mother's consent, gathered him up in her arms and gently hugged him to her. As she bent her head forward, her long hair fell round his face so that for a moment brother and sister were alone in a small secret place of their own. In that instant, Tis felt as if she'd been looking forward to this moment all her life. 'You're my baby brother,' she murmured softly. 'I'm your big sister, Tis, and I'm going to look after you always. What's his name?' she asked Ana, for her mother had refused to tell Tis what names she'd chosen for the baby in case it brought bad luck.

'We'll call him Davi,' replied Ana.

'Davi,' whispered Tis. 'Davi. Yes, I like that.' Gently she gave the baby to her mother and gazed enraptured as he took his first meal.

Yara and Tis were sitting talking on the step in front of Tis' house. Davi, now three, was squatting at their feet. Earlier in the day the girls had accidentally slopped some water on the ground when they were carrying the water bucket, so that the dirt was wet and Davi was amusing himself playing with it.

'What are you trying to do?' queried Tis. 'Do you

want me to help you?' and she looked with interest at the tiny mound of mud Davi was patting with his small hands.

'Our house,' replied Davi carefully. 'Come help me Tis,' he went on. Tis glanced at her friend who seemed to be preoccupied, wondering whether she would mind her helping Davi. She knew that Yara didn't like playing with him so hesitated before suggesting they both join in the game.

'What are you thinking Yara?' she queried. 'You're daydreaming about something aren't you?'

'I'm dreaming about being rich,' replied Yara, a faraway look in her eyes. 'Do you remember the beautiful lady in the car who gave us the chocolate ages ago? She was wearing that lovely yellow dress.'

'Yes I do,' replied Tis. 'There was a grumpy old man and a boy who was reading a book too wasn't there?'

'Well,' said Yara, 'I'd like to be like her. I want to wear lovely clothes and drive about in a big car like she did. I also want to eat chocolate every day, lots of it!'

'But what about me?' queried Tis. 'If you did those things you would have to go away, and what should I do without you?'

'You've got Davi now,' replied Yara shrugging her shoulders, and with that she got up and walked away down the village street.

'Oh Davi,' murmured Tis, 'why isn't Yara like she used to be? Ever since you were born she's been jealous of you. But she mustn't go away,' she added anxiously, 'I would miss her so.'

Watching Yara go, she thought sadly that for the last two or three weeks Yara had been behaving oddly. She'd seemed withdrawn and uncommunicative. Tis had come across her several times sitting on the step outside her house lost in her own thoughts. When Tis had asked her what she was thinking about Yara had snapped,

'Nothing,' and got up and walked away.

'What have I done?' Tis asked herself for the umpteenth time. 'She doesn't seem to want to be my friend anymore. We've shared everything and now she'll hardly talk to me,' and a sense of desolate bereavement swept over her.

'Tis play,' commanded Davi totally unaware of his sister's sadness. Tis got up from the step and squatted down beside him in the mud. Davi had given up trying to make a house and was now patting the mud with his little hands trying to make it level. He then picked up a nearby twig and poked a hole in the smooth patch and then another a small distance away from the first. After some thought, he placed another hole under the first two and sat back to admire them.

'Give me the stick Davi, I've an idea,' ordered Tis as she took the twig from him. Carefully she drew a circle round each of the top two holes. She then added a downward facing semicircle over each and lastly an upward curve under the lower hole. 'Davi,' she said, pointing first at the face in the dirt, and then at her brother's eyes, nose, and mouth. At first Davi didn't understand, but suddenly the face in the dirt made sense to him, and he chuckled delightedly. Tis laughed too. Brother and sister were so wrapped up in the joy of each other's company, that they didn't see Yara stop, turn round, and look back at them with painful longing.

That night Tis was in bed and asleep. In the early hours of the morning however, a sound woke her and she sat up wondering what it was.

'What's happening? What woke me?' she questioned, looking round the silent living room. Then she heard a noise from Yara's house next door. Quickly she got out of bed, padded over to the window and looked out. Dawn was just beginning to break, and in the dim light Tis made out the dark shape of a small truck parked outside. As she watched the door opened and Yara came out accompanied by the shadowy figure of a man. He opened the door of the pick-up and turned the headlights on. Yara scrambled in and he then went round to the back of the truck, put something in, and got into the driving seat. As he did so the light from the headlamps threw his shadow over Tis's window. She shivered as the darkness fell on her face, and a sense of dread wrapped itself around her heart as she stumbled back to bed.

'What a horrible dream,' she said to herself closing her eyes again.

However when she went to call for Yara in the morning she found that it hadn't been a dream at all.

'She's gone to Beleza to be a maid,' Yara's mother informed Tis sadly. 'I shall miss her, but she would go. The money will be good though,' she added, brightening a little.

'And she never even said goodbye,' mourned Tis to Davi. 'How could she go like that? She was my best friend. Shall I ever see her again?' Davi, who didn't really understand what was upsetting Tis, lifted a small hand and with his index finger, traced the track a tear had made on her cheek.

'Davi love you,' he chirruped and gathering him in her arms, Tis buried her face in his warm neck and hugged him.

'I love you too Davi,' she replied softly.

Chapter 5

A couple of years later, Carlos was sitting on the front steps of his shack surrounded by a tangle of wire which he was industriously bending and twisting with a pair of old, half broken wire cutters. Both children were leaning over him watching intently. Davi, now five years old and small for his age, had grown into a quiet, wistful child who idolised his big sister and followed her everywhere.

'Papai,' said Tis struggling in vain to bend a small length of wire with her fingers, 'how long before you get another job? Mamãe says the sugar cane crop has failed. They'll take you back in a couple of months though won't they?' she added in a worried voice.

'I doubt it, but we can't wait that long anyway,' replied her father. 'I've just got to find something else to do. But what?' he added in a voice made sharp by his desperation.

'But Mamãe and I can keep us going with the beads,' said Tis. 'Won't that be enough?'

'No,' snapped her father with uncharacteristic abruptness.

'How long before my car is ready Papai?' asked Davi for the umpteenth time, oblivious to the looming family crisis.

'Have patience little one,' murmured Carlos looking up. 'This car is going to be a masterpiece, and masterpieces take time,' and he recommenced his bending and cutting, glad to have something to take his mind off the anxiety that gnawed inside him like a cancer. Gradually as the children watched, a shape began to emerge from the tangle; first a body, then some wheels and a windscreen were skilfully added until at last there it was, a small toy car, fashioned entirely out of bent wire. Its little wire wheels even revolved, such was the skill of its creator.

'Go and see if your mother has a piece of string Tis,' said Carlos, 'and then we'll see this wonderful car set out on its travels.'

Tis skipped into the house and came back triumphantly waving a length of twine. One end was fixed round the front bumper and the small car was set down in the dust at the foot of the steps. Davi looked at it in awe. His eyes were round, and he stood very still gazing at the little vehicle resting on the dusty road. He'd never had a toy of any sort before so this was an amazing, new experience for him. Indeed, he was not even sure whether he was allowed to touch something so rare and precious.

'Take the string son,' said Carlos, gently putting it into his hand. Davi gave an experimental tug and the wire car moved a few inches along the road making him squeal with delight. Ana heard the noise and came to stand at the top of the steps looking with interest at the little group around the toy.

'That's a really fine car Carlos,' she said laughing. 'Does it really go?'

'Yes, it does,' replied Carlos proudly. 'It's the best car in the world.'

'Come on Davi let's take it for a ride,' encouraged

Tis and the two set off up the dusty track which wound its way between the neighbouring shacks, gaining confidence at every step. The little car trundled after them and they gradually picked up speed until they were both running. Turning round at the top of the street they came dashing back again kicking up the dust, laughing and shouting. All went well until they were near their home when the car bumped over a stone, rose a little way into the air and fell onto its side. Davi came to an abrupt halt, lost his balance and sat down hard on the road. Then as Carlos and Ana watched, he began to cough clutching his chest and bending over trying desperately to stop the spasms that racked his scrawny little frame. Immediately Ana ran to him, picked him up still coughing, and brought him back into the house.

'Fetch some water Tis,' she commanded. Tis ran quickly to the bucket beside the stove, filled a mug and brought it back to her mother. Gradually, as Ana soothed him, the coughing fit subsided and he lay exhausted on her lap. Carlos looked at his wife in consternation.

'How long has he had this cough Ana?' he asked, in a voice sharp with concern.

'About six months, Carlos,' said Ana sadly. 'I keep hoping he's going to grow out of it but it gets worse and worse. He needs a doctor, but how can we afford that?'

'As I came through Oliveira on my way home with Manolo, we stopped to get a drink there and I heard that the government has just opened a clinic in the town where the consultation is free,' replied Carlos thoughtfully. 'I don't think the treatment is free, but if we go at least we shall know what's wrong with him.'

'But how would you get him there?' asked Ana worriedly. 'That's about twenty kilometres away.'

'Walk,' retorted Carlos tersely, 'and if necessary, I'll carry him.'

So the next day, at dawn, father and son made their way up the village street, carrying a little rice in a plastic box, an old blanket and a bottle of water. As they disappeared out of sight, Tis turned anxiously to her mother.

'Do you think they'll be all right? I should have gone too, to help carry Davi when he gets tired.'

'I need you here,' replied Ana, running her hand distractedly through her hair. 'We must get on with the beads. It's all we have to live on now. I don't know how I'm going to stretch the food to feed four of us.'

As dusk began to fall, Carlos and Davi reached the outskirts of Oliveira. Both were weary beyond imagining and too late for the clinic that day.

'We'd better find where it is and then camp outside it for the night,' thought Carlos to himself. 'At least we'll be first then when it opens in the morning. Hi there!' he called to a man on the other side of the road who was carrying a bucket of water, 'can you tell me how to get to the new clinic please?'

'Go straight on until you reach the town centre,' replied the man in a surly voice. 'You can't miss it.' Davi meanwhile had collapsed at Carlos' feet too tired even to stand. Calling on his last reserve of energy his father picked him up and, with several rests, made his way to the town centre where, next to a food store, he found a small dingy one roomed building with a small sign on the wall saying 'clinic' in red capital letters. He set his son gently on his feet and looked about him for a sheltered place to make camp for the night. A few yards down the road a group of youths had gathered and were chatting and drinking. Several young women were lounging about the group, drawn to their company like moths to a candle, their shrill laughter clearly audible above the sound of the traffic. The town centre was thronged with people going home for the night and Carlos knew that it was only a matter of time before some of them would come back onto the streets looking for something to do for the evening.

'We can't sleep here,' he thought worriedly, 'it's too dangerous, but where can we go that's safe?' Leaving his son standing forlornly by the clinic door like an abandoned refugee, he walked round to the back of the building where he found to his delight that there was a yard. 'We'll sleep here,' he said to himself, going back to the street where he'd left Davi. The child was now slumped on the ground in a tired heap, so Carlos picked him up in his arms again and carried him. Just as they arrived at the open doorway a sudden gust of wind blew into the yard and the paper and plastic bags that littered the floor eddied round the small space. An empty coke bottle clattered towards them with an irritating desiccated sound only stopping when it reached Carlos's feet. 'This isn't good,' Carlos thought, 'but it's the best I can find so it will have to do,' and looking round for the cleanest corner he gently put his little son down on their blanket. Davi lay there, too tired even to sit up. Carlos knelt beside him. 'Would you like some rice Davi?' he asked gently.

'Yes please Papai,' replied the boy in a small tired voice. Putting his arm around the child's shoulders, Carlos helped him to sit up and eat a little of the rice they had brought. However, as he silently spooned the food into his son's mouth, he asked himself the question he had asked so many times before.

'Why, even though I work every hour there is in the day, can't I make enough money to feed my family?' No answer came, only silence. 'There never is an answer,' he muttered angrily to himself. When Davi had finished eating, his father gave him some water and after drinking some himself, looked at the meagre amount of rice left in the plastic box. 'I'd better leave the rest for Davi,' he sighed with regret. So trying to ignore the griping hunger pains in his belly, he lay down on the blanket, took Davi in his arms, and endeavoured to sleep. But sleep wouldn't come as the ground was hard and uneven and his mind full of dark, anxious thoughts. Presently the noise of shouting, and the sound of running feet on the road outside the yard made him fear for their safety, so abandoning all thoughts of sleep, he opened his eyes and watched the stars come out instead. As night fell, the sky became inky black, and each star shone down on him, cold, distant and remote. He could even see the pale smudge of the Milky Way forming a long ghostly arch across the heavens and, as he gazed up at it, despair gripped his heart. Finally, when all became quiet in the town, he fell asleep.

The next morning Carlos woke feeling dirty and very stiff.

'Where am I?' he said out loud as he sat up shaking his head, 'I'm so hungry,' was his next thought, but there wasn't enough food for them both. Davi however, seemed to have revived a little and sat up on the blanket to eat a little more of their precious rice.

'We'll go and sit on the clinic steps now,' Carlos said to him when he'd finished eating. So gathering up their meagre possessions, father and son made their way to the front of the building. 'Now we shall be first in the queue when it opens,' said Carlos as they sat down. Very soon a line of patients began to form behind them, and in no time at all it had wound its way right round the building. 'It did us some good sleeping here the night,' Carlos murmured to Davi, 'we can start straight back as soon as the doctor has seen us.' At last the door of the clinic opened and a nurse motioned to them to come inside.

As they stepped gingerly into the clinic's single room they could see a white coated doctor busily typing on a laptop. He made no move to speak to them so the nurse seated Carlos and Davi on two chairs facing him. They waited. Davi sat very still, legs dangling as he looked round the unfamiliar objects in the room with large frightened eyes. After a few moments the Doctor stopped typing and looked at them unsmilingly.

'What can I do for you?' he enquired in a business like tone and Carlos explained about Davi's cough. 'Weigh the boy, nurse, please,' commanded the doctor. Davi was picked up and placed on the scales where he stood trembling with fear. The doctor looked grave when he saw what the scales had registered, but made no comment.

'Come to me, child,' he commanded in a brisk voice. Davi, however, was petrified by the stranger in the white coat, so instead of obeying, he jumped off the scales and ran over to Carlos clutching at his father's knees in terror.

'Do as he says,' ordered Carlos. Slowly, and with great reluctance, the scrawny child made his way hesitatingly to the Doctor.

'Lift his shirt, nurse,' commanded the doctor and proceeded to sound the boy's chest with his stethoscope while the nurse stood behind him. 'Now the back,' he ordered, and Davi found himself turned round with his face pressed against the nurse while she held up his shirt. He could smell the scent of her clean uniform and stood shaking with fright as the cold metal end of the stethoscope prodded his bony ribs. As soon as the doctor had finished, Davi ran back to Carlos and buried his face in his father's lap. The Doctor turned back to his laptop and typed away for what seemed an eternity. He then looked up wearily and addressed Carlos.

'I'm afraid,' he said gently, 'that your son has tuberculosis.' Carlos knew what that meant and a cold numbness enveloped him. He heard, seemingly from far away, what must have been his own voice whisper,

'What can you do to save him?'

'Curing him is not a problem,' replied the doctor, 'if you have the money to buy the medicines,' and he mentioned the sum necessary to treat Davi.

'But I have no money,' replied Carlos miserably and he and the doctor gazed at each other in mutual despair. 'How long has he got?' The words hovered between them like the last glimmer of light before the coming of a black night.

'About six months,' replied the doctor. Carlos sat paralyzed with the awful news. This couldn't be happening to him. A dark mist seemed to cloud his brain and he looked at Davi in anguish. Dimly he heard the doctor say, 'I'm afraid there's nothing else I can do.' Slowly, as if in a dream, father and son stumbled down the steps of the clinic and out into the busy street.

Tis was glad when the sun came up and illuminated their room, since she'd been sitting with her mother in the half light of the early morning straining to see the beads she was endeavouring to thread. Since Carlos no longer had any income from the plantation, their job at home had become all absorbing, and they were both working away with a desperate concentrated energy.

'I hate these horrible beads!' Tis burst out vehemently at last. 'I must have threaded millions. Look at them!' and she stabbed at the small plastic bags lined up on the table. 'We'll never get to the end even if we work all day and all night.' Ana said nothing but looked sadly at her rebellious daughter. 'When do you think Davi and Papai will be home?' Tis went on, 'they've been gone two whole days.'

'They must come back today,' replied Ana trying to convince herself that what she said was true. They worked on wearily for another hour and then Tis said firmly,

'I'm going to get wood Mamãe.' Ana knew that

Tis really wanted to look for Davi and Carlos but she said nothing. The collecting had to be done alone now that Yara had gone, so Tis made her lonely way along the track out of the village picking up what few twigs there were along its margins. The road threaded its way between tall Jacaranda trees and round clumps of bushes, gradually gaining height until it reached a place where the ground fell away and a traveller could see down its length as it descended a long gentle incline. At the bottom, which was about half a mile away, it skirted a cluster of Acacias and so became lost to view. Shading her eyes against the morning sun, Tis gazed down the hill willing there to be someone coming. At first all she could see was a pony, loaded with bananas and pineapples, being driven down the track, but then, as she concentrated on the distant bend, two figures came into sight by the trees and began to toil up the road towards her. Even at that distance, Tis knew who they were, and dropping her bundle of sticks, flew down the road to meet them. How tired they were, how covered in dust, and how sad her father seemed! Tis knew instantly that something terrible had happened, but the grim misery on her father's face stopped her from asking questions. Instead she lifted Davi into her arms and cradling his head against her shoulder, walked slowly home.

They came so quietly up the steps to the house that Ana wasn't aware they'd arrived until they were actually at the door. One look at their faces was enough to show her that the news was bad so she busied herself putting Davi to sleep on his mattress and then came slowly into the room where her husband and daughter were sitting at the table.

'Well, what did the Doctor say?' she asked fearfully.

For a moment there was silence, then Carlos looked up from the bowl of food he was eating and said in a voice bleak with despair.

'He has tuberculosis and he's going to die, because we haven't the money for the medicine he needs.' There was a stunned silence then Tis jumped to her feet knocking her chair over.

'He can't die,' she shouted. 'I won't let him. Somehow I will earn that money if it kills me,' and she stumbled out of the house and sat down on the steps determined to do something to help. 'I will save him,' she said to herself over and over again, as if the mere repetition would make it a reality. 'I will. I will.' When her mind had quietened a little she crept back into the house where her mother and father were still sitting talking in low voices and went over to her bed. Taking down her two most precious possessions the shell and the hankie, from the shelf above, she walked softly back outside to her seat on the steps and sat looking at them. Carefully holding the shell in her hand she put her mouth to the opening and murmured softly into the waiting pink ear, 'If there's anybody there come and help me. I don't know who you were who covered my face by the boat, but please, please come again and help me save my brother.' She then cradled both shell and hankie in her arms, and rocking rhythmically back and forth, felt a little comforted.

Three weeks went by and on a hot sunny day, darkness again insinuated itself into the village, despite the radiant sunshine. It came, as before, in the shape of the well dressed man Tis had seen putting Yara into the pick up at the dead of night. This time, Thiago, for that was his name, came to the house, and for a long while talked to her parents, while Tis and Davi played outside with the wire car. After a while he left, got into his truck and drove away. Then from the open door came the unusual sound of her mother and father arguing. At last she could stand the suspense no longer and crept quietly into the room. When Carlos and Ana saw her they both fell silent.

'What's happening?   What did he want?' demanded Tis. 'Tell me. I'm old enough to know!'

'That man wants you to go to Beleza as a maid,' replied Carlos running his hands through his hair. 'He says he'll give us money when he comes to collect you. You will also send money back from your wages. But I don't want you to go,' he added in a low agitated voice.

'How much?' demanded Tis. He told her and a big smile lit up her face. 'With that money we can pay for Davi's medicine and he will get better. I'm going,' she said and nothing her parents could say would make her change her mind.

Consequently a few nights later, Tis climbed up into the same truck that had fetched Yara, clutching a plastic carrier bag holding all her worldly possessions. The following morning Davi cried and cried at the loss of his sister, refusing to be comforted. Carlos too left home that day to return to the clinic at Oliveira, torn between hope for Davi and dark, oppressive dread about what was going to happen to Tis.

Chapter 6

So Tis's journey began. As each kilometre passed she felt as if her heart was being torn out. It seemed to be attached to the end of a strong piece of elastic whose other end was securely anchored to her home and family. As the pickup truck sped on, the elastic appeared to stretch tighter and tighter.

'At some point it'll have to snap,' she thought desperately, 'and then what will happen to me?' But it didn't; the invisible thread was more resilient than that, and continued to link her to her parents and her beloved Davi, despite the fact that she was speeding farther and farther away from them with each revolution of the wheels. However, as the pickup fled into the night, so the anchor point in her heart ached more and more, until it was a pinpoint of pure pain. Tis sat and hugged her throbbing chest as shacks and ghostly trees, wild animals and weird outcrops of rock, all poured past in a blur of headlights. Twice they halted briefly in remote villages for Thiago to talk to shadowy figures who came out of the night and then disappeared again into the darkness. At last, as dawn began to finger the clouds, Tis, aware that the truck had drawn into a petrol station, fell into a deep, exhausted sleep, curled up on the front seat; a sleep which indeed, for a wonderful few minutes, stilled the wrenching pain of separation.

All too soon Thiago got back into the truck and off they set again. This time the journey was smoother as they had reached the beginning of the main highway and the pickup's engine purred along, consuming the kilometres and further stretching the umbilical cord of homesickness. When they entered the outskirts of the big city, Tis was astonished by what she saw and sat up straight with her eyes wide open, gazing around in wonder. Her only experience of urban life had been her own small village, but here she saw buildings so tall they seemed to reach the heavens. Tree lined avenues, fountains and shopping malls met her astonished gaze, and a river of multi-coloured humanity flowed along the wide pavements. Shoppers jostled with office workers, and Tis even glimpsed a young man seated on a stool playing a guitar while collecting money from the passing crowd. The traffic too, terrified her with its noisy cacophony of horns and roaring engines. On all sides they seemed to be hemmed in by cars and buses, until eventually they came to a halt in a dense traffic jam, where they spent so long that a street vendor sold Thiago a bottle of coke to drink while he waited to move on. At last the sheer noise and the overload of so many new sensations was too much for Tis, and she closed her eyes, covered her ears and longed for the peace and quiet of home.

When the traffic began to move again, Tis was aware that the truck was gradually climbing upwards and opened her eyes to look once more. Soon they turned a corner and there, spread out beneath them, she could see a wide silver estuary threading its winding path to the sea. The glimpse was only momentary however, as they immediately plunged into a maze of small streets and alleyways where they had to go more slowly. threading their way between   bicycles, market stalls, and piles of rotting pineapples. On several occasions the truck had to swerve to avoid groups of playing children, and the mangy dogs who were rooting about in the rubbish. Just when Tis thought she couldn't bear another minute of this journey, they pulled up in a filthy back alley. Silently, Thiago, who indeed had not spoken for the entire journey, got out of the truck and unlocked a door that gave onto the narrow street. He beckoned to her to join him. Tis looked at the shabby buildings with misgiving but obediently scrambled out of the truck feeling very stiff and sore from the long journey. Clutching her bag she reluctantly picked her way through the filth in the road and through the doorway. The door banged shut behind her and Tis heard the grinding of the key in the lock. Inside was a small dirty courtyard and ahead a tall, three storied building rose forbiddingly black against the blue of the sky. Thiago disappeared through another door into the house, and Tis stood looking round, feeling trapped and alone. For the first time in her life she was imprisoned in a confined space, and her immediate impulse was to go and beat her fists on the street door. Common sense told her that would be useless, so she stood, heart beating wildly and legs trembling, waiting to see what would happen next.

Moments later the door swung open and Thiago came out into the yard followed by a thin old woman. Her face was wrinkled and rubbery, like a slice of over baked aubergine, but the most striking feature was the mouth. This curved round a skull like jaw in a cruel thin line and was painted bright red. The old woman's hair was henna-orange and pulled severely back into a bun secured with large brightly coloured combs. However, it was the eyes that held Tis mesmerized, as they were reptilian in their blackness, merciless and icy cold.

'This is her?' The words fell like shards of glass

into the silence of the courtyard, the voice dry and arid. 'She's thin, but I suppose she'll fatten up a bit.'

'She may be thin, Tia,' replied Thiago smugly, 'but she's unspoiled goods.'

'Ah,' the old woman let out a satisfied sigh, a brittle sound that despite its brevity held a world of menace. 'Just what those whoring foreigners are always asking for. What's your name girl?'

'Tis,' stammered the frightened child, and shrank back as a skinny arm grasped her shoulder, and bony fingers pinched her cheek. She was then turned this way and that as if she were a dead chicken in the market being inspected for its suitability for the cooking pot.

'That's no good for a working name. We shall call you 'Little Flower.' You're small enough for that. Get in,' and she motioned Tis to go before her through the door into the house.

Tis entered a dingy kitchen, which looked out onto the yard. It smelt of stale food and she noticed that the sink was piled high with unwashed plates and mugs. Off this was a tiny storeroom with a thin soiled mattress on the dirty floor.

'You sleep here,' said the old woman sharply, so, not understanding quite what she was supposed to do, Tis immediately squatted down on the mattress. 'Can you do housework?' The question came abruptly and she had to think carefully before she replied, as she felt so tired and confused.

'I can clean and cook,' she murmured looking

down at the floor.

'Good! You can start now,' said the ice cold voice. 'Get up you lazy slut. It's not time for bed yet.' Leaving her meagre belongings on the mattress, Tis followed the woman into the dirty kitchen in a daze. 'There's the rice,' the old woman said crisply, pointing to a large sack propped up against one wall. 'Beans are in that cupboard. I'll show you how much to cook.' With that she tipped a huge quantity of rice into a grubby pan on the stove.

'That would feed our family for a week,' thought Tis dully to herself. 'But I must do my best if I'm to please her.'

'We eat at five,' snapped her new mistress. 'Make sure it's ready and have plenty yourself. Someone will come and carry it in for you,' and with that she was gone. Tis set to work feeling tired, disorientated and utterly dismayed. Her back ached, her small arms ached and her head ached with the oppressive heat of the kitchen but at last it was cooked and taken into the adjoining room by Thiago. When the empty plates came back Tis realised that there must be at least ten people in the house.

'That's a lot of people for one family,' she thought listlessly 'I wonder who they are?' She set to work washing up the plates and pots in the grubby sink and with her last reserve of energy scoured the rice pot until it shone. She then lay down on the smelly mattress in the storeroom cuddling the shell wrapped up in the handkerchief and fell into an exhausted sleep.

The next day passed in a similar fashion. At

mealtimes Tis could hear voices, but since she was not allowed out of the kitchen she had no idea what was going on, even in the next room where the other people in the house ate their meals. Some of the voices she could hear were girls' voices and once or twice, one particular one seemed to awaken a distant memory in her mind. It was as if a lovely song from years ago had threaded its melody back into her consciousness, but she couldn't put a name to it.

'I'm sure I know that voice,' she thought to herself, but she was so busy that she didn't have time to puzzle out where she could have heard it. As she cleaned, swept and prepared meal after meal, Tis consoled herself with imagining a picture of Davi, tall and strong, and without his dangerous cough. Just the thought itself gave her energy, kept her tired legs working, and her small hands preparing the endless round of beans and rice.

The following afternoon, Tis was scraping dirty plates into a bowl on the kitchen table when the door from the dining room burst open and in came, not the cruel, desiccated old woman, but a group of three girls. They were laughing together, but they stopped as soon as they saw Tis, and stared at her curiously. Tis noticed that all three had their faces painted with bright lipstick and dark eye shadow. The smell of the cheap scent they were wearing wafted round the kitchen mingling with the omnipresent cooking odours. One of the girls gave a start as she looked curiously at Tis. Suddenly she stood quite still, and for a long moment stared in anguish straight at her.

'Oh no! Not you too Tis!' The words came out

in a distressed whisper.

'Yara!' cried Tis. 'You, here. But how? I don't understand. Are you a maid here too?' Yara moved swiftly across the room and caught Tis in her arms.

'Oh Tis,' she said in a broken voice, 'I prayed he wouldn't find you. That you would be too thin for him.'

'Yara, Yara,' wailed Tis in bewilderment, 'what's the matter, what's this place and why is it so bad for me to be here? I only came to earn money to pay for medicine for Davi. He's ill.' Yara, bereft of words, stood looking sadly at Tis. Eventually she took her gently by the arm and led her out of the kitchen.

'Come to our room,' she said dully, and led the way through the dining room and up a short corridor into a hallway in the centre of the house. 'The Turtle is out, so the place is ours for an hour. That's our name for the old hag you're cooking for.'

Off the hall, Tis could see five small rooms which all appeared to be bedrooms. The hall itself was empty except for two couches, which were draped with faded red velvet. A short corridor seemed to lead to the front of the building and Tis could hear the sounds of a busy street outside. Behind a closed door was a staircase, which led to the upper part of the house. Quickly, Yara led the way up the stairs to a large room on the second floor, which was the girls dormitory, sparsely furnished with bunk beds and a washbasin. There were no chairs or cupboards in the room, and the only light came from a single high window, which was heavily barred. Yara sat down on one of the lower bunks pulling Tis down beside her. The two other girls, whose names were Yaritza and Magdalena, sat on the opposite bunk and looked questioningly at them.

'Tis lives next door to me at home,' said Yara in a quiet voice. 'She and I are best friends.'

'What's the matter with this place Yara? Tell me,' whispered Tis in a small voice. She could see that this Yara was not the Yara she remembered. The friend she used to know, and with whom she had spent so many happy days at home, was carefree and full of laughter. Everything they'd done was fun because she'd been full of energy and vitality. Now a lot of that joyful energy appeared to have drained away and what was left had been converted into intense, desperate anger. For a few seconds Yara remained silent, and then she seemed to come to a decision.

'There's no easy way to say this,' she said at last with deep sigh. 'This is a brothel Tis, and you're here to work as a prostitute, not a maid.' Tis felt as if an ice cold hand had taken hold of her heart.

'But Yara,' she said in a voice so small and trembling, that she didn't recognise it as her own, 'why do we stay? Can't we go home?' Yara laughed a bitter laugh.

'There's only one way out,' she said, and that's guarded day and night by Alexio the doorman. He's very fat, but he's also extremely strong and nobody gets past him.'

'Anyway,' queried Magdalena, 'where would you go? How would you get back home? Have you got your bus fare?'

'Believe me,' added Yaritza, 'If there was a way we could escape, we would. We wouldn't stay a minute longer in this hellhole. Anyway, the moment we set foot outside the house they'd come after us. We shouldn't get very far and then we'd be beaten,' she added glumly.

'One day I shall escape,' said Yara. 'I only hope it won't be too late.' These last words hung in the air like a wisp of poisonous gas, but nobody dared explain their meaning to Tis, who was too afraid to ask. A thought suddenly occurred to her and she said hopefully,

'But surely it's against the law to keep a brothel here in Brazil isn't it Yara?'

'Yes,' replied Yara, 'but the police turn a blind eye to it. I guess 'The Turtle' gives them money, and we have to entertain several policemen each week for nothing. Besides, it pretends to be a strip joint. I only wish it were,' she added wryly.

At that moment the door opened revealing the Turtle who looked very cross.

'Magdalena, why aren't you in the window?' she rapped.

'Sorry,' said Magdalena sullenly, walking reluctantly from the room to take her place in the shop window on the street, which advertised the pleasures on offer inside.

'What are you doing here Little Flower?' snarled the Turtle turning to Tis.

'Tis is an old friend of mine,' Yara said, speaking up for her. 'May she come and share our room please?'

'I suppose so,' replied the Turtle grudgingly. 'Now get back to the kitchen immediately. Lazy slut!'

Numbly Tis followed her down the dark stairs and through the waiting room into the kitchen.

'Sweep the floor,' ordered the Turtle. 'You forgot to do it yesterday.' As if in a daze, Tis fetched a broom from the cupboard and began to sweep the kitchen. It was indeed dirty, but Tis was too shocked to notice the bits of food and dust scattered over its surface. After the last spider and an unwelcome lizard had been shooed out into the yard along with the crumbs, Tis sat down at the kitchen table and put her head in her hands. Gradually fear and dread began to rise inside her as she allowed herself to think through the implications of what Yara had said. What was she going to do?

'Papai,' she murmured, 'please come and rescue me. Please.'

Later on that evening, when all was finished in the kitchen, she crept into the waiting hall. Several of the girls were sitting on the sofas, and the doors to some of the rooms were tightly closed. Yara was there and gave Tis a tired smile.

'Mine's the bunk by the window,' she whispered. 'The spare bed's underneath.'

And so, Tis joined the whores of the Sparkling Delight Brothel and lay in bed and thought of home, the ache in her heart throbbed as the night sounds of the big city wrapped the sad house in an impersonal blanket of noise.

Somehow life went on. Each day the sun continued to rise, and the air was still there to breathe, but Tis went around in a state of constant terror. Fear had so gripped her being that her mind was almost paralysed. She could think of nothing but the next thing she'd been asked to do. The kitchen became like a refuge, and she worked ferociously all day long, cooking and scrubbing until it began to look much cleaner than when she'd arrived.

'If I'm a good cook and cleaner,' she thought to herself as she scoured the sink in a desperate frenzy, 'they'll let me stay in the kitchen.' The Turtle, who was standing by the open door talking on her mobile phone glanced up, and noticing Tis's industry, smiled a cruel smile.

'Good,' she said to herself as she finished her call and went into the dining room, 'at least the housework's being done properly.' Thiago, sitting at the dining room table reading a newspaper, looked up as the Turtle entered.

'Why is 'Little Flower' still working in the kitchen?' he enquired.

'Because,' replied the Turtle, 'first of all she's far too skinny, and secondly I haven't been offered enough for her yet. I'm waiting for a rich tourist to come. There are several who visit us regularly and they pay much more than the local boys for a virgin.'

'Does she know that?' queried Thiago.

'She knows,' replied the Turtle shortly. 'Why do you think she's working so hard?' she enquired, laughing sadistically. 'And Thiago,' she went on, 'you paid far too much for her. She's thin and nervous. I don't think she'll last long. I've seen her type before. Waste of money,' she added as an afterthought. 'Although,' she continued thoughtfully, 'we might sell her on but I don't think we'd get much for her. She'd better stay.'

That afternoon the Turtle went out again, and Yara and Tis were able to snatch a few moments together on the top bunk.

'It's lovely when the old Devil goes out,' remarked Yara fiercely. 'It's as if the house stops holding its breath. I hate her!' she added vehemently. Tis, feeling frightened and depressed, sat looking listlessly out of the barred window, barely hearing what Yara was saying. Seeing her friend's misery Yara put her arms round her holding her close. 'Listen Tis,' she commanded, 'I'm giving you some of my strength. Can you feel it going into you?'

'I suppose so,' murmured Tis uncertainly, 'but Yara what am I going to do? It will kill me, I know it will.'

'Think of the happy times we had together; fetching the water and the firewood, and even making bracelets,' commanded Yara. 'It'll help you cope.'

'I'd give anything to be back home now,' whispered Tis, 'even threading beads,' she added with a flicker of a smile.

'Is my mother all right?' queried Yara. At this question, Tis stopped worrying about herself for a minute, since Yara's mother had died soon after her friend had left home for Beleza.

'Do I tell her?' she thought, panic stricken. 'No I shan't. Then she won't be sad.' So she answered as firmly as she could. 'Yes, fine.'

'Do you remember the time we were given chocolate by that lady in the broken down car?' Yara queried, trying to think of something else to cheer her friend.

'Yes I do,' replied Tis, brightening a little. 'I saved mine until late in the evening and shared it with Mamãe.' As she said this, such a vivid picture of her mother came into her mind that she buried her head in her hands moaning piteously.

'Tis, Tis what is it? Are you in pain?' queried Yara anxiously holding her close.

'I just want to be at home with minha mãe, [my mother]' whispered Tis in a trembling voice. Yara sat up very straight on the bed and looked down at her.

'Look at me Tis,' she commanded. Tis looked, and saw that Yara's face wore an expression of desperate seriousness. 'Tis, I promise that I'll get us out of here, and somehow I'll take you home again. Just hang on. I will do it. I will, I will.' As she said this she clenched her hands and made her back as strong and straight as a young pine tree. Watching her, a tiny seed of hope germinated and took root in the numbness of Tis's heart. There it grew into a little plant that although small, sustained her through many months of torture. Yara would do it. Yes she would. Yara had always been able to do things.

'Thank you Yara,' said Tis quietly. 'I believe you.'

One evening, after the other girls had gone to the hall to wait for the men to come and hire them, Tis found she couldn't sleep. Usually she fell asleep straight away, worn out with all the hard work in the kitchen, but that night there was thunder in the air, and the room was especially hot and stuffy. Feeling thirsty she climbed out of her bunk and tiptoed to the door. Silently she made her way down the stairs and opened the door at the bottom, meaning to go through the waiting room and into the kitchen at the back of the building for a mug of water. This was the first time she'd been in the waiting hall in opening hours, and she shrank back into the shadows and watched what was happening through the half open door. She saw three of the girls sitting on the couches. They were dressed in loose cotton wraps, which seemed to be their only clothing, and these hung seductively open as they lounged tiredly in dejected invitation. As she watched, the far bedroom door opened and a fat man came out, doing up his trousers as he came. He was dressed in working clothes of jeans and grubby T shirt, and even across the hall Tis could smell the dank reek of stale sweat and dirt that clung to him. His stomach wobbled as he walked and his forehead was wet with perspiration.

'See you tomorrow night,' he remarked cheerfully to the Turtle who manned a desk near the entrance corridor. 'I'll have her again. She's good,' and passing through the corridor he went out into the street. Seconds later Yara appeared from the same room, and sat down on one of the couches where she began to wipe her thighs with the edge of her wrap. Panic hit Tis like an enormous tidal wave. She flung the door wide open and fled across the hall to the entrance corridor leading to the front door of the brothel. The Turtle looked faintly surprised as she sped past and then smiled viciously to herself. Tis hurtled down the passage and came up short behind the vast form of the doorman, Alexio.

'Let me out! Let me out!' she screamed, and beat on his back with her small desperate fists. Alexio turned and looked down at her.

'Trying to escape Little Flower?' he said in menacing tones. 'Not tonight, I think,' and grasping her by her clenched hands half carried, half dragged her back up the passage. When he came to the desk he stopped, the girl still writhing ineffectually in his grasp. The Turtle lent towards them and fixing Tis with her implacable gaze said in a steely voice,

'If you ever do that again I will beat you to within an inch of your life. Do you understand?' All the fight went out of Tis and she collapsed onto the floor weeping uncontrollably feeling utterly helpless and alone. 'Get back to your room,' commanded the Turtle. Slowly Tis got to her feet, dragged herself across the hall and up the stairs to her bunk. Once there she lay rigid in the darkness willing herself to die. However death cannot be summoned so easily but eventually his little brother, sleep, came to her instead, to give her exhausted mind a brief respite from the bitter reality of her life.

Months crawled by and Tis was again in her bunk. She had come early to bed exhausted by the day's cooking and cleaning and was lying curled up on her mattress asleep dreaming of home. Suddenly she was aware that someone was shaking her. Opening her eyes she gazed confusedly at the ugly face of the Turtle bending over her. Thiago stood by the door with a small predatory smile hovering round his lips.

'Get up Little Flower,' commanded the Turtle. Tis climbed sleepily from her bunk not sure what was happening. 'Take your clothes off,' ordered the old woman. Tis knew then what was coming and shrank back against the hard iron of the bunk clutching her shirt around her. Again came the command and the Turtle loomed over her, a dark menacing presence. With fumbling fingers Tis undid the buttons of her shirt and took it off, then her skirt fell to the ground leaving her naked and vulnerable. She stood there whimpering in terror, clutching the cold metal frame of the bunk. 'Wash!' The word stung like a whiplash. Tis stumbled over to the basin and did her best to comply, but her hands were shaking so much that the soap kept falling to the ground. 'Hurry up,' snarled the Turtle, and hard fingers dragged a comb through her hair and smeared her small mouth with lipstick. 'Put this on,' came the harsh command and a cotton wrap was thrust into the girl's trembling hands. Tis slipped her arms into the sleeves and clutched it tightly round her slight body desperately trying to cover herself. 'Out you go,' growled her tormenter, pushing Tis in front of her down the stairs. As they crossed the hall, the Turtle caught hold of her arm in a vice like grip and forced her into one of the bedrooms. Once inside, she grasped the wrap, wrenching it off, and threw Tis onto the bed. 'Lie there,' she ordered in a hard fierce voice 'and keep still if you don't want to be beaten. Open your legs wide. No, wider. Keep them like that if you value your life. Try to look happy for God's sake!' She went out, closing the door firmly behind her.

Tis lay on the bed gazing up at the room's single light bulb, trembling uncontrollably, her stomach knotted and her breath coming in short gasps. She felt utterly vulnerable and alone. No cowering puppy in the midst of a circle of tormenting boys ever felt more terrified and defenceless. The minutes ticked by and she could hear voices arguing in the hallway outside. Was it five minutes, was it an hour? She never knew, but at last the door opened a little way and she heard a loud, coarse, male laugh and a snatch of conversation spoken in English. Then the door closed again as someone entered the room. Tis shut her eyes tightly and held her breath. Footsteps crossed the room and she could hear heavy breathing. Someone was looking down at her. Then large strong hands caught hold of her bent knees wrenching her thighs even further apart and upwards and holding them wide open. Tis held her breath and pressed her back into the mattress to try and get away from the pain but the hands pinned her firmly to the bed. Desperately she tried to wriggle free but it was no good. She clenched her teeth, straining every muscle in her body, her head rolling from side to side in terror but there was no escape. After what seemed an eternity she heard a grunt of satisfaction and her legs were released. The footsteps retreated and the person went out closing the door. Silence. Waiting.

Chapter 7

Aidan left school early because the 'Spring Onion' had a cold and was too ill to teach.

'Good thing too,' thought Aidan. 'I don't want his germs. It's no wonder he catches cold he's so thin.' He had decided to take the woodland route home. This took longer, but it was a warm spring day and the walk appealed to him. So, shouldering his school bag, and stuffing his tie in his pocket, Aidan set off along the track feeling happy and relaxed. The wood looked beautiful now that the trees were coming out in leaf, and the sun shone through their interlacing branches creating welcome patches of dappled shade. He had only gone a short distance when the path made a sharp turn and entered a long avenue of horse chestnuts. As he rounded the bend Aidan stopped short in astonishment, for the way ahead was covered with a blanket of pure white as if it had been snowing. 'No, not snow,' thought Aidan, 'it must be horse chestnut flowers. This would make the 'Spring Onion' feel better.' Coming towards him over the white carpet was a pretty young woman. She was dressed in blue jeans, and long fair hair hung down either side of a beautiful oval face. As he watched, a fluffy black standard poodle bounded out of the trees and fell in beside her. Aidan began to walk forward again and the two passed each other on the path. After a few more steps, he stopped, turned and looked back. The young woman had also halted and was bending down to kiss the poodle's fluffy topknot as it stood looking up at her. Her long hair was falling over her face like a golden curtain and brushing the top of the dog's head as it gazed at her adoringly. 'Lucky dog,' thought Aidan. 'Wish I could change places with you and be kissed by that girl.' He continued on his way, but his cheerful mood changed and restless depression took its place. He thought regretfully that there was not much chance of meeting any nice girls when he was condemned to go to a boys' school. How he longed for a really pretty girl friend. 'At the rate I'm progressing,' he thought sourly, 'I shall still be a virgin when I'm ninety. In any case,' he added disparagingly, glancing down at his long skinny body. 'What girl is going to look twice at me? I've got the muscles of a prawn!'

He was still feeling moody when he turned into his driveway only to see his Uncle Rhys' large saloon car parked behind his mother's small hatchback.

'All I need,' thought Aidan angrily and gave his uncle's tyres a kick as he went past the car. 'I wonder what he wants.' The idea then occurred to him that he could perhaps slip into the house and creep upstairs to his room. 'Then I won't have to talk to him,' he thought, but his mother heard his key turning in the lock and called out as he opened the front door. When he entered the lounge Aidan could see that she was pleased about something as a small smile was hovering round her lips, and she was getting on well with his uncle which was unusual.

'Darling, Rhys has a proposition to put to you,' she said.

'Hello Uncle,' said Aidan curtly.

'Aidan,' replied his uncle, who appeared to be trying hard to look less poisonous than usual, 'how would you like to come with me on my next business trip to Brazil. I could do with the company. You seemed to enjoy it when you came with your mother a few years ago. I'm going straight after your final exams so you won't miss any schooling.' and he looked enquiringly at his nephew. To his great surprise, Aidan found himself saying, 'yes.'

'Anyway,' he thought, 'it'll be something to do while I'm waiting for my 'A' level results, and then it's off to medical school and goodbye Rhys.'

Accordingly on a sunny day in high summer a plane taxied down the runway at Heathrow and took off, bound for Brazil. Aidan, seated next to his Uncle, felt a little flutter of excitement as he watched the airport disappear from view and contemplated two weeks of adventure stretching out in front of him away from the safe company of his mother.

The journey was long and uneventful. For much of the time Aidan watched the inflight films, and Rhys beavered away on his laptop. During their first meal Aidan tried to think of a safe topic of conversation, for he knew from bitter experience that Rhys didn't approve of the way he lived his life, and would have preferred his nephew to spend every night out clubbing. Finally, in desperation he said,

'Uncle, what exactly is it that you do? I know you're a Civil Engineer but I'm not sure what that involves. Tell me.'

'I used to work for a Civil Engineering firm Aidan,' replied Rhys, 'but I've my own consultancy now. You should be a civil engineer,' he added. 'It's a challenging career, long hours but plenty of opportunity to enjoy yourself too. I don't understand why you want to be a doctor,' he went on. 'As far as I can see it's all sick and shit.' Then as a shadow passed across his normally brash face he added, 'and you have to tell people they're going to pop off.'

'I do believe he's scared of dying,' Aidan said to himself in surprise. 'He's not as brave as he makes out to be. How odd.' Their conversation was cut short by the arrival of the air hostess with the meal trolley and after Rhys had finished his food, and drunk his coffee he reclined his seat to its fullest extent, much to the annoyance of the passenger behind, and proceeded to go to sleep. When he began to snore with his mouth wide open Aidan would cheerfully have disowned him. 'Two weeks with Uncle Rhys, I must be mad,' he thought dismally. 'But what does he mean 'enjoy yourself'?' he mused. 'I've never seen him do anything sporty. Anyway he's too fat for that and he's not a culture vulture. So what is it he does?' There was no answer to this question so he began watching another film, glad that he didn't have to talk for a while.

Aidan sat under a yellow umbrella on the wide terrace gazing at the view. The hotel was perched high on a hillside, and down below were numerous other hotels half hidden in the trees. At the foot of the hills ran a broad river, and he could see where this met the sea in a wide sweep of silver and blue loveliness. Ships large and small speckled the waters of the estuary and there appeared to be some sort of port almost directly below him. The sky was a vivid blue and the atmosphere, which was moisture laden, seemed to have a softer feel about it than the air at home. On the next terrace down was the hotel pool where a fountain played, and as the water tumbled back down again the morning sun turned the falling spray into a misty rainbow. Although this was early, there were already a few guests in the swimming pool and a couple of children in costumes came running past him. Aidan had got up because he couldn't sleep. The journey had been a long one, and the drive from the airport a nightmare of honking horns, and manic traffic. At times, Aidan had closed his eyes and gripped the edge of his seat so hard his hands had hurt. However, tired though he was, he'd found it difficult to get to sleep and now he'd woken early. Rhys was still in bed. Aidan supposed that a seasoned traveller like his uncle had worked out how to sleep despite jet lag. He was however, pleased Rhys wasn't there, and that thought made him feel guilty, since his uncle was paying for this trip. He supposed that it was Rhys' loudness and lack of sensitivity that got to him the most.

‘He charges through life like a perpetually aggravated rhinoceros,’ he said to himself, ‘an unpredictable one at that.’ Once or twice indeed, some of the things Aidan had said to him on the flight had seemed to amuse his uncle, but most of the time he'd been visibly irritated. During their second meal he'd also been a little too inquisitive about Aidan's non-existent love life, which had puzzled him. Rhys had never shown the least interest in this before. ‘It's none of his business,’ he thought crossly. ‘What does the fat old fool know about love anyway? He's not even married.’

At that moment a waiter emerged from the hotel, and approaching his table, enquired in broken English what he would like to eat. In a few moments Aidan found a large slice of pink water melon and a basket of hot rolls placed in front of him. As he spread the butter watching it melt invitingly into the warm bread, he began to relax a little and to enjoy the perfect day and the beautiful scenery. An hour later, Rhys lumbered out from the hotel, tousled and sleepy and sitting down ordered a huge breakfast. As he crunched and munched his way through his fourth roll he enquired what Aidan would like to do that day.

'I've got business to attend to, Aidan,' he said. 'Why not take a taxi to the main shopping centre and get the feel of the place again. Do you remember it from when we were here a few years ago?'

'Not really uncle,' replied Aidan. 'You've taken me to several places since then and the shops all seem to merge into one. I need to buy some presents though,' he added, 'so that sounds like a good plan.'

A few days later uncle and nephew were again sitting on the terrace relaxing after their midday meal. Over the estuary a formidable bank of storm clouds were gathering, moving inexorably towards the sun like an invading army.

'There's a carnival in town tomorrow,' announced Rhys glancing up at the darkening sky. 'Let's hope this has gone by then. Would you like to go?' and he looked enquiringly at Aidan.

'Cool, uncle,' replied Aidan enthusiastically. He'd been getting bored with a diet of shopping malls and cinemas. He'd even tired of the beach with its constant parade of bikini clad girls who only served to remind him of his loneliness. If only Jake had been with him he would have spent more time on the bustling streets with their vendors, street musicians and dancers but he'd found these a little scary on his own. The carnival therefore sounded like a brilliant way to pass the time.

'Don't wait up for me this evening though,' Rhys went on. 'I'm going out to a business meal.'

After dinner, Aidan went up to bed. He soon fell asleep but woke about one o'clock in the morning feeling thirsty. His room, which was at the front of the hotel, was dimly lit by the lights outside his window so he had no need to put on his bedside lamp but got straight out of bed and padded across to the wash basin for a drink of water. Wandering over to the window, glass in hand, he glanced out at the road below. As he watched, a taxi turned into the deserted street and to his surprise Aidan saw his uncle get out looking dishevelled and very drunk. He lurched up the hotel steps helped by the taxi driver and Aidan winced as he heard his uncle's loud laughter and saw him stumble against the hotel door.

'Should I go down and help him?' he wondered. However he dismissed the idea saying to himself that Rhys would be angry if he did. So he watched until he was sure the night porter had let his uncle in and then went thoughtfully back to bed.

So the days went by. Aidan was now sleeping well, and waking one morning at the end of his holiday, he lay lazily in bed, hands behind his head, feeling completely at home in his opulent surroundings.

'Amazing! I must have slept for about nine hours,' he said to himself in astonishment 'and if sleep "knits up the ravelled sleeve of care," as Shakespeare seemed to think it did, then it must have knitted me a complete woolly jumper in the night!' Laughing drowsily at his own wit, he climbed into his shorts and t-shirt before making his way onto the terrace for breakfast. 'I could get used to this,' he thought wryly, as he looked round and found a waiter hovering at his elbow with a large glass of iced orange juice on a tray before he'd hardly sat down. Later, Rhys joined him, looking decidedly the worst for wear, and after he had satisfied his gargantuan appetite he sat back in his chair, rubbed his protruding stomach lovingly and asked,

'Like to visit a National Park today Aidan? It's a sort of cross between a safari park and a small wildlife reserve,' he explained. 'Bit like Whipsnade. There's an excursion you can join which takes you there in a bus from the town centre. It'll give you an opportunity to see a bit of the countryside. It's just the sort of place,' he added, 'your father would have gone to. He liked animals, can't think why. I shan't come. Not my cup of tea. Got business to do anyway.' Aidan jumped at the idea, as this was the last full day of the holiday.

'I wonder if he really has a meeting or whether it's the thought of all those animals' he pondered. 'Either way I'm glad he's not coming.'

The excursion started from the city centre, and Aidan got onto a smart tour bus along with a mixture of rich Brazilians and sightseers like himself. He had taken the precaution of grabbing a bottle of water, some chocolate and a snack from the hotel, which he carried in a small backpack. As the coach made its way along increasingly worsening roads, he munched on a chocolate bar and mused on the vast differences between his world and this new country where he felt so out of place and alien. The bus eventually arrived at a large compound where it drew up in a cloud of dust. The tour then transferred to the small, dilapidated buses, which were to drive them round the reserve. These were furnished with uncomfortable metal seats and to make matters worse, everything was covered in a layer of fine red dust. Many of the passengers tried to wipe this away but it was an impossible task and there was much grumbling as they gingerly lowered themselves onto the seats.

'I wish I'd put my black chinos on,' Aidan thought regretfully as he looked at a red smear on his cream trousers. He tried to clean it off with his hankie but this only seemed to make it worse. In the end he gave up and instead looked around him at his fellow passengers. In front of him sat a rich Brazilian mother and her little boy. The latter was about four years old and was dressed in a neat matching outfit of linen shirt and trousers, topped off with an expensive pair of miniature dark glasses. These gave him a rather sinister appearance. Indeed, with his slicked down dark hair, he looked just like a miniature member of the Mafia. Aidan watched him closely as the child pressed his small nose hard against the grubby windowpane. The bus started off and they jolted and bumped their way to the park's special monkey section, passing through a complex barrier, which their guide told them was to prevent monkey escape artists from getting out of their enclosure. They came to rest under a large tree and soon the windows were festooned with monkeys who hung down from the roof and climbed up on the wheels to peer in.

'Are we looking at them, or are they looking at us?' Aidan wondered and was particularly amused by one upside-down monkey who stared at the small child in the seat in front with its tiny face pressed close to the glass. This made the little boy very excited and he jumped up and down on his seat shouting,

'Vai embora, vai embora,' which Aidan presumed was the Portuguese equivalent of "go away."

'Embora would make a good name for you,' he thought to himself and smiled at the small boy's exuberance. Following the monkey enclosure the bus swayed and rocked its rickety way round the rest of the park seeming indeed, to travel several kilometres. Often the animals were hidden in the bushes, but much to Aidan's delight they did see some agoutis and even a giant anteater. Embora greeted every sighting with the same exuberance, which began to irritate Aidan. 'I wish you were less of a pain,' he sighed to himself. 'I'll be glad when we get back and you're home in your luxury apartment or wherever you live. I'd be grateful too for a padded seat and a smooth ride,' he added, wriggling uncomfortably. 'Top marks to the man who invented foam rubber!' When they got back to the entrance compound he was therefore relieved to sink down onto his dust free seat in the luxury tour bus that was to take them back to the city. By now Embora was really tired, and curled up with his head on his mother's lap, he went to sleep, much to everyone's relief.

Aidan sat back, ready to enjoy the journey home in the comfort of the air-conditioned coach. As the bus sped along, he gazed out at the passing scenery and whiled away the time eating his remaining chocolate bars and drinking water from his bottle, feeling relaxed and sleepy. At first all went well, but then he became aware that the tour bus was slowing down and that an odd noise was coming from the engine. Slower and slower it went until at last it lurched off the main highway onto an unmade road and painfully chugged its way to the edge of a large village. There it came to a juddering halt on the dusty forecourt of a ramshackle garage. The driver stood up, mopped his forehead and in halting English announced,

'Bus broken, must mend it.'

'How long is that going to take?' demanded a portly American seated at the front.

'Not long, not long,' replied the driver waving his hands in the air. 'Very quick, one hour only,' and again he waved his hands over his head. Now that the air conditioning was no longer working the bus began to get very hot and, worse still, Embora woke up and began to cry. In desperation Aidan decided he would go for a walk to see if he could observe at close hand, how ordinary rural Brazilians lived.

'It's an opportunity too good to miss, and anyway I can't survive even an hour of cross passengers and fractious children,' he said to himself and set off towards the straggle of houses that marked the edge of the village. In no time at all he'd reached the main street, but even here the houses were well spaced, and everywhere he looked Aidan could see scrawny chickens scratching in the dust and skinny dogs sleeping in the shade. Although it was very hot, a few village boys were kicking a ball around in a half-hearted manner but they stopped when they saw him, and stood and stared until he had gone past. Some of the houses were built of concrete he noticed, but the majority were ramshackle shacks that were obviously homemade. Half way along the village street he came upon a small shop but it proved to be full of boxes and sacks of local food, most of which he didn't even recognise. Nobody much was about, but since it was the hottest part of the day, Aidan reasoned that they were all indoors sheltering from the heat. He wandered aimlessly on, until the houses began to thin out and it seemed that there was nothing else to see. Up ahead however, he could see a large shady Jacaranda surrounded by the last two or three shacks. Drawing nearer, Aidan saw that these dwellings were even more dilapidated than those in the main village and obviously belonged to the very poorest in the community. Still, nobody about. Then a small movement caught his eye at the side of one of the shacks and he strolled over to investigate. He found himself looking down at the huddled form of a young boy curled up in a small patch of shade. His little body was painfully thin and covered in dust and sores and when the child, sensing his presence, turned his head and looked up at him, Aidan was startled to see a pair of huge eyes round which crawling flies clustered. The boy gazed dully at him, but just how long child and tourist looked at each other Aidan was never able to say. It could have been a couple of seconds but it felt like eternity. As he gazed down, he only knew that the spinning world seemed to stand still and become focused on the tiny collected heap of misery at his feet.   A fly buzzed in his ear, a dry, irritable, predatory sound that seemed intensely close, yet infinitely far away.   Never had Aidan seen anything like the utter wretchedness of the small human at his feet.   Nor had he observed such poverty or such desperate sickness and he suddenly felt a deep and overwhelming desire to do something to help. But what could he do?   Then he remembered the last vestiges of water in the bottle in his bag and wrenching it out he unscrewed the cap and crouching down by the body tipped it gently over the upturned face.   The water fell on the child's forehead and trickled down over his cheeks making dark furrows in the dust and grime.   Hot tears welled up in Aidan's eyes as a feeling of utter helplessness overwhelmed him, and putting the now empty bottle beside the little form he rose clumsily to his feet and stumbled back to the village, all thought of rest and shade forgotten.

When he arrived back at the garage it was with profound relief that he saw another tour bus coming down the track in a cloud of dust, and soon all the passengers were transferred to the new vehicle for their return journey. Aidan sat on the coach in a state of shock hardly noticing his fellow travellers who were hot, grumpy and complaining.   He'd never thought that poverty looked like this, and his mind hurled a hundred desperate questions at him.

'Where are the child's parents?   Have they died and left him there?   Should I have done anything about him?   But what could I do?   How, in a country where there is so much wealth,' he thought desperately, 'can things like this be allowed to exist?'   Then the realisation dawned that this was what happened to the very poor in this society.

The city he'd been enjoying was actually an artificially created world: a rich man's playground where the rich got richer, and the poor got poorer, and where, no doubt, there were slums in which even more appalling things happened to the sick and frail. While all these thoughts were swirling round in his head he could see the face of the child in his mind's eye, like a perpetual water mark on his sight, through which the houses on the outskirts of the city swam like mirages.

Eventually the tour bus arrived back in the city centre and Aidan dragged himself to the hotel and out onto the terrace. A waiter brought him a drink, and Aidan looked at the man with new eyes.

'Where do you come from?' he thought. 'Are you coping with life or have you come from a poor village too?' Then his gaze strayed to the pool on the next terrace, where two children were standing under the fountain, letting the water stream over their faces and down across their plump little bodies. What a contrast! Half unconsciously words began to form themselves in his mind and taking a pen and paper out of his bag he began to write them down before he forgot them. He'd been good at English at school, and in moments of stress or joy had jotted down scraps of poetry. He'd never shared these with anyone, as he was sure they were rubbish. As he wrote and rewrote, some of the tension went out of him and in an odd way he felt as if he was doing something positive about his horrible experience. For a long while he wrestled with the words, changing and replacing them until at last he felt as if the poem was as near perfect as possible. In order to get some appreciation of how it sounded he read it over to himself in a quiet undertone.

The Garden Of Sparkling Delight

Which of the sky's legion of
Bright raindrops would I be?

Would I drop into the limitless ocean?
There to ride breaker and spindrift,
Lazing gently in warm ocean currents.
Then to slide down the tectonic escalators of the world
And rupture forth at length in a
Dense carbonated gas cloud?

Or to daintily alight on a
Green-leaf-landing stage,
And diamond-glisten in the dawn light,
A painted beauty by great Mother Nature.
And so to enter the osmotic dance of life?

Perhaps an upland watershed calls?
Haunt of wild plover and smoking mist.
To bounce past rock and peaty pool,
Gravel-shallows and minnow-darting deeps,
To slow town-fringed rivers and muddy estuaries,
Chuckling along the sides of yachts,
Or jetting round the speedboat's screw.

But here's a starving, upturned, dirty face,
Round eyes too huge, patterned with flies and sores.
To trickle gently down that face,
One single, universal tear,
Soothing, caressing, healing.'

He'd just finished saying the poem to himself and was having second thoughts about a word in the last stanza when Rhys eased his great bulk down on the chair beside him.

'Had a good day then?' he enquired. 'What's that you're writing?' and before Aidan could stop him he grabbed his notebook and read the poem. 'What on earth brought this on?' he enquired, as if his nephew had suddenly begun to exhibit the symptoms of measles. Aidan could detect the exasperation in his voice, so he told him of the break down, the village and the sick emaciated child.

'That child really got to me,' he said wretchedly, the feeling of helplessness engulfing him once more. 'I guess the whole country is full of little children like him,' he added miserably staring at his hands and shaking his head in despair.

'Don't give them a second's thought,' snapped Rhys sharply. 'They're only rubbish. Rubbish of the world. He'll be dead by tomorrow. His family will be much better off without him.'

'But he's a human being!' exclaimed Aidan in astonishment, looking his uncle full in the face and searching in vain for some hint of compassion, 'Doesn't that count for anything?'

'Thousands more to take his place,' retorted Rhys in exasperation. 'Just rubbish! Rubbish that's all they are. Don't waste your time on them Aidan. But I can see you don't believe me. I'll leave you to your misguided sympathy and your silly poems.' And with that he strode off into the hotel muttering, 'Poems! What rubbish!' under his breath.

That evening Rhys came down to dinner with a determined look on his face. Aidan didn't notice, as he was still too shocked by the day's experiences. Half way through the meal as they were waiting for the dessert trolley, he gave Aidan his bedroom door key and asked him to fetch a book from his bedside. As soon as he was out of sight, Rhys leant over and slipped some powder into Aidan's glass of wine. Dessert over, he sat back in his chair, lit a cigarette and announced,

'It's our last night Aidan. Why don't you come out with me and paint the town red?'

Normally Aidan would have said 'no' to this request after seeing his uncle's late night return earlier on in the holiday, but unaccountably he'd begun to feel happier as if he really didn't care about anything. 'Let's finish this bottle of wine Aidan,' he continued, 'and then you can decide,' and he looked shrewdly across the table, like a gardener who examines his tomatoes to see if they are ready to pick. By the end of the bottle, Aidan was more than content to do anything Rhys suggested and even the face of the little child had miraculously disappeared from his memory.

Half an hour later, they were travelling in a taxi, which wound its way up the hill behind the hotel and into the poorer part of the city. Aidan, sitting on the back seat, was in a contented haze and wondered idly where the car was taking them.

'Not that I really care,' he thought. 'I don't care about anything,' and smiling happily he lolled back in his seat thinking that Rhys wasn't as bad as all that. In fact, he couldn't really remember what he disliked about his uncle. Sometime later he was dimly aware that the taxi had stopped. Rhys came round to Aidan's door and helped him out keeping a steadying hand under his elbow. Aidan tried to take his arm away but his uncle gripped him even tighter, marched him across the road and knocked on what appeared to Aidan to be a shop door. 'We're going shopping!' he thought happily to himself and waited placidly on the road while Rhys had a conversation with someone just inside. They were then admitted into a hallway where Aidan could see several scantily clad young women sitting in a row on a couple of couches. 'What are they doing here?' he thought. 'Perhaps this is a meeting we've come to, and not a shop after all.' Rhys dumped him on an empty chair and had a long conversation with a fearsome looking woman sitting behind a desk. Glancing blearily at the girls again Aidan saw that they all wore brightly coloured wraps. The colours made his head spin but as he looked closer he was fascinated to see that apart from these garments, they were naked. Sexual excitement began to rise inside him as he glimpsed bare thighs and breasts. 'It's a dream,' he said out loud feeling suddenly more alert than he had all evening. 'I'm going to talk to them,' and he half rose out of his seat. At that moment his uncle came back to him, rubbing his hands together in a satisfied way.

'Go in there, boy,' he ordered catching hold of Aidan's arm once more. Rhys then steered his nephew into a room, and shut the door firmly behind him.

Aidan stood in the doorway and tried to take in the amazing scene that met his startled eyes. On a bed, on the far side of the room lay a young woman. She was naked and lay with her legs apart and eyes tightly closed. To Aidan, in his confused state, it suddenly seemed that the moment he had imagined so many times in his erotic day-dreams had suddenly become a reality. Uttering a grunt of animal pleasure and anticipation, he scrambled hastily out of his trousers and threw himself onto the bed between the legs of the prone female body, totally taken over by his desire to make love to this wonderful dream woman. As the first passionate exultant strokes of his virgin lovemaking began, the girl beneath him began to twist and turn. Without thinking, he grasped the slight body tightly, holding it in a vice like grip and pushed deeper and harder. Then the screaming began. He'd never heard such an awful sound before. It was a high piercing continuous shriek that knifed through his head into the very centre of his brain. Appalled he rocked back on his heels and gazing down with startled eyes at the girl beneath him, saw to his horror that she was bleeding and writhing in agony. Quickly he struggled off the bed, and catching the handkerchief out of his shirt pocket, threw it over the contorted face. At that moment, the door opened and a small woman, one of those who'd been sitting on the couch in the outer hall, hurled herself into the room, also shrieking, but this time in anger. Before he'd time to draw breath, she threw herself on him, and although small, propelled him out of the door and into the waiting room with considerable force, hurling his trousers after him. Aidan staggered across the room and collapsed onto a chair where he lapsed into a state of near unconsciousness.

In the room Yara held Tis and rocked her backwards and forwards repeating fiercely over and over again.

'I'll get you out of here Tis. I will I will!' But Tis was beyond hearing and lay in her arms, broken and violated, clutching the handkerchief over her face, rigid with pain and terror.

Chapter 8

Emily stood in Terminal One arrivals at Heathrow Airport, her heart singing because very soon Aidan would be home again.

'It's been so quiet,' she thought. 'However am I going to manage when he leaves for medical school in the autumn and I have to start disentangling my life from his? Why did you have to die Andrew?' she murmured. 'I need you so much. I don't know how I'm going to cope on my own.' Knowing that the plane had landed and that he would soon appear however, Emily put these sad thoughts aside for the time being and allowed her heart to begin its welcome song once more. At last, little groups of travellers began to trickle out of the custom's hall and she scanned each face excitedly, wondering, as she always did in airports, where all these folk had come from, and hoping that someone who loved them was waiting for them. 'They all look so tired and dishevelled,' she thought as a particularly weary woman stumbled past her pushing a loaded trolley, 'but that's only to be expected when they've been journeying for so long.'

At last Rhys, large and lumbering, came into view followed by the one person in the world she was really longing to see – her son. However, as he came closer she felt a pang of worry, as he seemed more than normally tired. He was also dragging his feet and looked dazed and ill. Reaching up she hugged him tightly to her, sensing that indeed there was something the matter as there was a tension in him that seemed at odds with his obvious tiredness. It was like hugging a taut wire stretched near to breaking point.

'What's the matter with Aidan?' she said sharply, turning to Rhys.

'Oh, he's just a bit weary,' replied her brother-in-law dismissively. 'Nothing a good night's sleep won't put right.'

However in the morning the situation hadn't changed. Aidan said very little when he eventually came downstairs, and after having drunk a cup of tea went straight back to his room shutting the door firmly behind him. It was Sunday, and Emily waited in vain for him to reappear.

'Perhaps he's just very jet lagged,' she said to herself, when she came in from the garden at lunch-time and discovered that he was still upstairs. By the time five o'clock came she was seriously worried so went up to his bedroom and knocked on the door. When she went in she found him lying on the bed, wide-awake, staring fixedly at the ceiling, his face white and drawn. Sitting down on the end of the bed she looked anxiously at him.

'What's the matter darling?' she enquired gently trying to keep the concern out of her voice.

'Nothing much, mum,' he muttered. 'I've just seen one or two things that have upset me that's all.'

'Would it help to talk about them?' asked his mother.

'Well, perhaps a bit,' he replied hesitatingly, and he told Emily about the little boy in the village. 'It was dreadful mum,' he said desperately. 'There was no one there to help him but me. Where were his parents? I think that he was nearly dead when I found him,' he added. 'Should I have picked him up and taken him with me? But, where to? Oh mum, what should I have done?' and he looked at her pleadingly, his face a picture of misery. Emily thought for a minute before replying. She wasn't sure what she'd expected to hear but it certainly wasn't this. What should she say? How could she comfort him? At last she said tentatively,

'I don't see what else you could have done Aidan. You were all on your own. You're not trained to deal with a critically ill child, and you were in a strange country. A doctor would have known exactly what was wrong and what could be done, but at the moment, you don't have that knowledge. I would have been just as confused,' she added as an afterthought, reaching out and clasping his hand reassuringly.

'But I should have done something, anything,' sighed Aidan miserably. 'All I did was tip water over him and write a stupid poem. How pathetic is that?' Emily tried her best to reassure him with every argument she could think of but nothing she said seemed to lift her son's spirits.

'What did Rhys say?' she asked eventually when she saw that her words were not helping. Aidan told her in a voice loud with anger. There was a silence as Emily digested this information then said almost to herself, 'I could never understand how two brothers could be so different. Your father would never ever have said anything like that. He cared deeply about people, all people.'

On Monday morning Emily left for work with a heavy heart. Aidan, who'd been woken by the sound of the car starting, desperately tried to go back to sleep, but each time he closed his eyes he saw either the fly covered face of the sick child, or the contorted body of the girl on the bed in the brothel. Indeed, he had thought about nothing else since Rhys had woken him in his hotel room on the morning of their departure and bundled him into his clothes. All the while his uncle had been packing his case he'd sat slumped on his bed aware that Rhys was angry with him but he'd been too confused to work out why. The first part of the long journey home had felt like a bad dream to Aidan, as although he knew his head was aching badly, he none the less found it difficult to keep his eyes open. His brain indeed seemed to be full of foam, and his legs and arms too large for his body. Gradually, as the airplane droned its way across the endless sky however, his mind had begun to clear and he'd been forced to face the events of the previous night. Where had he been? Who was the girl? Why had she screamed? How had he hurt her so badly? The questions had buzzed round his head like a cloud of hornets. At last he'd turned to Rhys and demanded,

'Uncle, what exactly happened last night?'

'We went to a brothel boy, but you weren't quite up to it,' his uncle had replied abruptly.

'Who was she, the girl in the room?' he'd persisted 'and why did she scream?'

'Just a new whore,' Rhys had said dismissively. 'Don't worry about her. She'll get used to it,' and with that he'd firmly turned away from his nephew and begun working on his laptop.

Aidan had lapsed into silence, feeling black hatred for his uncle well up inside him. How dare Rhys take him to a brothel without even asking him! How had he ever got him to agree to it? Had he been drugged in some way or just drunk? All these and a thousand other questions had swirled round his confused brain for the entire trip home. However, the worse thing of all was that he couldn't get the girl out of his head. Her shrieks still reverberated in his ears even now, and the thin line of blood trickling down her inner thigh had got into his dreams, where it became a scarlet river that he'd endeavoured to dam with his hands, only to fail. He'd woken from one particularly vivid nightmare, where he'd been trying frantically to get help, shaking and sweating. For a long time he'd gazed into the darkness of the night feeling like the poor tormented wretch in Edvard Munch's 'The Scream', who having been chased halfway over a narrow bridge across a black abyss, then sees some terrifying apparition coming towards him from which there is no escape.

Aidan eventually decided that if he couldn't rest then he must get out of the house, so he dressed and set out for the centre of the city. It was a long walk but he felt his head had cleared a little by the time he arrived. Just as he reached the shopping centre with its bustling lunch-time crowds, he heard the cathedral clock strike twelve. Aidan was an atheist and his only experience of religion had been at his Church of England primary school, but the thought occurred to him that he might find some peace of mind in the cathedral, so he made his way into the close and up to a side door that gave access to the building. He couldn't remember the last time he'd visited the magnificent old church, so before going in he stopped and gazed up in awe at the great towering mass of stone above him and then at the line of disapproving statues over the doorway who were glaring critically down over the close. His attention was caught by the enormous flying buttresses holding up the tower and he'd begun to speculate about how much weight they must be bearing, when a party of teenage school girls rounded the corner of the cathedral and crowded into the entrance porch ahead of him, talking and chattering.

'They sound like a flock of angry geese,' he thought absently as he heard their teachers trying to hush them into silence. After they'd gone inside and all was quiet again, Aidan noticed a sign over the door, which read - 'Welcome to the Cathedral church of St Peter and the Holy Indivisible Trinity.'

'Wow! Who on earth are that lot and will they be around inside?' he wondered wryly.

Slowly, he pushed open the heavy wooden door and stepped in. He'd expected the interior to be empty and silent but the reverse was true. It took him some moments to realise what was happening as he observed several hundred teenagers milling around, crowding round tables set up in the nave. The air was filled with the subdued hubbub of their voices and he realised with dismay that the building had been taken over by the local schools for a university fair. Dismally he sat down on an ugly chair near the almost deserted Cathedral shop and thought bitterly that the one place he might have found rest had been temporarily ruined by education!

He closed his eyes, for he was desperately tired. The ubiquitous chatter at once seemed more like the restful murmur of the sea on the shore, than an irritating distraction. The sound rose up to the lofty, vaulted ceiling of the nave where it curled and spiralled round the arches and corbels, and spilled down again in wave after wave of gentle, soothing, anonymous noise. Somehow, despite the presence of so many people nearby, the murmuring of their voices began to sooth him and in the cathedral's ancient womb he fell asleep.

Awakening some minutes later, he stumbled to his feet and made his way along the side of the nave to the quiet depths of the chancel. There were no students here, and the sound of their voices soon began to fade. Around this central area ran a long, wide corridor complete with various effigies and tombs, one of which was being industriously cleaned by a white haired volunteer. On looking closer, Aidan saw that the tomb belonged to Gervaise, Duke of Rouen, who appeared to have been recently renovated, as he was resplendent in bright crimson and silver armour. The scent of polish and ammonia hung heavy in the air.

Glancing to the right as he ambled past the spring-cleaned Duke, Aidan came to a sudden halt, his eye lighting on a most unusual scene. At first he thought two people were sitting by the wall, but no, it was a holy family group - Joseph, Mary and the infant Jesus in his manger. Mary was kneeling parallel to the wall at right angles to the long side of the manger and the baby Jesus, his arms wide open in welcome, was facing Aidan. However the most astonishing thing about the group was that father - Joseph, kneeling at the back of the manger, seemed somehow to enfold mother, baby and manger in a protective, all-encompassing embrace. Aidan stood and gazed at the little group. Then he hunkered down on the step of Gervaise's tomb, his arms round his knees, and scrutinized the sculpture more closely. Somehow the figure of Joseph seemed to represent all the powerful, loving strength of the perfect father. This man was determined to protect, to cherish, and to keep safe both mother and baby. The baby seemed indeed, to be grafted onto Joseph's body in some way as an integral part of him.

'Why, oh why, did my father die when I was so young?' he thought miserably, feeling alone and isolated. 'How wonderful, it would have been, to have had a man like Joseph to guide and comfort me all these years. He would have understood how I feel now,' and his heart went out in deep longing for the protection of a father's love. 'That's what fathers are all about,' he mused, as his eyes filled with tears of grief for what he'd never experienced.

Hastily brushing his tears away, he wandered on a bit further and found his attention attracted by the flickering lights of several small candles. Going closer he saw that this was the place where visitors were expected to light candles and say prayers. There were in fact some of their petitions written out on scraps of paper and stuck to a board with map pins. Distractedly, Aidan read them, feeling sorry for the many people who were so ill. Then he found one that made him so cross, he reached over and detached it from the board. It read,

'Please pray for my husband, Denis. God come to him in these bad days, and help him to forgive me, and to find love again. Amy.' He wondered what Amy had done, although he could guess, and his heart went out to poor Denis. It seemed to Aidan, as he turned the tiny scrap of paper over in his hand, that the answer to Amy's prayers lay with herself. Only she could put things right. No divine intervention was needed at all. How convenient it would be for Aidan if his own troubles could be resolved so easily. Reading some of the other prayers he concluded that many of these poor folk were feeling as tortured as he was.

'Will these prayers do any good?' he wondered? He doubted it very much.

Pondering on the ill health and anxieties of these unknown petitioners caused Aidan's own feelings of despair to surface once more and the merry-go-round of his tormenting thoughts began again. In order to divert his mind, he picked up a blue laminated notice from a pile beside the prayer stand, sat on a seat and read what was on it. This is what it said.

'Father God cherishes every sparrow.
He searches for every lost sheep.
He folds in His heart every lonely child and dries every tear.
May this God, who is like the warmth of the sun, and the strength of
the hills, cherish you, embrace you, and fill your life with His healing
today and always.
Amen.'

'Fat chance,' said his sad heart crossly. 'If God's so clever he can do all that, why doesn't he go and cherish that dying village child?' and he stumbled angrily up some steps, past the flickering candles into a little side chapel and sat down. The seat on which he rested was tucked out of sight of the main corridor and he sat hunched up for a long time, a heap of sad, disconsolate misery, while his soul descended to depths of blackness and despair he'd never dreamed existed. No cherishing God, no warm sun, no enfolding arms, just the pain of guilt and remorse and a desperate longing to be comforted.

Suddenly, he became aware of a touch, light as a feather, on his shoulder. He glanced up to find himself looking into a wrinkled old face, crisscrossed with myriad lines. Straggly white hair haloed a bald head speckled in brown sun spots, and a tortoise neck seemed to grow out of a clerical collar several sizes too large for it. He could see too that the rheumy old eyes, which gazed down at him, were full of sympathy and concern.

'Come with me,' said a deep, quiet voice and Aidan found that his arm was being gently held. He was led through a low door, into a tiny, dim stone cell, illuminated by one high window. The room was sparsely furnished with two wooden chairs and a prayer desk, on which a small pile of books rested. The walls were equally bare except for a picture of the crucifixion. Although the window only let in a little light, Aidan could see that his mentor was a very old emaciated clergyman, dressed in a rusty black cassock. A thin hand, disfigured with arthritis, motioned him to one of the chairs and when the two were seated the old man said gently,

'My name is James, what's your name my son?'

'I'm Aidan,' he replied wonderingly.

'You have a wonderful namesake,' mused the priest almost to himself. 'What a humble, brave and kind man the first Aidan was. But tell me your troubles friend, for you surely have them.' His gaze rested on Aidan with infinite kindness, making him feel that he could trust this unknown clergyman who had apparently appeared out of nowhere in order to talk to him.

So Aidan found himself pouring out his troubles. He told him of the trip, of his enjoyment of the city and its sights, of his visit to the Safari Park and the discovery of the sick, fly encrusted child. And then in a lower voice, and one that halted and stumbled, he recounted the events of the final night, sparing no detail however painful and sordid.

At last he stopped speaking and silence fell between them. After a while Father James quietly said,

'And how do you feel my son?'

'Responsible and helpless for the child Father,' replied Aidan 'and desperately guilty for raping the girl. I've asked myself again and again whether it was really my fault because I'm sure my uncle drugged me, but each time I come back to the fact that it was me. I did it. How could I have done such an awful thing! That must be what I'm really like deep down inside. I can never ever forgive myself Father,' and putting his head in his hands, he groaned.

Silence fell again but it was a healing silence this

time. Aidan was aware that the very act of telling someone all the dreadful things that had happened had quietened his mind and steadied his inner being. Then the old priest spoke softly again,

'Your guilt,' he said gently, 'we can do something about, but your sense of responsibility you will have to work out for yourself. Look up.' Surprised at the command, Aidan raised his head and found himself looking at the picture of the crucifixion. 'Have you any faith?' enquired Father James.

'No, none.' replied Aidan. 'I'm a scientist.' A ghost of a smile illuminated the priest's face for a second.

'No matter, you may not have found God but he will find you,' he replied. 'What do you see in this picture?'

'Why, that must be Jesus being crucified,' replied Aidan looking thoughtfully up at the mangled remains of the young body on the cross.

'What about the other two crosses?' enquired Father James gently.

'Well I guess they are the two thieves aren't they?' asked Aidan hesitantly, feeling unsure of the exact details of the crucifixion.

'Yes they are,' said James. 'One died not knowing forgiveness, but the other one was found by God in the moment of his most extreme need. He could not go to God, but God came to him. Now go and sit in the garden I will show you, and you will know what you have to do.'

Aidan allowed himself to be led out of the small cell, round the outer corridor of the chancel behind the high altar, and out into a beautiful cloister garden, but when he turned round to thank Father James, the priest had disappeared. In the centre of the garden a fountain played, its water sparkling in the midday sun and up above him the massive walls and spire of the cathedral rose up like a vast protecting bulwark. There was no one about, and Aidan, sitting on a bench in the sunshine, felt the deep peace of the centuries seep slowly into his mind. It enfolded him like a soft shawl, placed tenderly round a newborn baby. At last, feeling more tranquil than he had done for three days, he made his way slowly back into the cathedral and sat for a long time in front of the sculpture of the holy family. The white haired spring cleaner and the students had all gone home, and he and Gervaise seemed to be alone together.

'What shall I do?' he said at length to the tiny welcoming baby in the manger. Faint and far away, like the echo of a beautiful chord, came the answer:

'Comfort my world.' And Aidan hid these words in a secret place in his heart and felt strangely forgiven.

Chapter 9

As soon as she had hustled Aidan out of the room, Yara lifted Tis in her arms and staggered through the open door, across the waiting area and up the staircase to their dormitory. Each stair was a challenge, as Tis grew heavier with every step she took, but Yara's burning anger gave her the strength to struggle up to the top and kick open the bedroom door. Once inside, she summoned a last burst of energy, and laid Tis on her bunk. In the comparative seclusion of the bedroom she did her best to care for her by fetching some old rag and wetting it under the tap. Then she gently bathed her friend's bruised thighs. Tis lay on the bed, eyes tightly closed moaning, her slight body rigid and her head turning from side to side as if it were trying to escape on its own to some place of safety. As she attended to her friend, Yara spoke to her constantly in a low voice. It was a one sided conversation alternating between gentle endearments such as a mother would give to a small child who has fallen and injured itself badly, and outbursts of incandescent anger.

'Who do they think they are? These pigs?' she hissed through clenched teeth, her hand shaking with rage as she tenderly soothed battered muscle and torn flesh with a cool compress. 'They buy us like cardboard cups, use us, then fling us away. How dare they!' The door opened softly and there stood Thiago, listening to the tirade. He smiled to himself as he watched Yara at work.

'Come downstairs Yara!' he ordered curtly after a few seconds. 'There's a customer waiting.'

'No,' she replied vehemently, 'I'm staying here. Tis needs me. That foreign bastard crucified her.' Then she looked straight at Thiago and said in a voice white hot with fury. 'This life will kill Tis. You know that don't you!' Smiling in amusement, Thiago padded across the floor and taking Yara roughly by the shoulder pushed her to the door.

'Shut up and come down,' he said menacingly. 'There's a customer waiting.' Being a strong man he had no difficulty in forcing Yara out of the dormitory. He began pushing her down the stairs but Yara resisted, struggling against his hands screaming and spitting at him. The girls in the hall looked up when they heard the commotion, as did a young man who'd just come in from the street. Seeing this, Thiago struck Yara hard across the face, and shoved her roughly down the last few stairs. Holding her firmly by the arm he said to the newcomer. 'You want a challenge mate? Here's one, a real firebrand!' The man looked at Yara and a smile of anticipation lit his face.

'She'll do,' he replied lecherously. 'We'll go to room one,' and walking over to Yara he twisted her arms behind her back and marched her into an empty bedroom. Thiago watched until Yara, still struggling and spitting was safely inside and then, smiling cruelly, went quietly back up to the prostitutes' bedroom where Tis was lying half conscious and alone on her bunk.

'You need to be taught a lesson Little Flower,' he said softly. 'I shall enjoy giving it to you.' Silently he glided across the room to where she lay.

Morning came at last, and Tis awoke from a sleep

that was more like unconsciousness than rest. Gradually the awful memory of the previous night came back to her, as did the pain when she tried to move.

'How can I do this? How?' she said over and over to herself. 'Please let me die. Please, please.' Gradually she became aware that she was clutching something tightly in her right hand. What was it? She uncurled her fingers and found a large crumpled handkerchief, which dropped onto the mattress beside her. Glancing down she gave a little cry, caught the handkerchief up again and looked at it intently. There in one corner were the initials AV, and twining round them were two little fishes worked in blue and red embroidery silk.

'But this is my handkerchief,' she gasped scrabbling under her mattress where she'd hidden her shell, and the hanky that had been put over her face on the beach so many years before. To her astonishment, she found that both of them were still there.

'But these are exactly the same,' she said to herself in wonder comparing them. 'The same letters, the same little fishes. I've got two now. I suppose they must be common where that dreadful man came from.' In a daze, she folded the second handkerchief carefully and put it with the first one back under the mattress.

That day The Turtle was forced to make the mid day meal herself as Tis was too ill to even get off her bunk. Feeling cross and frustrated she hurried around the kitchen preparing the food and pondering on what had gone wrong the night before. After a while Thiago wandered into the kitchen looking for a snack.

'Why are you preparing the food, Tia?' he asked harshly.

'Little Flower is sick,' replied the Turtle shortly.

'Is she too sick to work tonight?' Thiago asked apprehensively, wondering if the old woman had found out about his own abuse of Tis the previous evening.

'I've been thinking about that,' replied the Turtle, 'and I don't think she's ready yet. I don't know what went on with the English boy, as I was in the kitchen while he was in the bedroom. When I came back I found him slumped on a chair with his trousers in a heap at his feet. I had to help him on with them. Neither he nor the fat old man with him said anything after that. They just went. The only thing I can think of is that she was too scrawny.'

'Yes she is,' replied Thiago who knew at first hand just how thin Tis was, 'but do you really think that was the reason?'

'Yes I do,' replied the Turtle. 'That young foreigner certainly didn't like her and I'm sure it was because she's so thin. What else could it be? She's going to have to fatten up before men find her sexually attractive, and besides, I've nobody else to cook and clean at the moment. I don't want to have to pay a woman to come in to do that do I?'

'Why not sell her?' suggested Thiago thoughtfully. 'I've got a friend who's just got rid of one of his girls. She was too ill to work. Maybe he would buy her off us cheaply. But then,' he added, 'I guess she would be too thin for him too and she would be too old anyway. He deals in children, not girls as old as Little Flower.'

'I don't suppose he'd be interested,' agreed the Turtle, 'and I'd still have to find a cook. Anyway there's another thing,' she added, 'after a while we can pass her off as a virgin again to some other foreign pig.'

So Tis had a reprieve, but the next day there was a new cross waiting for her. She'd just carried the pots of beans and rice into the dining room and had seated herself painfully at the table next to Yara, when the Turtle came into the room. Seeing the two friends sitting together she said shortly,

'Sit next to me Little Flower.' Wondering what was going to happen, Tis did as she was told. The old woman then proceeded to put a large helping of food onto a plate and pushing it under Tis's nose said curtly. 'Eat this. All of it.' Tis looked at the mound of beans and rice in dismay.

'I can't eat that much,' she whispered in despair. I'm not hungry!'

'If you don't eat it, Alexio will beat you. Won't you Alexio?' the Turtle added, as the doorman came lumbering into the dining room.

'My pleasure,' he answered in a matter of fact way. 'Eat up. You're as scrawny as a starving chicken. I'm not surprised that foreigner didn't want you,' and he sat down and began to attack his own food with gusto. Both Tis and Yara then immediately understood what was happening.

'If I eat this,' Tis thought to herself in desperation, 'they'll make me be a prostitute, but if I don't, I shall be beaten. What can I do?' Slowly, spoon by spoon, she managed to shovel the food into her mouth. The Turtle watched her coldly like an evil scientist who dispassionately checks a person he is experimenting on, to see how close to death they can be pushed without actually dying.

After she had finished cleaning up, Tis fled upstairs to the bedroom. Yara, who was lying on her bunk, looked up as her friend came into the room. She had been deep in thought and was abstractedly twisting the belt of her wrap in her fingers pulling it this way and that as she tried to think up a way of helping her friend. Tis scrambled up beside her. 'Yara, what am I going to do?' she asked desperately. 'The Turtle is trying to fatten me up. That means I'm safe for the moment but the minute I get fatter I shall have to be a prostitute. Help me please!' and she clutched Yara's arm in despair.

'I know,' Yara replied bleakly. 'The only thing I can think of is that when The Turtle isn't looking, Yaritza, Magdalena or I will take a little food from you. The others will help too as we all hate her so much it will be good to spoil her plans. I can't think of anything else,' she added miserably putting her arm round her friend.

More than a year passed in a succession of indistinguishable, dreary days. Tis cooked endless meals, cleaning and scrubbing with desperate energy in order to make herself indispensable in the kitchen. In the afternoons, Yara sometimes helped her so that the two of them could be together. So the Sparkling Delight began to shine with cleanliness even if it didn't sparkle with happiness. But despite her best efforts in the kitchen and her determination not to eat very much, at last Tis began to look more nubile.

'You begin work this evening Little Flower,' remarked the Turtle casually one day as Tis scuttled across the waiting hall after clearing up the evening meal. She stopped short half way up the stairs, frozen with horror. It had come at last. She'd failed.

A little while later, her legs trembling with terror, Tis crept down the stairs holding tightly onto Yara's hand. Gingerly she sat down on the couch with her best friend on one side of her and Magdalena on the other. Keeping very still she closed her eyes, willing the punters not to notice her. She heard the street door open and Alexio's loud voice saying something she couldn't quite catch.

'Yara,' she whispered, 'someone's coming in.' Yara squeezed her hand encouragingly and Tis heard the Turtle shout,

'Magdalena, go to room two.' Magdalena got up and walked across the hall to the bedroom. Tis groaned. Then almost immediately she heard footsteps approach the couch. Shrinking back against the cushions she desperately clutched Yara's hand. A foetid odour of stale sweat mixed with cigarettes, enveloped her and in terror she opened her eyes and found herself looking up into an eager, lustful male face, glistening with sweat and anticipation. Then the man grasped Yara's arm and before Tis could cry out her hand was wrenched out of her protector's, and she was left on her own. Five minutes went by as Tis watched the entrance corridor in pure terror. Who would come in next? All too soon, a fat middle aged man ambled into the hallway. Tis saw him speak to the Turtle who muttered something to him and pointed across the room. With horror she saw him look straight at her. Squaring his shoulders he came strutting over to her couch.

I'm told you need some lessons Little Flower,' he sneered. 'Come. I'll give you your first with pleasure,' and grasping her firmly by the arm he marched her into the bedroom. 'You won't need that,' he rasped harshly snatching at her wrap and pulling it off. For a long minute he looked appraisingly at Tis, who stood naked, and trembling before him. 'Get on there,' he commanded. With faltering steps, on legs that threatened to buckle under her, Tis went over to the bed and lay down watching in revulsion as her tormentor took off his large trousers and came slowly towards her a cruel smile hovering round his lips. And so, for the third time in her life, Tis found herself spread-eagled with a semi naked male body on top of her. But this one didn't give up so easily as the first, and again and again she felt all the breath squeezed out of her as he thrust her repeatedly into the hard mattress. She felt as if she was suffocating and when at last it was over she drew a deep shuddering breath surprised that she could still breathe at all. She didn't notice the fat man stuffing himself back into his trousers however, as the unaccustomed smell of the semen made her gag with disgust. She then became aware that he'd smeared it over her thighs and even her breasts. Tentatively she touched it with her finger and then, grasping the sheet, scrubbed at it in a frenzy of revulsion. Seeing what she was doing her tormentor said in a satisfied voice. 'You won't get many punters as good as that whore, even though they're younger.' Filled with loathing and trembling with shock, Tis scrambled off the bed as fast as her shaky legs could manage and made for the corner of the room where she brought back all the beans and rice the Turtle had stuffed into her earlier in the day. It lay in a noxious puddle round her feet and it was now the turn of the fat man to be revolted, his satisfaction at his sexual prowess turning to anger. 'You'll never be decent whore,' he shouted. 'I want my money back,' and he stormed out of the room banging the door behind him. Tis slumped down on the floor in a wretched, miserable heap, seeing an endless succession of days and nights stretching out in front of her, black with pain and never ending abuse.

'I can't do this. I can't, I can't,' she murmured brokenly. 'Not even fit to be a prostitute! I wish I was dead. Yara! Oh Yara please come and rescue me!' But there was no friend to help this time. Yara was busy in another bedroom and instead it was the Turtle who came angrily into the room.

'Get the bucket and clear up this disgusting mess Little Flower,' she commanded. 'If you do that again, Alexio will beat you. Then go back to the couch.'

So the night went on, with punter after punter coming and going in a never-ending ordeal of torture. Finally the last one left, and Tis was left lying in total exhaustion on the bed, the smell of semen filling her nostrils; not for her the perfume of tender love, but instead the smell of vicious torment. Trembling and in pain, she crawled up the stairs into the dormitory where she went over to the washbasin and began frantically to sponge herself with shaking hands. At that moment, Yara came into the room. Seeing what Tis was doing she came quickly across and gently removing the cloth from the girl's stiff fingers, began to wipe the semen and vomit away with quick, deft strokes. Looking at her friend, Tis saw that tears were streaming down her face.

'Oh Yara,' she whispered brokenly 'what can I do? I shall die.'

'No you won't,' retorted Yara fiercely catching her breath on a sob. 'Remember, I'm stronger than you are and I'm going to rescue you. They're not going to steal our lives from us Tis. I won't let them.'

But as the days turned into weeks and the never ending abuse continued, Tis did indeed begin to die. At first it didn't show particularly, because it was happening so slowly inside her. Gradually however, she began to lose the power to think and to relate to the other girls, even Yara. Her emotions became numb and cold, and nothing seemed to matter anymore. Her only relief was in the deep, exhausted sleep, which descended like a dark shroud in the early hours of each morning, after the last customer had departed. Eating, washing, talking, all became automatic actions as if performed by someone else who was living in the shell that was her tormented body. Any free moments she had between waking and work, she sat on Yara's top bunk, cradling her shell and gazing out of the barred window above the bed with eyes that were lifeless and traumatised. There were no tears, no cries. The black well of unhappiness where she now lived was too deep for these. Profound, black depression engulfed her and she knew that she would never feel clean again as long as she lived. Her only consolation was the memory of that glorious experience at the seaside when she'd sat in the warm shallow sea and the water had covered her small body, softly and lovingly caressing those tender secret parts which were now being tortured each night by the rough, dirty hands and bodies of her tormentors.

To add to her misery, Tis also had to take her turn in the brothel's window, into which one of the girls was locked each afternoon so that the passers-by could see the delights, which were offered inside. There they had to sit; mere bodies for sale to the highest bidder with no more worth that a chair or a table.

'Smile Tis,' said Alexio threateningly as he pushed her into the cramped shop window one afternoon a few weeks later. 'Just remember what happed last time you were looking so miserable and the old woman saw you.'

'How could I forget,' Tis thought dismally. 'You beat me you bastard.' As if reading her thoughts Alexio remarked,

'Yes, I beat you, and remember I enjoy beating you Tis. Why not give me that pleasure again?' and with a cruel smile hovering round his mouth he bolted the window hatch behind her. It was stiflingly hot, and Tis sat bolt upright, her jaws aching from the fixed smile she was trying to maintain. She didn't even notice the passing crowds or the expressions of the men who leered at her through the glass, their faces distorted by the window-panes, as her mind was empty of all emotion. Suddenly she became aware of a flicker of movement in the corner of her prison and looking down saw a small lizard, one tiny foreleg raised for instant flight.

'Lucky, lucky lagarto,' she murmured to the lizard. 'You're free, and I'm a prisoner. You're clean, and I'm dirty. I'd give anything to change places with you. If I were a lizard,' she thought miserably, 'I would run and run, away from this hateful city straight back home. There I'd live in a crack in the wall and gaze at my beloved family. Each day I would creep out and watch them. Just being in the same room would be enough.' At the thought of her parents and Davi, her eyes filled with tears and her lips began to tremble. Hastily she brushed them away and resumed her plastic smile, but her mind was far away and her heart was as cold as ice.

Chapter 10

The tiny gear wheel dropped onto the floor for the fourth time, and Chinn swore with exasperation. He'd been working on the bicycle now for about an hour, and was feeling very frustrated. As supervisor in the bike shop he got the most difficult jobs to do, and although this meant that he earned more money, some of the bikes were almost impossible to mend they were so old. He stood up, rubbed his back and looked round. The workshop was cramped and smelt of oil, dirt and sweaty bodies. Tools hung in racks on the walls, and the floor had a thin coating of oil all over it, which made it slippery on wet days. Near the door, a couple of trainees were busy renovating old bikes for resale and since they seemed to be working hard, he thought he'd take a short break to ease his aching back, so he fetched himself a cup of water and lounged on an old box by the open street door, his back against the wall of the shop.

The workshop was situated on a steep hill, and Chinn watched the dense throng of humanity that was the poor of the city, toiling incessantly up and down, going about their weary business. His mind turned, as it often did, to his home so many hundreds of miles away. This heaving anthill, where even the weeds had to fight to survive, was in stark contrast to the tranquillity of the countryside where he'd been brought up. He remembered with a sharp stab of homesickness, the beauty of the brilliant green paddy fields near his house and the tree lined tracks, jewelled with wild flowers, over which at certain seasons of the year an ever changing kaleidoscope of painted butterflies fluttered. Imprinted on his memory too, was the breath taking sight of the sun shining through the early morning mist as he and his father walked to their day's work in the fields, and if he concentrated hard, he could almost feel the squelch of the mud as it oozed in between his toes when he paddled along the river's edge. Even the sounds were different from city sounds. Here the rain made a hard unforgiving noise as it bounced off brick walls and concrete roads, beating a heavy-metal tattoo on the corrugated iron roof of the workshop. But at home, it sang a tender song as it caressed the leaves and grass, and sank gently into the thirsty earth. The many miles that separated him from his family seemed like an unbridgeable distance to Chinn.

'I might as well be on another planet,' he thought sourly. Loneliness welled up inside him, a bitter all enveloping ache, and he longed with all his heart, to be back with his family as they ate their evening meal by the light of a flickering oil lamp in the small shack he'd called home for so many precious years. Looking out at the anonymous crowd hurrying up and down the street he realised that the biggest ache in his heart was to be with people he belonged to; his mother, father, his younger brother and two sisters as well as his frail old grandmother. An invisible cord bound them all together and gave each of them a sense of self that was warm and secure. With sadness he recognised that he would never be able to go home again, since they depended on the money he sent them, and even then they only just managed to survive.

However there was yet another thing worrying him that morning. He'd always known he was different, and had finally plucked up the courage to go across the city to a gay bar on the other side of the city on his infrequent days off. He'd tried very hard to hide this from the trainees in the workshop, for he'd heard their conversation about the prostitutes they visited, and the girlfriends they took out on festival days. He knew that once they discovered that he preferred men, his life and work would be a misery and he'd be the butt of jokes and constant teasing. Indeed, only yesterday he'd overheard big, clumsy Bruno whispering behind his hand to the newest trainee, Luiz, and had caught the words 'queer,' and 'poof,' followed by a nasty snigger. When they'd seen him watching them they'd stopped talking and guiltily resumed their work on the bicycle they were repairing together.

'They must have guessed. What am I to do?' he thought desperately as he gazed unseeing at the passing crowds. At that moment a fat, belligerent looking man stopped inches away from him, took a packet of cigarettes from his pocket, lit one and puffing happily continued on up the street. As Chinn idly watched him he crossed over and went into a building that advertised itself as the Sparkling Delight Striptease Club. 'I've seen you before,' thought Chinn. 'So that's where you work.' Indeed in the small shop window he could just make out a scantily clad girl lounging in a seductive pose intended to entice the passers-by into going inside. Luiz had taken great delight in telling Chinn only the day before, that in fact, the place was actually a brothel, not a striptease at all, and he thought wryly that it was a great pity he felt no desire to sample the so called sparkling delights that were on offer inside. Then an idea suddenly occurred to him. It popped into his head and surprised him so much that he sat blinking, his cup of water forgotten in his hand. 'Why shouldn't I go and visit the brothel anyway? No one would know why I was really there. I could just chat to a prostitute and leave. Then Luiz, Bruno and the other lads would believe that I was just like them.' The more he thought about it the more it appealed to him as a way out of his problems. Taking a large gulp of water and smiling to himself, he went back inside to his bike.

That evening, as the trainees were packing up to go home, Chinn casually asked Bruno,

'Are the girls any good in the Sparkling Delight, Bruno? You seem to go there a lot so they can't be too bad.' Both Luiz and Bruno looked very surprised at the question but nonetheless they gave Chinn an intimate description of their favourite prostitutes and how much they cost.

'You thinking of going then?' enquired Luiz, an impudent grin on his cheeky face.

'Thought I might go this evening,' replied Chinn with an assumed air of nonchalance.

'Best of luck,' commented Bruno laboriously winding his arms into what he mistakenly thought was a seductive pose. 'You can tell us all about it in the morning Boss,' and with that the two made their way out of the door laughing conspiratorially together.

Chinn went back to his room, washed and changed and with a pounding heart and trembling legs made his way up the hill to the Sparkling Delight, feeling anything but sparkling. Minutes ticked by as he stood in the shadow of a shop doorway on the opposite side of the road, trying to pluck up the courage to go in. Darkness was falling and the neon sign above the brothel window was suddenly illuminated as somebody inside switched it on. Chinn, oblivious of the traffic and the hurrying crowds, found himself gazing at a gross representation of a half naked woman bent into an impossible pose on the sign, outlined in orange and green flashing lights. For a while he stood mesmerised and repelled by the grotesque, pulsing female body, but eventually he realized that he either had to enter and face whatever was inside, or go home. Giving himself a good shake he crossed the street, pushed open the door, and was confronted by the fat man he'd seen earlier in the day, who appeared to be the doorman. He was sitting on a chair just inside the entrance but ignored Chinn who walked nervously past him into a waiting area. There he found himself facing a repulsive, reptilian old woman seated behind a small desk who silently held out a bony hand for his money.

'Good thing Bruno told me how much these girls cost,' Chinn thought to himself thrusting some notes into the waiting claw.

'Choose who you want,' commanded the crone in a hard, brittle voice pointing to a row of girls sitting on two couches at the other side of the hall. Chinn turned to look at them. His mouth went dry and he broke out in a sweat as he gazed in horror at the four girls listlessly regarding him across the waiting area. They were of different ages and dressed in a variety of loose wraps, but in his panic stricken state they all looked the same. A thousand fearful thoughts chased each other through his head.

'Why have I come? How do I know which one to

choose? What shall I do?' Suddenly he noticed that one of the wraps was covered in a pattern of butterflies, and thinking of the butterflies at home, he pointed at the girl who was wearing it and said in a strangled voice, 'I'll have that one.' When the butterfly girl rose from the couch he could see that she was small and slender. As she walked in front of him across the hallway to the room, with head bent and shoulders hunched, even Chinn, in his agitated state, sensed her weary dejection. Without glancing at him she lay down on the bed and clenched her fists, every muscle in her body taut and quivering. The wrap had fallen open as she climbed onto the bed and revealed to Chinn's startled gaze a figure that was almost childlike in its proportions. Gazing helplessly down at the vulnerable form on the bed, he suddenly realized that the girl was more frightened than he was. Wonderingly he put out a hand to touch her but she shrank back, eyes starting, nostrils flared as a patient, conscious on the operating table, shrinks from the surgeon's approaching blade. Mystified he sat down beside her on a chair and said softly 'Don't worry. I don't want to touch you. Can't we just talk? What's your name?' The girl looked at him in astonishment and said in a surprised voice,

'Little Flower, but my real name is Tis.'

'Where do you come from, Tis?' asked Chinn gently. Tis told him the name of her village and then in a puzzled voice enquired,

'Why don't you want to have sex with me?' Chinn gazed at her, desperately searching in his mind for words that this girl might understand. At last he blurted out,

'I prefer men to women.' There was a silence that

seemed to Chinn to go on endlessly and he looked down at his feet in embarrassment, wishing with all his heart that he was somewhere else.

'But why have you come here to me then?' she eventually enquired when she'd grasped the logic of what he'd said.

'It's because,' he replied, 'if I don't pretend to be like most other men, the boys at my work will make my life hell.' A sudden thought then struck him and he hastily added, 'Please don't tell anyone what happened in here tonight, will you?

'No, of course I won't,' said Tis softly. 'You're in trouble like me aren't you?' She sat up on the bed and, fastening her wrap tightly round her, regarded him for the first time. Chinn, short and stocky with spiky black hair and untidy clothes, looked back at her nervously.

'Please stay a long time,' she pleaded impulsively, 'then I won't have to go back to work so soon.' Chinn was surprised. He'd intended to get out of the room as quickly as possible, but this pathetic request suddenly revived an early memory of a time at home when one of his little sisters was lying ill with a fever. He could still hear her voice pleading with him not to leave her. In an odd way the prostitute on the bed reminded him of that incident and he felt a strong desire to protect this terrified girl welling up in his heart. He looked at her again, deep into her eyes this time, and saw there an expression of intense wistfulness and despair. Rarely had he seen such naked suffering mirrored in a human face.

'Tell me about yourself then,' he said at last, so Tis

poured out the story of her life at home and the reason for her arrival at the Sparkling Delight brothel. As she talked about her mother, father and little brother, Chinn sensed a depth of misery and longing that matched his own. Suddenly there was a sharp knock and the door opened slightly.

'Are you going to pay for another session?' rasped the Turtle's voice. Hastily Chinn jumped to his feet knocking the chair over in his anxiety.

'I'm just coming,' he said through the crack. Turning back to Tis, he muttered hurriedly, 'I'll be back to see you again Little Flower,' then he pulled open the door, scurried gratefully across the hall, and escaped out into the street.

Chinn slept badly that night, and in consequence arrived slightly late at the workshop. Usually he got there first in order to prepare the list of tasks for the day, but on opening the street door he saw that both Bruno and Luiz had already arrived, and were pretending to be very busy cleaning two bikes that had just been repaired. When they saw him they both grinned and Luiz enquired salaciously,

'Had a good night boss? Who did you have then?' and he leered at Bruno, a knowing expression on his face. Recognising that this was a test question, a sense of relief swept over Chinn as he realised that he knew Tis's working name.

'Little Flower,' he replied with an assumed nonchalance.

'Oh her,' sneered Luiz. 'I only have her if all the other girls have gone. She's not much good. They must have been having a busy night. You should try another one next time.'

'That's a good idea,' replied Chinn, privately resolving to have Tis each time he went. To his great surprise, he realised indeed that he actually wanted to go back and talk to the strange little flower, which drooped so sadly in the garden of Sparkling Delight.

The following week Chinn visited the brothel again making sure that he let Bruno and Luiz know where he was going. On his way he bought a bag of sweets from the stall near the bike shop and with these in his pocket entered the hallway and paid his money to the intimidating woman at the desk. Looking her full in the face this time, he announced confidently,

'I want Little Flower.' There were only two prostitutes sitting on the couch and after a quick glance she said harshly,

'Little Flower is busy. Take another. They're both good.'

'No, thank you. I'll wait,' replied Chinn firmly sitting down on a wooden chair next to the desk. Five minutes later, the door to one of the side rooms opened and, to his surprise, out lumbered Bruno followed by Tis who stumbled across to the couch and sat down, looking both hopeless and depressed.

'Hello Boss,' he said to Chinn stopping at the desk. 'Don't have her she's rubbish,' and with a dismissive laugh he sauntered out. Chinn breathed a big sigh of relief saying quickly,

'I'll take Little Flower now.' Getting up he went hastily across to Tis and slipping his arm round her waist, helped her into the vacant room. They sat down side by side on the bed. Fumbling in his pocket he retrieved the sweets and held them out to her. 'Here,' he said gently, 'I've brought these for you.' Wonderingly, Tis took the packet.

'No one's ever done that for me before,' she whispered looking at the multicoloured sweets, and a tiny smile illuminated her face like a small ray of winter sunshine brightening a dark room. Opening the bag she held it out for him to take one. 'Please tell me about yourself,' she asked. 'You heard about me, but who are you?' So Chinn described his mother and father, younger brother and sisters, and his old grandmother who lived with them. He also spoke of his intense homesickness.

'I'd give anything to be back home,' he said sadly. 'In a way I wish I was stupid, but you see I was clever at school so they sent me to do a course in bike repair. Then I came here to Beleza so I could send money back to keep my family. We're very poor.' Tis nodded sympathetically.

'We are too,' she said. 'That's why I'm here,' and an involuntary shudder shook her slight frame and her eyes filled with tears.

'Every day I think about each person in my family and what they might be doing,' Chinn added glumly, 'but I wonder sometimes whether I shall ever see them again,' and he ran his hands through his hair making it stand up on end like a bristly black brush.

'Me too,' said Tis dejectedly. 'I want to know if

Davi is still alive,' and she buried her face in her hands and groaned.

'We both want the same things don't we?' said Chinn wonderingly. 'Look, I'll come and see you as often as I can Tis, so we can talk together. Perhaps that will make us feel a bit better.' With that he began to tell her about the workshop and the trainees, the room where he lodged and the people who lived and worked near the shop. 'If it hadn't been for Bruno and Luiz, he said finally, 'I wouldn't be here. They're not bad lads. Just young and silly,' he added smiling. Tis listened intently to what he told her, realising for the first time since she had come to the brothel, that there was a life outside its walls.

'Please come again soon,' she begged as he got up to go.

'I will Tis,' he replied looking at the forlorn figure still sitting on the bed. As he walked down the hill back to his room Chinn began to plan his next visit. 'I can talk to her,' he said to himself. 'I don't have to be careful what I say,' and his heart felt lighter at the thought.

So began an odd friendship that benefited both of them. They spent many sessions curled up on the bed together in friendly talk, often sharing sweets but also sharing a deepening companionship; two forlorn, sad souls, reaching out to each other for mutual support.

'You're happy these days,' remarked Luiz to Chinn one morning as he caught his Boss whistling while he cleaned some small cogs.

'Oh, am I?' replied Chinn surprised. 'I suppose it's because I've been working so hard I've got a rise. You should try it sometime,' he added looking sternly at the young man. 'But that's not the only reason,' he said to himself. 'It's because of Tis that I've been working harder. I'm not so lonely anymore. Oh yes,' he added under his breath as he turned away, 'It's also because you think I'm like you,' and he smiled a satisfied, secret smile.

Not long after her first encounter with Chinn, as Tis and Yara were cuddled up together on the top bunk, she told her friend about him.

'I like him Yara,' she said wistfully. 'He's as sad as I am but please don't say anything to the others because I promised not to tell a soul. Oh! But now I've told you,' she added miserably.

'It's great news Tis. I'm amazed that one of those awful men could actually be kind. I won't say a word to anyone. Don't worry,' promised Yara. 'I had a feeling you were just a tiny bit happier. Perhaps this is where our luck is going to turn,' she added 'and I'll find a way for us to escape.'

'O Yara, let it be soon, let it be soon' whispered Tis in a desperate voice. 'I shall die if I stay here much longer.'

Chapter 11

The April rain spat viciously against the bedroom window and roused Kirsty from a deep sleep. Drowsily she stretched out her hand for her alarm clock, but as her fingers groped in the half-light, its bell began to shrill.

'Oh no!' she groaned, glancing towards the window and registering the fact that it was raining, 'not six o'clock already, and wet, today of all days!' A thought slowly sat up in her brain, stretched, and announced in a small, satisfied voice,

'Yes, but today's the day. I'm going to be a nurse at last. Real hospital, real patients, real everything!' A tingle of excitement ran through her body and she smiled to herself as she stretched the night out of her limbs. Then a procession of worries sent the excitement right away. They marched through her mind like a long line of monsters each more scary than the last. 'Shall I like it, I wonder? I've been planning for this day for so long, but what if I'm no good? What if I make a stupid mistake?' And worst monster of all – 'what if I miss some obvious symptom and someone dies? That would be dreadful!' These, and a succession of related anxieties, all clamoured for instant attention as she lay in bed staring at the rain making rivulets down the window-pane.

'Don't be so silly!' said her sensible self at last. 'Just get up, put on your uniform, have breakfast and go.'

Three quarters of an hour later, washed, dressed and breakfasted, Kirsty hurried down the road to the hospital, still fretting distractedly about the coming day.

At the entrance she met a fellow student nurse also going to her first ward placement.

'Hi there Nadia,' said Kirsty as they fell into step, 'how do you feel? It's scary isn't it? All that theory and a couple of outside placements don't seem to have done much to calm my nerves.'

'Me too' replied Nadia. 'I just hope I don't kill somebody. What if my hand shakes so much, I can't give an injection?'

'What ward are you on?' enquired Kirsty, as they hurried to the lift.

'Men's surgical,' replied her colleague, grimacing.

'Poor old you,' sympathised Kirsty. 'That's a tough one to start on. I'm on gynae.'

They reached the lift and waited with a group of other nurses for its arrival. Most of these were second or third years who stood in silence, too sleepy to talk much. Nervously, Kirsty checked the names against the list of floor buttons although she already knew that her ward was on the fourth floor. Up went the lift and as the doors opened and closed, the butterflies in her stomach flew in closer and closer formation. All too quickly the fourth floor came, the doors opened for the final time and she found herself walking quickly down the corridor to her ward. By now all the worries were forgotten and a feeling of excited anticipation had taken their place.

The day passed in a constant bustle of things to do. Kirsty was immediately immersed in helping her patients with their activities of daily living such as eating, drinking, checking skin integrity, and the constant round of observations of blood pressure, temperature and pulse. As she was being given her list she noticed that the Sister looked at her closely.

'Why is she watching me like that?' she wondered. 'Does she think I'm about to make a mess of things? Well, I'm not going to,' she added fiercely. 'When I do my report it's going to be perfect. All the care plans will be immaculate and there'll be no crossings out on the charts.' So she squared her shoulders and set off to find her first patient who was a young woman about her own age. 'I'm Kirsty,' she said smiling down at her. 'I'm your nurse and I'm here to look after you.' The woman in the bed, who looked tired and worried, gazed up at her, a small answering smile hovering round her lips for a second.

'Hello,' she said in a weary voice. 'Not more temperature taking.' All went well for Kirsty until the last detail was entered on the chart.

'What if I've filled it in incorrectly?' she suddenly thought in panic, fishing it out of its holder again to check that the name and the information she'd just written down were right. 'Perhaps I should do it all again just to make sure?' said a fearful voice in her head but she resisted it firmly and returned the chart to its place, trying to look as if this was the correct thing to do. 'This will all be easier when I get used to it,' she said to herself, as she glanced abstractedly at the young woman in the bed who was lying back on her pillows, eyes closed. Suddenly into her head came a vivid picture of her mother, who had died of cancer in her last year at school. 'I wish you could see me now mum. You'd be so proud of me,' she thought sadly, turning her head away so that the patient shouldn't see her eyes filling with tears.

When she sat down at last to eat her lunch in the hospital restaurant, Kirsty realised she was very tired. Her feet ached and her mind bulged with all the new information she had to remember.

'That was a hard morning's work,' she said to herself. 'But, I enjoyed it. What a relief!' and she drank the last of her coffee feeling happier than she had all day.

On the Thursday of her final week on the ward, Kirsty was working on the high dependency unit next to the sister's office. In the first bed was a young woman who'd already had three miscarriages and had been rushed in the night before with a threatened fourth. She lay quietly in the bed and, to Kirsty's surprise, was amazingly calm.

'She couldn't be calmer if she were in a hotel room waiting for room service,' she thought as she took her temperature. 'I'm sure I shouldn't be so relaxed if I were in her position.' On the bedside locker was a picture of a handsome, dark haired man. 'Is that your partner?' she enquired.

'Yes,' replied the woman smiling.

'Have you been together long?' asked Kirsty, trying to put her at ease.

'Four years,' came the reply. 'Four happy years!' and the woman seemed to glow with an inner radiance.

'How lovely to be so much in love,' thought Kirsty enviously, who'd been out on several dates in her last years at school, but had found that most of the boys were shallow and immature. 'He's very handsome,' she remarked out loud. 'What's his name?'

'Alex,' replied the patient and smiled again. 'He'll be in after work.'

The patient in the next bed couldn't have been more of a contrast. She was a very elderly, emaciated woman who Kirsty knew had advanced ovarian cancer. She lay in her bed, quite still, looking small and insignificant, almost an irrelevance in this high-tech hospital. Even with Kirsty's limited experience, she could see how ill she was. Her colour was poor, her white hair lank, and her eyes, which were opened and unfocused, seemed dull and lifeless. It was obvious indeed that the little flame of life, still flickering in her body, was having a hard time staying alight. One thin, wizened arm lay on the counterpane, and Kirsty looked at it in dismay knowing that she had to give the old lady a pain relief injection.

'That's really going to hurt her,' she thought to herself and shrank from the task of inflicting yet more pain on someone who was already suffering. The only thing that consoled her was the thought that the injection would give the old lady relief for a while.

She was still thinking about the same patient and the uncomplaining way she'd accepted the injection when she walked to the lift on her way to the restaurant for her morning break. Surprisingly, it was empty when it came, and Kirsty was about to press the button for the tenth floor when a young man hurried up. He'd just pulled a packet of peppermints from his top pocket and as he bundled in, they slipped out of his hand and fell on the floor at her feet. Quickly he knelt to retrieve them and as he did so, glanced up into her face. Recognition flooded his features.

'You're the girl in the anorak on the biology field trip!' he said half to himself. Time rewound to a patch of warm heathland, and the aromatic scent of wild thyme. Looking down, Kirsty saw the same gentle, sensitive face, which had imprinted itself on her memory so many months before. Even the dark unruly hair was still unruly and she found her heart unexpectedly missing a beat.

'The boy with the peppermints,' she said laughing. 'You never did give me one you know.'

'Have one now,' said Aidan cheerfully, getting to his feet and holding out the packet. 'What's your name? I've forgotten what the biology teacher said you were called. Mine's Aidan.'

'Kirsty,' she replied. 'But what are you doing here?'

'Going to the restaurant for coffee,' replied Aidan, as the lift got to the tenth floor and they stepped out. He then looked at her quizzically saying, 'I'm a very new first year medical student and you appear to be a very new student nurse. Care to join me?'

When they reached the restaurant, Kirsty collected her coffee and, as if in a dream, joined Aidan at one of the tables.

'Where are you living?' he asked.

'In a house share down the road,' she replied. 'What about you?'

'Me too,' he said. 'I'm slumming it with another couple of students. Will you be working on the same ward for a while?'

'No. Just until the weekend,' she replied.

'Why don't we meet here for coffee at the same time tomorrow then?' he enquired.

'Yes,' said Kirsty, 'that's a great idea.' And with that they began to chat about the hospital and their respective courses. 'I'd best be going now,' she said at last looking at her watch and picking up her cup. 'My break's nearly over,' and she rose from her seat at the table. Aidan glanced at his own watch.

'Mine too,' he agreed. As they walked back to the lift, Kirsty was surprised at how easily they chatted together.

'Anyone would think we'd know each other for years,' she thought with interest. When the lift came it was nearly full so they had to squash close together. Standing so near to Aidan she felt a little frisson of pleasure run through her body, which caused her to look thoughtfully at his retreating back as he strode off to his next lecture. Still pondering what had just happened she turned and walked quickly back to her ward.

At the agreed time the next day, Kirsty sat at the same table nervously watching the door. Minutes ticked by. Was Aidan coming? Her fingers began to trace patterns in the sugar spilt on the tabletop as she subconsciously tried to calm her anxiety. Relief washed over her as the door opened and she saw him come in, stop, and then glance round the restaurant obviously looking for her. She waved and got up from her seat joining him at the counter where they both collected their coffee. Again the time passed unnoticed as they talked together.

'I'd better be getting back to the ward now,' said Kirsty at last rising. Then to her great surprise she heard him say,

'Are you doing anything tomorrow? I've got a day off.'

'I don't think so,' she replied saying to herself, that even if she had been, she would have cancelled it.

'Let's meet for a coffee then?' said Aidan, naming a coffee bar on the sea front.

'What time?' she enquired.

'How about ten o'clock?' he replied. 'If you give me your mobile number I'll text you if anything crops up to stop me.' They exchanged numbers and it was a thoughtful and excited Kirsty who made her way back to work once more.

'Mmm,' she sighed as she opened the door into the ward, 'I wonder where this is going?'

The next morning found them drinking coffee again, trying to make conversation in a cafe near the sea. The place was crowded, and Kirsty was acutely aware of all the people who were chattering at the different tables. Oddly enough, instead of the anonymity she usually experienced in crowded places she felt as if everyone was watching them. Indeed the elderly lady on the next table had put her newspaper down soon after they'd taken their seats and seemed to be staring fixedly in their direction.

'I do wish we could get away from these people,' she thought desperately. At last, when they'd drunk their coffee she said 'It's a bit crowded in here, Aidan. Why don't we go for a walk by the sea? It'll be much quieter.' However, on reaching the promenade they found that too bustling with Saturday morning shoppers and trippers. Elderly people were also out in droves making the best of a fine day, and several seemed intent on running them down in their mobility scooters.

'Why don't we walk on the beach? It might be safer,' suggested Aidan. 'That last scooter driver had murder in mind.' Kirsty laughed, and readily agreed, as the shore by contrast was quiet. This was not surprising, as it was too cold to swim and the beach was covered with pebbles. The only other people present were a clutch of hardy mothers who were sitting propped up against the breakwaters, while their tough little children dug gritty holes at the water's edge. Kirsty could also see an elderly spaniel nosing up and down among the detritus on the shingle in the mistaken impression it was a bloodhound. The tide was going out and small waves were running up the beach and disappearing into the pebbles with a hiss and a sigh. Seagulls wheeled and screamed to each other, and the air was fresh, stimulating and deliciously salty. The two of them began to wander along by the sea, blissfully unaware at last of the crowds on the promenade. After a minute or two, Aidan looked out over the water to the horizon, took a deep breath and asked,

'So what have you been doing with yourself since

we met on the field trip?' Kirsty began to talk, telling him of her life and her ambitions. She spoke about her father but made no mention of a mother. Feeling that she had chattered too much, she asked Aidan the same question and soon the conversation was flowing freely, and with an ease that neither would have thought possible a few moments before. Gradually their separate histories met and mingled like the confluence of two small rivers, melding together until each felt that they knew what the intervening years had meant to the other.

'Isn't it odd,' remarked Kirsty thoughtfully, in a break in their conversation, 'you and I are mirror images of each other. Do you realise that? I only have a father, and you a mother.'

'Yes I suppose we are,' replied Aidan. 'It hadn't occurred to me.' Why don't we go somewhere this evening?' he added as they turned to walk back along the beach to the town.

'Sounds good,' replied Kirsty, trying hard not to seem too keen. 'Where shall we go?'

'There's a night club near the hospital,' said Aidan. 'We could try that if you like?'

Later that evening, as they sat at a table sipping their drinks, Kirsty began to wonder whether they'd made a mistake in coming somewhere so noisy. The rooms were rapidly filling up she noticed, and becoming uncomfortably warm. Loud music swirled round them like so much acoustic wall paper, and they were constantly being jostled by people pushing past their table to go to the bar. Half an hour passed during which Aidan began to look increasingly desperate. Eventually he shouted above the din,

'Are you enjoying this, or would you rather go somewhere quieter?' Kirsty looked at his face and could see by his pained expression that the music and the loud voices were grating on him.

'I didn't think you were the clubbing type,' she thought. However out loud she said, 'Let's go,' and the two made their way out into the cool fresh air. The wind had dropped and the night was calm and still. Without saying anything they found their feet going once more in the direction of the sea. The promenade was deserted now. The shoppers and the maniac scooter drivers had all gone, and the trippers were safely in their homes. The tide was going out once more and tiny waves crept up the beach to break unseen in the darkness like the sighing of lost souls on the shores of the underworld. Bright pools of light illuminated the promenade, but a few feet out over the water an impenetrable wall of darkness began. There was no moon and clouds hid the stars, so the endless expanse of sea which was murmuring out in the bay, was hidden and secret. Aidan and Kirsty walked to the edge of the promenade and gazed into the black night.

'Spooky! Isn't it?' said Kirsty shivering. 'It's such a deep cold nothingness out there, and I can't see through it. Even here on the prom the lights are only just keeping it at bay.'

'Yes but then,' said Aidan slowly 'if you were to go through that darkness and on and on, eventually the dawn would break and you'd burst out into the sunlight! Take my hand. It'll seem less spooky then,' and he gave a cheerful chuckle. A small cold hand slid into his and he rubbed it gently.

'My, it's frozen!' he remarked. 'Let me see if I can warm it up a bit. Let's walk.'

Later that night, when safely in her warm bed, Kirsty found it hard to sleep. Suddenly she seemed to be heading into a relationship. She felt like someone who is quietly walking down a road, turns a corner, and finds themselves caught up in a fast moving carnival crowd. It took her breath away but she knew she was very glad it had happened.

The days sped by in a flurry of lectures, practicals and study. Aidan and Kirsty spent most of their free time together, and when they were apart, the text messages flew back and forth constantly.

'You must come and meet my mum the next time we have a couple of days mutual time off,' Aidan announced to Kirsty a while later, on one of their many shared coffee breaks. 'You'll get on well with her. I know you will.'

'You don't know that Aidan,' replied Kirsty taken aback, 'she might hate me,' and she remembered with anxiety all those things her own mother had told her about her strained relationship with her in laws.

'No she won't,' he replied emphatically. 'I just know you'll like each other. I'm free next weekend are you?'

'Well yes, as it happens I am,' she answered hesitantly.

'That's decided then,' said Aidan happily. 'If that's ok with you that is?' he added hopefully. He looked so much like a puppy that is trying desperately hard to please that Kirsty laughed and gave in.

'Ok' she said smiling. 'We'll go.'

Emily sat in a patch of sunshine in her conservatory waiting for Aidan and Kirsty to arrive. She felt very anxious. Would she like Kirsty? When Aidan had told her he was bringing his girlfriend home, she had suffered an amazing set of emotions. She was so glad for Aidan, as he was a quiet, lonely person, but at the same time it seemed that a bit of her very being and existence was about to be taken from her. Would Kirsty like her? She had worried and fretted endlessly over how to entertain her and had even bought a new set of matching sheets for the single bed in the spare room. However, all the preparations for the visit were now finished so she lay back in her lounger and closed her eyes. How tired she was. Gradually the sun warmed her as she lay listening to the barely audible sounds drifting in through a partially opened window. The distant sound of a car, the children playing next door, all these made a soothing symphony that gradually lulled her off to sleep. A little while later, Kirsty and Aidan entered the garden by the side gate and peeped into the conservatory.

'Your mother's really beautiful Aidan,' whispered Kirsty, looking at the elegant woman asleep on the recliner. Quietly, Aidan opened the door and went in. Kneeling beside her chair he gently touched his mother's shoulder.

'We're here mum,' he said.

The first ten minutes of the journey back on Sunday afternoon passed in silence as Aidan, who was driving, concentrated on negotiating the route through the suburbs. He hardly noticed the local shops and new housing estates they passed, as he was busy fretting about what Kirsty thought about his mother and his home. However, when they reached the motorway and the car was cruising along, he took a quick glance at her sitting beside him and enquired,

'Well, what do you think then? Do you like her?'

'Yes I do,' replied Kirsty smiling. 'I like her a lot. We got on well together. You know she was just as nervous about me as I was about her. She even told me that she'd bought a new set of sheets for the spare bed because I was coming.'

'Really!' he said in surprise. 'Why should that make any difference?'

'Oh, it's a woman's thing,' replied Kirsty laughing. 'You wouldn't understand, being a mere male!'

'I'm so glad you liked her though,' he said seriously. 'She's very important to me.'

'Has she never thought about marrying again?' queried Kirsty. 'She's beautiful. You know Aidan, I'm surprised she hasn't been swept off her feet by somebody before now.'

'She says,' replied Aidan thoughtfully, 'that no one could ever be like my father, but I'm no judge of that as he died when I was very young. I have a mental image of what he must have been like but I've no way of knowing whether it's correct. You can't tell much from old photos,' he finished sadly.

'I wish you could have met my mum too,' said Kirsty thoughtfully, tears beginning to fill her eyes. 'That can't happen now,' she went on, surreptitiously trying to brush them away. 'But when are you coming to meet my dad? I'm afraid our house isn't as tidy and nice as yours since my dear old dad isn't much of a housekeeper now mum's gone, and I'm not at home anymore to help him.'

Kirsty was quite right about her dad not being much of a housekeeper. The house, when they arrived a couple of weeks later, had a definite lived-in look which appealed to the male in Aidan, perhaps even more than the tasteful feminine home he'd grown up in. Small touches of Kirsty's mother persisted however, in faded curtains and dusty ornaments, like the lingering smell of old potpourri.

'Dad won't be back until this evening,' said Kirsty, 'he's at a business meeting he can't cry off. Why don't we go swimming this afternoon?'

'Ok,' agreed Aidan without much enthusiasm. He wasn't very keen on the idea, but was happy as long as he could be with Kirsty. So borrowing a pair of trunks for Aidan, the two made their way to the local leisure centre.

'See you by the pool,' said Kirsty as she disappeared into the women's changing room. Aidan hurried into the men's changing area and was soon engaged in a tussle with a recalcitrant locker, which ended up eating his pound coin, and refusing to shut. In desperation, he went to look for an attendant, but it was quite some time before he emerged onto the noisy poolside. He scanned the bobbing heads in the water for Kirsty, and eventually located her sitting on the edge of the pool, dangling her feet. Her hair was glowing in the sunlight from an adjacent window and Aidan's heart did a somersault as he looked at the lovely curve of her neck, the sensuous swell of her breasts and the attractive whiteness of her fine skin. She seemed to him like a Dresden china ornament, delicate and beautiful, and he vowed to himself that if their relationship became any more permanent he would treat her with infinite care and respect. Nothing should be allowed to harm her in any way. As he gazed, his mind suddenly flipped to another scene and he found himself looking down at a thin, slight, discarded figure spread-eagled on a dingy bed in a hot, fetid room. Desperately he shook his head to get rid of the image. He then noticed that Kirsty was looking at him, so forcing himself to smile, he walked round the edge of the pool and sat down beside her.

'You look as if you'd just seen a ghost,' she remarked.

'Perhaps I had,' replied Aidan abruptly. 'Let's swim, shall we.' The two slid into the water where Kirsty turned out to be a strong swimmer, gliding up and down the pool like an energetic mermaid. Aidan, who was only really a holiday indulger, splashed around, made one or two excursions up to the deep end, and then propped himself against the side watching her swim powerfully up and down. Eventually she came and stood with him and Aidan was painfully aware of her body close to his in the water. He longed to put his arm around her but was aware that such behaviour was frowned on in swimming pools. At last, to his relief, even Kirsty had had enough swimming and they scrambled out and made their shivering way back into their respective changing rooms.

Kirsty's father had still not returned when they arrived at her home, so the house was chilly and deserted.

'Let's light the fire and have our tea in front of it,' suggested Kirsty. 'It will be a cheerful welcome for Dad when he gets in. I expect he'll be tired and cold.' So Aidan lit the fire, which had already been laid in the grate, while she bustled about the kitchen, cutting bread and raiding the cupboards and fridge for cakes, butter, cheese and biscuits. They piled the food on a tray with a pot of tea, mugs and milk and sat close together in front of the fire on the hearthrug to make toast.

'I don't think I've ever made toast by an open fire before' said Aidan. 'This is a new experience for me. It's great.'

'Oh yes,' agreed Kirsty smiling happily, 'Dad keeps threatening to get rid of the fire but he knows I love it. It makes the room look beautiful don't you think?' Aidan had to admit she was right. In the daylight the lounge had looked dusty and faded but now the firelight had smoothed away the neglect, and overlaid it with a mantle of dancing golden light and shadow. The room had indeed, been transformed into a deliciously warm place of intimate cheerfulness.

'Hush, for a moment. Listen!' commanded Kirsty, and they both fell silent. Then he realised what Kirsty was listening to - the faint crackling, rustling sound coming from the grate. 'That's the fire talking to itself,' laughed Kirsty. 'That's what I used to say when I was small, and I thought, if I really listened hard, I might understand what it said.'

'What would it say if it could talk then?' asked Aidan quizzically. Kirsty sat back on her heels with a piece of bread impaled on the toasting fork in her hand, and thought hard.

'You know,' she mused slowly, 'I think it would tell tales of nomads under the stars, huddled round a bright, sparkling fire for warmth; or perhaps it would remember the days when the coal was a prehistoric forest, and gigantic dinosaurs roamed beneath the branches.' She paused and gazed into the white, hot depths of the fire. 'What do you think it says then?' she enquired at last.

'I think,' replied Aidan, and then paused. 'I think,' he repeated, 'that you look really beautiful sitting beside the fire, waving a bit of bread around on the end of a toasting fork.' Both of them laughed at this, Aidan because he was surprised at what he had just said, and Kirsty because, like most women, she was under the mistaken impression that men only like them when they are immaculately groomed. Just then, there was the sound of a key in the front door, but both were so absorbed in each other and the buttered toast, that they didn't hear it.

The door into the sitting room opened, and Kirsty's father put his head round. The tableau that met his eye was one of cosy, exclusive intimacy. There was his only child, and a dark haired, long legged man, sitting on the hearthrug in front of a cheerful fire, eating buttered toast, with mugs of tea beside them. He drew back his head sharply and stood quietly on the other side of the door breathing deeply, a forlorn lonely figure. However he was also a courageous person so he took a deep breath and pushed the door open with a flourish.

Looking up, Aidan saw a short, bearded, rotund man, with a bald head, framed in the light from the hall. The corners of his eyes were crinkled with a road map of tiny lines, down which the laughter of the years had constantly travelled; the highways of merriment and good humour. The eyes themselves were brown, and the bronze beard streaked with grey. Both young people scrambled to their feet.

'My dad – Stephen. Dad, this is Aidan,' Kirsty said, and the two men shook hands. 'Come and get warm Dad, and I'll make you some toast.'

'Thank you love,' he said simply, and sat down.

Chapter 12

A few weeks later, Aidan and Kirsty were staying with Emily for a short break. Aidan usually felt completely at ease in Kirsty's company, but for some reason, which he couldn't explain, a feeling of restlessness was causing him to be preoccupied and withdrawn so he was not enjoying himself. On the third night he couldn't sleep and in desperation got out of bed, padded over to the window and looked out. His bedroom had a view over the garden but the night was cloudy so all he could see was a vague outline of branches moving in the wind against the dark backdrop of the sky. Again the restless feeling swept over him. It was almost as if he were about to take an important exam. Suddenly he realised what it was. His subconscious mind had been grappling with the question of whether to ask Kirsty to marry him. What was the answer? The thought reared up and expanded in his brain filling every corner of it: a megalith of huge proportions. He returned to bed and lay still and tense, staring into the blackness trying to make up his mind. As the hours ticked slowly by, this single question whirled round and round in his head like a racing car on a perpetual circuit. But as the sky began to pale with the coming of the dawn, he still didn't know the answer.

At long last he fell into a troubled doze, and woke an hour later feeling tense and irritable. The day was cold, windy and wet and Aidan racked his brains for something to do indoors.

'Why don't we go into town?' suggested Kirsty as she sat at the breakfast table spreading butter on a slice of toast. 'I haven't seen the cathedral since I went there on a school trip years ago. I like old churches. They have such a peaceful atmosphere. At least we shall be out of the rain,' she added cheerfully.

'Good idea,' replied Aidan, who hadn't been back to the cathedral since meeting Father James. So when they'd tidied away the breakfast things they drove into the city and soon found themselves in the dim, echoing depths of the ancient church. Aidan was glad however, that this time there were no students to spoil the atmosphere of calm tranquillity.

'Come and look at this lovely sculpture,' he suggested after a few moments, taking Kirsty's hand and leading her up one of the side aisles to the holy family group that had so enthralled him on his previous visit. Kirsty was enraptured, and sat down on the steps of Gervaise's tomb to study it properly.

Eventually Aidan got tired of waiting for her and drifted into the chancel. There he saw a huge horizontal mirror with its reflective face angled upwards.

'That wasn't there last time,' he said to himself. 'I wonder what it's for?' and walking over he peered down at it curiously. What he saw amazed him, for he found he was looking at his own face superimposed against the vast emptiness of the roof. There it swam, like a small boat set adrift on a dark ocean. How alone. How forlorn. Was this how it was going to be forever? If so, he couldn't bear it. At that moment, the road of life seemed to stretch endlessly out into the future and he could see himself, a tiny insignificant figure, trudging down it all alone. But as he stood there feeling utterly depressed and lonely something miraculous happened, for another image suddenly appeared in the mirror and came to rest beside his own. Then a gentle, reassuring voice said,

'Looking at the roof? It's beautiful isn't it?' and there was Kirsty's face smiling at him: a burnished sun to his pale moon. The darkness fled, and a warm comforting glow seemed to seep into every part of his body. Then he knew. This was the reassurance he'd been waiting for and he grasped Kirsty by the hand.

'Come with me,' he commanded, and led her into the watery sunshine of the cloister. Finding a reasonably dry seat, they sat down. There was nobody about, the rain had seen to that, but even if there had been, Aidan wouldn't have cared. Taking both Kirsty's hands firmly in his own and looking directly into her face he said fiercely,

'Kirsty, I've something to ask you. Will you marry me? I can't live without you!' Kirsty smiled gently at him, her eyes sparkling with tears.

'Yes,' she replied simply. 'I can't live without you either, Aidan.'

A while later they ambled back into the cathedral where, to Aidan, it now seemed to be a place of warmth and comfort, not isolation and loneliness. He found indeed, that a deep joyful peace had replaced the restlessness that had been tormenting him all night long.

'Come on. Let's go and have one last look at the Holy Family before we go,' insisted Kirsty, so they made their way across the nave towards Gervaise's tomb. Nearing the sculpture Aidan saw gliding towards them out of the shadows, a dim figure in clerical garb who he suddenly realised was Father James. As he passed them the old man said quietly,

'So you've found her then,' smiled serenely, and disappeared out of sight behind a pillar. Aidan dropped Kirsty's hand and turned to follow, but when he rounded the same pillar there was nobody there.

'Odd,' he thought, 'where did he go?' and he began to hunt for him among some of the adjacent pillars and tombs. Since Gervaise's was directly in front of the holy family he then wondered whether Brother James had passed behind it and out into the nave, but there was nobody there either. Indeed, the cathedral seemed to be completely empty at that moment. After a few frustrating seconds he gave up the search and went back to Kirsty who was still studying the sculpture of Mary and Joseph.

'I'm going to be like that Father,' he said to her, squeezing her hand. 'I want to protect you, cherish you, and live with you forever.' Kirsty turned and smiled at him with eyes full of love and happiness.

Hand in hand they eventually wandered back down the nave and out into the cathedral close where they found that the sun was still trying to shine, making the old flagstones of the surrounding paths look like polished back marble. A range of medieval buildings faced them, as they stood in a happy daze not sure where to go next. Suddenly, Aidan noticed that one was a jeweller's.

'Look over there,' he said to Kirsty pointing. 'That's a jeweller's. Why don't we go and buy an engagement ring?' As they got closer to the shop they could see that it was a very narrow building crammed in between two much larger ones.

'I think that house is holding its breath,' laughed Kirsty when she saw it. 'It's the only way it could ever fit into such a narrow a space.' She paused thoughtfully and then continued, 'Aidan, when we've chosen the ring, can we go back to the cloister and put it on please? After all that's where you asked me to marry you.'

Aidan awoke in the early hours of the next morning and lay wondering not only where he was, but why the bed seemed so cramped, and his back and legs so cold. Almost immediately a jolt of painful joy arced through his whole body as he realised that he was in bed with Kirsty, who was now deeply asleep. He also saw that most of the duvet was on her side of the bed and that he was teetering on the edge, in danger of falling on the floor at any moment.

'The practicalities of making love in a single bed!' he murmured, grinning broadly, and thinking back to the times they'd come across this problem before in his student house. Gently, he extricated himself from the remnants of the bedclothes and went softly along the landing to his own room. He now felt really wide-awake so he padded across to the window and looked out. Unlike the previous evening, which had been dark and cloudy, this was a night of cold, tranquil beauty. The moon was high in the sky, bathing the whole garden in its pale radiance and a halo of sparkling frost outlined each twig on the old cherry tree outside his window, causing him to catch his breath in wonder. Even the grass was white with gleaming rime, and nothing moved in the deep shadow of the bushes and trees. 'How beautiful,' he thought, hardly daring to breathe for fear that the slightest sigh might shatter the loveliness of the scene.

'I think I feel a poem beginning,' he murmured, and wrapping himself in his duvet he took pencil and paper and began to write of his love. But nothing he wrote down satisfied him. Every simile and adjective that came into his mind seemed too trite and sentimental, like an over iced cup cake, and somehow he couldn't find the right words to combine the beauty outside his window with his love for Kirsty. Yet he felt that in some profound way they belonged together.

Suddenly a memory from his primary school days of the story of Adam and Eve in their own perfect garden popped into his head. He didn't believe for a minute that they'd ever existed, but he did recall that the story had impressed him, even at the age of six. He still vividly remembered the large mural his class had created in the assembly hall of the Garden of Eden. His contribution had been a misshapen green bush covered with improbable flowers that had eventually come to roost for a while on the side of the fridge.

'I suppose we must have been doing a topic on green issues,' he murmured. But thinking about the story now, he realised why the writer had imagined that woman was made out of man, as it encapsulated exactly the sort of oneness he felt with Kirsty. 'Perhaps the author had a partner that he loved, like I love her,' he mused, smiling in the moonlight. 'And I wonder,' he pondered, 'if old Adam was more amazed when he first glimpsed the beautiful Garden of Eden, or when he saw Eve for the first time lying beside him?'

After that, the words tumbled out of his brain and onto the paper in a torrent. At last, he put his pencil down and read through what he'd written;

Softly he awoke.

All around him divine sleep hung gently in the air.

The magic hues of Eden wove and scattered,

In the pellucid breaking of another day.

But Adam was unhappy.

His vital sense of unity had gone.

Uneasy, he glanced around to

Sense the cause of his distress.

And then he saw her.

Breathless, he gazed as at some radiant dawning,

Bred of the rainbow shades of jewel shattered sunbeams.

Gently the voice of God stole through the garden.

'She's yours my son.

She was made from you.

She desires to be one with you again.

Adam, reach out and touch the sentient form beside you.'

Amen

And all the birds of Paradise carolled their joy.

Adam had found his mate.

Later that day he showed it to Kirsty. With tears in her eyes, she said,

'I think that's the most beautiful poem I've ever read Aidan. You found me, and I found you.'

Aidan often thought about that particular poem as the years passed. It seemed indeed to perfectly encapsulate that first fine careless rapture of new love; and, although time changed the depth and quality of their relationship, that singing high note of joy continued to sound in their lives like the reverberating clang of the mighty cathedral bell, as year followed year.

Chapter 13

Yara woke feeling very strange indeed. To her astonishment she found she could see bits of her face she had never seen before except in a mirror. She also discovered that her jaw was tender when she poked it. Easing herself carefully off her top bunk, she padded across the bare room to the mirror on the wall where she looked in horror at her reflection. Dawn was breaking and the other girls were all asleep, but there was enough light to see that the face that stared back at her didn't look like hers at all, for one side was grossly swollen. Then she tried wiggling her tongue around her mouth and discovered a painful patch of gum encircling one of her top back teeth.

Yara slipped on her work wrap then went down to the kitchen to get a drink, and think about what to do. She sat down at the kitchen table and sipped her water carefully, grateful that there was nobody about. She'd been aware of a nagging pain in her face for the last few days and now reasoned that she must have a tooth abscess. Thinking back to when she first arrived at the Sparkling Delight brothel, she dimly remembered another girl in a similar condition being taken to the dentist to get the tooth extracted. She felt very frightened at the thought. Would it hurt? How long would it take? These and a hundred worrying questions went round in her head as her tongue continuously poked and prodded the affected gum. Then a daring little thought crept into her brain and she contemplated it with growing enthusiasm.

'Perhaps,' she mused, excitement growing inside her, 'this is my chance to escape and get help for Tis!'

That help was needed was beyond doubt. Tis seemed to get thinner by the day, and had almost totally retreated into some hidden place deep inside. She never smiled, rarely talked, and spent any leisure time gazing into space. 'It's now or never,' said Yara grimly to herself, and began to plan her moves carefully.

An hour later when the Turtle came into the kitchen, she found Yara with her head in her hands moaning theatrically.

'What's the matter with you, Yara?' she enquired sharply. The girl slowly sat up so that the Turtle could get the full impact of her misshapen face. 'Oh Drat! You've got an abscess. You'll have to go to the dentist and have the tooth out. No man would want to pay for such an ugly girl.'

'Will that hurt?' Yara enquired in a quavering voice, pretending to be frightened. 'Perhaps if we wait a day or two it will improve.'

'I can't afford to have you lounging about doing nothing, you lazy slut,' retorted the Turtle tartly. 'Alexio can take you this morning.'

'But how can I go out?' Yara enquired innocently. 'I can't walk through the streets in this wrap. I should look stupid.'

'Stay here. I'll get you some street clothes,' grumbled the Turtle, and Yara inwardly hugged herself knowing that the first obstacle to her escape had been successfully overcome. Coming back into the room a short while later, the Turtle thrust a faded old t-shirt and a pair of grubby jeans at her. 'Put these on, then go and wait in your room,' she commanded.

Trying hard to look unhappy, Yara took the proffered clothes and making a big show of being in agony, drifted slowly back upstairs. As she mounted each step, the excitement that had been growing inside her became almost unbearable and she had to stop herself from skipping into the dormitory. The other girls were still sleeping, tired out from their night's work. Yara had decided that it would not be a good idea to tell everyone what she was going to do, in case someone gave her away, but she knew that she had to tell Tis what she had planned. Kneeling down beside her friend she gently put her arm across the sleeping girl and whispered in her ear.

'Tis, wake up.' Tis groaned in her sleep and turned onto her back. Yara, looking down at her, saw again how thin she had become. The heart shaped face was gaunt, and the high cheekbones were much too prominent. Fear gripped her.

'Pray God I'm not too late!' she thought desperately. 'Tis,' she whispered again more urgently. 'Wake up!' Slowly Tis opened her lacklustre eyes and gazed at Yara.

'What's the matter with your face Yara?' she murmured.

'Listen Tis,' said Yara urgently. 'I've got an abscess on my tooth and the Turtle is going to send me to the dentist this morning. She's given me some outdoor clothes and I'm going to escape and get help for you. Somehow I shall get back home and fetch your father to get you out of here.' For a brief instant a smile flickered across Tis's face.

'Oh Yara, that's wonderful. Tell them I love them so much, so very, very much,' she murmured brokenly, and a tear trickled down the thin cheek and dropped onto the pillow.

About an hour later, Yara and Alexio set out on their walk to the dentist. As they stepped out of the door, Yara realised with a sinking heart, that she knew nothing of the streets that surrounded the Sparkling Delight brothel. She'd only ever seen the immediate view from the shop window, since none of the prostitutes were allowed outside. Alexio gripped her tightly by the shoulder and for an instant she wondered whether she would ever be able to get away from him. However, Yara was both courageous and resourceful, so there was no doubt in her heart that she would indeed escape somehow or other. With a throbbing face and a head whirling with the unaccustomed proximity of so many people hurrying about their daily business, she meekly allowed Alexio to lead her through a maze of unfamiliar streets. Strange smells, loud music coming from numerous bars, and the swirling colours of the noisy jostling crowds left her feeling anxious and disorientated. With irritation she dimly registered the fruit sellers and the shoe blacks peddling their wares, the garish colours of the bright advertising boards and the trundling rubbish carts, as they distracted her from her desperate efforts to remember their route.

'I've got to remember the way we go,' she thought desperately. 'I must avoid the brothel at all costs,' but despite her best efforts she soon became totally confused by the number of twists and turns they made. Her concentration was further interrupted by the constant need to avoid people since she and Alexio, who was now holding tightly onto her arm, took up a lot of space on the narrow roadways. 'Where are we now?' she wondered desperately, 'and where shall I go when I escape? Perhaps I shall be able to get away when we get to the dentist,' she thought at last. However, when they eventually arrived, they were shown into a tiny, dirty consulting room where Alexio sat so close to the only door, that even a mouse could not have squeezed past him. The dentist, a small, furtive man, who knew exactly what Yara was, as he'd done several back street abortions for the brothel, disdainfully extracted the offending molar, wrongly attributing her trembling to the fact that he had not given his patient any local anaesthetic. This was on the Turtle's orders, as she wanted the extraction done as cheaply as possible. He then thrust a small bag of salt into her hand, telling her to wash her mouth out three times a day for three days. Yara thrust the bag into the pocket of her jeans and holding a wad of paper hankies to her aching face, stood looking out of the surgery window while Alexio paid the dentist, his vast bulk still blocking the room's only doorway. He then grasped Yara's arm once more in a painful grip and the two began their walk back to the Sparkling Delight.

'If you're listening God,' prayed Yara desperately as they went down the steep street from the dentist's house, 'please, please help me!'

A short time later Alexio stopped, grunted and put his free hand into the pocket of his greasy jacket, searching for a cigarette. Finding that he had none, he looked around for a place to buy some more. There was a small shop across the road, and gripping Yara even more firmly, he led her across the street and into the shop, leaving the door open. As the shopkeeper handed the cigarettes across the counter, Alexio momentarily let go of her in order to get some money out of his pocket. In a flash, Yara whisked away from him and was out of the open door before he realised what was happening. No Olympic sprinter ever got off the starting blocks with more speed or enthusiasm, for this was a race not only for freedom but also for the life of her friend. Frantically, she dashed up the road and dived into the nearest alleyway she came to. Tearing down it she dodged and twisted in and out of a maze of streets not knowing where any of them went. Behind her she could hear the shouts of the hunt and the sound of running feet. Her heart raced. Her breath came in painful gasps and she knew that she could not run much further. Bursting out of another alley, she momentarily halted to see where she should run to next and to her despair saw that her blind flight had brought her back, like a homing pigeon, to the street where the brothel stood. There was the Sparkling Delight, further up the hill to her right and, as she glanced at it in panic, she saw the back of the Turtle disappearing inside. What was she to do?

Desperately, she looked across the road and saw a cycle repair shop with a man sitting outside the door on an empty upturned box having a quiet mid-morning smoke. It was Chinn. Instantly recognising him, Yara dashed across the road.

'Quick, hide me Chinn!' she gasped. 'I've just escaped and they're hunting me.' For a moment Chinn didn't recognise Yara's swollen face, but after a second light dawned and grasping her by the arm he hustled her inside the workshop. Fortunately, this was empty as both Bruno and Luiz were out delivering bicycles to customers. Bikes awaiting repair were propped up against the walls of the workshop and cans of oil and small parts littered the floor but there seemed nowhere where she could conceal herself. 'Where can I hide?' she panted looking round in despair. For a second, Chinn hesitated then seizing an oily boiler suit hanging on a nail he thrust it at her.

'Put this on,' he ordered. 'Be quick. We'll pretend you work here.' With fumbling fingers Yara scrambled into the overall.

'What about my hair?' she gasped.

'Here's my cap. Put it in that,' he rapped, dragging it off his head and holding it out. 'Quickly, come over here and crouch down by this bike. Rub the spokes with this rag.' Rapidly Yara did as she was told, stuffing her long dark hair into the greasy crown of the baseball cap. Chinn took a step back surveying the scene. 'Rub your hands on the floor Yara,' he directed. 'They're far too clean. Then dirty the back of your neck. If anyone comes in, upset that can of oil and I'll come over and shout at you. That will give you an excuse to cower on the floor away from them.' Taking a last hurried glance round the work shop, he returned to his station on the upturned box, and with trembling hands took out another cigarette. A couple of minutes passed during which Yara's breathing became more regular. Then they heard the sound of hurried footsteps as Alexio lumbered up to the door of the workshop panting hard. Yara's heart began to race and her whole body tensed. She felt an overwhelming urge to turn and look at him but mastered it with a tremendous effort.

'Have you seen one of our girls,' he snarled, stepping inside. 'The bitch has just escaped.' Assuming an air of total innocence that he certainly didn't feel, Chinn replied,

'No I haven't,' and looked straight into Alexio's fat sweating face. There was a long pause. Yara was quite sure that she could feel his eyes boring into her back, so in desperation tipped over the oil can.

'You careless fool!' shouted Chinn. Haven't I told you time and again to put that can back on the shelf? Now look what you've done! That's less wages again for you this week my lad and he moved across the workshop in order to put himself between her and Alexio.

'If you see her let me know.' shouted Alexio, and turning, lumbered out. The two conspirators breathed a collective sigh of relief.

'You're amazing, Chinn!' exclaimed Yara, eyes bright with merriment. 'We really tricked him didn't we,' and catching hold of his hands, she danced him round and round, the joy of freedom welling up inside her and overflowing in ecstasy. At last they both stopped to catch their breath and Yara became serious again. 'What should I do now do you think Chinn?' she asked anxiously. 'I can't go out into the street. Someone from the Sparkling Delight will see me.' He thought for a second or two and then replied,

'We've a back door. You can go that way. But what are you going to do now?'

'I've got to get help for Tis,' replied Yara. 'She's fading away. I must get home and fetch her father.' And she told him where Tis lived. Chinn whistled.

'That's a long way!' he exclaimed. 'Have you got any money?'

'No I haven't,' she wailed looking at him desperately.

'Look,' said Chinn, 'I'll give you what I can. Then go to the bus station and catch a bus home. While you're gone, I'll keep an eye on Tis. I've been worried about her too. She's getting so thin.' The words hung between them and the two looked at each other, both thinking the same thought but afraid to put it into words in case it made the thought come true. Chinn shuddered, fished in his pocket and handed Yara a wad of well-used notes. 'You'd better get going,' he said briskly. 'You mustn't be here when my lads get back. They'd be sure to tell someone.'

Chinn took Yara to the back door of the work-shop which opened onto a small side alley, and gave her directions to the central bus station. Yara took a few steps down the hill her heart pounding with excitement and apprehension. Then she stopped and turned to wave at Chinn who was still standing at the door.

'Thank you,' she called. 'Thank you, Chinn. Look after her,' then she turned and ran down the hill still wearing the oily boiler suit and Chinn's cap. 'No one will ever recognise me in this,' she thought to herself as she sped along. Suddenly the wonder of her escape overwhelmed her once more. She was free and despite the pain in her face, she could have shouted out loud for pure happiness. She felt like a caged bird that had woken one morning to find its prison door open and flown up into the sky to wheel and turn in an ecstasy of joy. She also revelled in the feeling of being her own person once more, in charge of her own body. Rejoining the crowds on the main thoroughfare, she was forced to slacken her pace, but she hurried along at a brisk walk and every now and then her feet, which seemed to have a joyful life of their own, gave a little hop and a skip. Having seen little of the city when she'd been brought to the brothel she looked around her at the shops, the bustling crowds, and the ever moving traffic wishing she had the time to stop and explore.

Her happiness was somewhat dampened however, when she arrived at the bus station and enquired about a ticket to the stop nearest to her home.

'But I haven't got that much!' she wailed in dismay looking up into the disinterested face of the booking clerk when he told her the price.

'Make up your mind,' he ordered. 'Do you want this ticket or not?' There was a long queue of people behind her waiting to be served, so Yara stepped out of the line to think. She stood turning her money over and over in her hands while the uncaring crowds swirled round her. By now her head was beginning to ache as well as her face and she put her hands over her ears trying to block out the incessant noise of the tannoy and the shrill cries of the small boys selling water. Desperately, she glanced round seeking inspiration, but all she could see in her immediate vicinity was a small, bewildered looking family from the country, surrounded by their belongings wrapped in plastic bags, who looked as beleaguered as she was herself. For the third time she counted the money Chinn had given her and realised with dismay that he'd only given her enough to get about a quarter of the way home. At last, she took a deep breath saying resolutely to herself,

'I shall buy a ticket, go as far as I can, and see what happens next.' So she rejoined the queue and when her turn came she gave the ticket clerk all her money, bought a ticket and boarded the bus. 'Surely after my luck today something will turn up,' she thought as she sat down. 'Hold on Tis. Help is coming.'

Chapter 14

The early September sunshine woke Emily on the morning of Aidan and Kirsty's wedding. It came peeping in at her as she lay in bed in her hotel room thinking about what was to come. Rubbing the sleep from her eyes, she got up and went across to the window to see what sort of day it was. To her relief the sky seemed to be cloudless and the hotel garden lay basking in the stillness of an early autumn morning. Opposite her window was a copper beech tree and she became aware of the motionless form of a squirrel looking directly at her, like a small grey sentry.

'This is going to be a perfect day,' she said to herself, trying to shake off the one sad thought that kept returning like a black thread in the gold of her happiness, for she knew that this was the point where she had to give her son into another's keeping, and step back from his life forever. In one way this made her heart ache, but in another respect she felt consoled that a younger woman was taking on the task of caring for him. 'He's so precious,' she said to herself. 'I'm glad there'll be someone to look after him when I'm old.' After marvelling that two such contradictory emotions could be felt at the same time by the same person she gave the squirrel a friendly wave and got back into bed to think about the coming events of the day.

The wedding was going to be an expensive one, not however, because either herself, Stephen, Aidan or Kirsty necessarily wanted it that way, but solely because Kirsty's mother had set aside some of her personal money specifically for Kirsty's marriage. When she was dying the thought that she would be providing the perfect day for her daughter had been a great comfort to her. Because of this, all four of them had decided to respect her wishes and spend the considerable amount of money she'd set aside for the occasion.

Accordingly, after the ceremony in a quaint Norman church, a small party of guests were going to a beautiful, country house hotel for the reception. There they had hired the old panelled library and also the dining room for the meal. The house, set amidst spacious formal gardens complete with ornamental fountains and statuary, was situated on high ground above the river Thames, and it fitted their requirements perfectly.

Emily's thoughts went back over all the arrangements she'd helped to make in the preceding months. She'd indeed felt touched that Kirsty had wanted her advice on her wedding dress, flowers, and the bridesmaids' dresses for her two little god-daughters.

The morning whirled past in a flurry of hairdressers, and last minute arrangements, and Emily soon found herself sitting in the church waiting for the bride to come. Her best friend, Rachael, and her husband Sean were to keep her company so she didn't have to be on her own, but they had not yet arrived so she sat looking round the church trying to impress every detail of it on her memory. In front of her sat Aidan with Jake, his best man, almost unrecognisable in their morning suits. The two had remained friends all through their school days and still met up regularly. Emily had never seen either of them look so beautifully groomed before and thought wryly, that she probably never would again. The small congregation chatted expectantly to each other, patiently waiting for the bridal party to arrive. As she looked at them she was relieved to see that the only toddler present was fast asleep with his head nestling in his father's arms. Glancing up at the carved angels who decorated the cross beams of the ancient building she wondered just how many weddings they'd witnessed over the last few hundred years. However none could possibly have been as beautiful as this one was going to be, of that she felt sure. Five minutes later Rachael and Sean took their seats besides her and they conversed in excited undertones until a sudden bustle at the back of the church alerted them to the fact that the bridal party had arrived.

Soon the glorious sound of the Bridal March filled every corner of the old building, and all eyes turned as Kirsty, dressed in an elegant full length, ivory, lace dress with puddle train and with a short veil covering her beautiful face, walked up the aisle, through a cloud of love and smiles to take her place beside her husband to be. Looking at Stephen as they passed her, Emily realised that the same conflicting emotions were troubling him as had visited her in the early morning hours.

As the last triumphant notes on the organ died away the marriage service began, with the elderly presiding clergyman taking the couple through their vows with the precision of a well-oiled, ecclesiastical machine. After that, time seemed to speed up and hymns, readings and register followed each other in quick succession and before she knew it, Emily found herself processing down the aisle on Stephen's arm. Surprisingly she found herself thinking what a comfortable person he was. The thought had scarcely entered her head before they emerged from the dimness of the sanctuary into the morning sunshine and her heart gave a leap of joy as the bells in the tower broke into a glorious paean of praise which floated over the countryside, announcing to the whole world that Kirsty and Aidan were now, and forever, married.

The photographs were going to be taken on the lawns at the reception so the guests got into their cars for the drive to the historic country hotel. When they arrived at the imposing gates, Emily was amused at how grand she felt as Sean drove up the wide driveway, bright with beds of chrysanthemums and dahlias glowing like jewels in the September sunlight.

'Now I know what royalty feels like,' she thought as they alighted from the car underneath a cover portico. She was however, also conscious that she felt tired and that a lot of the day was yet to come. They were immediately ushered into the library where a middle aged fire burned gently in the grate, while at the same time, French doors were open onto the long terrace which overlooked the large formal garden with its geometric pattern of clipped hedges and flower beds. The ground then dropped away into a steep wooded valley, at the bottom of which wound the silvery river Thames. When the photographs were over and Emily had done her duty greeting the guests, she was glad to escape for a brief moment to relax with a drink in one of the library's comfortable, old leather chairs. Looking round her she thought that the room was the perfect place for a wedding reception. It was both charming and tranquil, which was probably because it had been used as a place of quiet refuge for several hundred years. Huge oil paintings of children hung round the walls, collected by the family who had once owned the house. These, for the most part, were of fat and ill-favoured little girls, and stiff, aristocratic boys. Emily much preferred the two little modern bridesmaids in their matching ivory silk dresses and wide pink sashes who were beginning a cheerful game of hide and seek. She noted with amusement one rosy, diminutive face firmly clasped in two tiny hands with lips that were counting to twenty, while the other small girl took refuge under the long white cloth that was on the drinks' table.

Then the music began. Aidan had told her that two friends of his were going to play, and Emily had imagined some sort of loud modern group. However, there were only two performers, a young woman flautist and a man playing a guitar. The combination was perfect, and she listened, mesmerized, to the beautiful melody played on the flute which glided soothingly round the old room, while underneath the guitar slid from key to key weaving a constantly changing kaleidoscope of deep brown sound. These effortless cadences seemed to wind their way among the guests, helping them to relax after the excitement of the ceremony.

'I'm sure,' thought Emily, 'that those chubby infants and haughty young aristocrats in the paintings, were they here, would be amazed at all this. How just right everything is.' Even the photographer was perfect she thought, as he unobtrusively moved among the guests, trying to capture, as if in amber, the elusive, intangible feel of the day in all its mellow beauty. Momentarily, she closed her eyes. A little while later she became aware that someone was bending over her and opened them again to see Stephen looking concernedly down at her.

'How about a breath of fresh air on the terrace, Emily?' he enquired. 'I do hope you're not too tired by all this.'

'Just catching my breath,' she replied, taking his arm. 'This is a beautiful place for a wedding isn't it? I'm so glad we came here.'

'Yes it is,' he replied and guided her out into the afternoon sunshine. Down in the valley below a light mist was spreading over the river and looking at it, Emily said with a sigh,

'I think your dear wife would have thoroughly approved of everything.'

'Yes,' he replied sadly, 'I think she would.' He paused for a moment, a faraway look in his eyes and then added, 'You must come and stay with me soon you know. We shall both be lonely now our young folk are wed. Would you like that?' Emily surprised herself by saying without a moment's hesitation,

'That would be lovely Stephen. I could see by your face in church that you've the same conflicting emotions that I have about dearest Aidan and Kirsty. How can we be both so happy and so sad at one and the same time?'

After a gentle promenade on the terrace they were ushered back inside and into the lovely historic dining room for a late lunch.

'This beautiful and elegant room must have seen some amazing dinner parties,' thought Emily as she took her seat, 'and no doubt many of the world's great politicians and socialites have dined here. But has there ever been such a joyful occasion before for two such lovely young people? I don't think so.' And so the meal began. Each item on the menu, when it came, was beautifully presented and served, and the guests laughed and chatted and enjoyed the food and the atmosphere. Course followed course and finished with pineapple beignets. When her dessert was placed in front of her Emily thought it looked like a tiny golden atoll afloat on a white china sea. 'What a pity this lovely occasion ever has to end,' she said to herself looking at the happy faces gathered round the huge old table.

'What are you thinking?' Kirsty asked, breaking in on her reverie. 'You were miles away.' With a jolt Emily came back to the present and seeing her new daughter-in-law's radiant face said,

'I was just thinking how lovely you look Kirsty. I think you're the most beautiful bride I've ever seen.'

'I think,' replied Kirsty laughing, 'that maybe you're a tiny bit prejudiced.'

The rest of the day passed in a flurry of speeches and entertainment, and Emily eventually reached the sanctuary of her hotel room in the early hours of the morning feeling very tired. She was too exhausted even to hang her wedding outfit in the wardrobe and tumbled it onto a chair where it hung forlornly, its job done. Thankfully she got into bed, but just as she was reaching for the switch on the bedside light an image of her dead husband, as he had been on their own wedding day, drifted into her memory.

'You'd have enjoyed it Andrew,' she said drowsily to him. 'And you'd love your new daughter-in-law. She's kind and thoughtful just like you. But oh, I miss you so very, very much.'

Chapter 15

As the last few houses of the city disappeared, Yara began to take stock of her position. The fact that she could only get a quarter of the way home troubled her immensely. It then occurred to her that perhaps she could hide somewhere in the bus, so the driver wouldn't see she had stayed on board after her designated stop. However, a quick glance round the interior showed that this would be impossible, since the bus was full of men, women and children and every conceivable hiding place was occupied by their luggage.

'Maybe some of them will get out soon and that'll leave a space where I can crouch down out of sight,' she said to herself, but as the long straight road unfolded in front of them and stop followed stop, the bus became, if possible, even more crowded. Yara also realised with dismay that the driver had an encyclopaedic memory and allowed nobody to go beyond the stop for which they had paid. Sitting next to her, by the window, was a very fat, smelly old man who spent the entire journey eating endless packets of biscuits and bags of crisps out of a large paper carrier bag, and although Yara looked hungrily at him, he steadfastly refused to take the hint. He was however a messy eater, so she was able to pick up and eat the fragments that landed on her lap. She did this ostentatiously, looking pointedly at him hoping he would relent and give her at least one biscuit but it was all to no avail. It seemed, indeed, as if he found her presence offensive as he kept glancing at her and sniffing loudly. The thought then occurred to her that perhaps the old man didn't like the look or smell of her greasy boiler suit.

'Serves him right,' she said crossly to herself. 'Mean old Fatty!'

When the bus arrived at the filling station on the main road, which was near the village on her ticket, Yara shrank down in her seat trying hard to be as inconspicuous as possible. After several passengers had alighted the driver got up, scratched himself, belched and then walked down the gangway towards the back of the bus. When he got to Yara, he grinned evilly, took her by the arm and roughly hustled her out of the exit. Several other would be stowaways were treated in the same fashion and came tumbling down the steps after her like refuse out of an upturned garbage bucket.

The bus pulled away in a cloud of dust, and Yara found herself trailing after a small group of passengers who were walking to their homes in the nearby village. In a very short time they had reached a dusty square, where she saw a ramshackle shop lolling dispiritedly among the houses and shacks. Having nothing better to do Yara wandered disconsolately into it. It was only the third shop she'd ever been to in her life, and was much larger than the one in her tiny village at home. At first she looked at the variety of goods on sale in amazement, not even sure what some of them were, but her curiosity waned fast as she began to realize the perilous nature of her position. Aimlessly she poked about amongst the sacks of beans and rice desperately hungry and thirsty, having eaten nothing since breakfast, which seemed hours ago. To add to her misery her jaw ached unbearably so she cradled it in her hand to try and ease the pain. Not knowing what to do she began to make her way out of the shop but had to stand aside for a tired looking woman, who stared at Yara's odd clothes with interest.

'Please, where is the nearest tap?' asked the girl in desperation.

'There's one outside,' replied the woman, pointing back the way she'd just come. Yara drank eagerly from the rusty tap poking out of the shop wall and her thirst satisfied, wandered off into a maze of poor dwellings. She felt almost too tired even to think. All the adrenaline-fuelled energy of the morning had evaporated leaving her feeling shaky and dispirited.

Dusk was falling and the sun was setting gently in the west in a mellow, golden haze. Gradually the sky darkened to velvet black and a breeze brushed away the last vestiges of the scorching heat of the day. Yara shivered, and was glad of the greasy overall. As she stumbled aimlessly down an alley, little lights came on in some of the shacks and from a larger building nearby she heard the harsh sound of raucous laughter and drunken shouting. Overcome by extreme weariness she eventually squatted down, out of the breeze in the angle made by two walls, holding her aching face in her cupped hands. Desperately she tried to work out a plan but her brain seemed to be functioning in slow motion. Most of the time all it would do was to replay scenes from her dramatic escape. She felt again her terror as she fled down the narrow alleys desperately trying to get away from Alexio and always, as if burned onto her retina, she could see Tis's tortured face, which seemed, in her weariness, to be entirely composed of two sad, lifeless eyes. Sleep overwhelmed her at last, and she relaxed on the bare ground in an untidy sprawl.

A few hours later, she was roughly awakened by a heavy body falling on top of her, and the sound of angry swearing. Yara screamed and struggled to her feet. Looking down she saw, by the light of the moon, a dishevelled man sitting in the dirt rubbing his elbow.

'Fool!' he bellowed, getting up with difficulty. 'What are you lying there for? You nearly killed me!'

'I'm lying here because I've nowhere else to go, you stupid man,' Yara yelled back angrily.

'Why don't you go home?' he questioned loudly, still rattled by his unexpected fall.

'I can't go home. It's miles away,' snapped Yara. 'I've run out of money and I don't know anyone here.' There was a pause before the man said more quietly,

'You'd better come home with me and sleep on my porch then. It'll be safer. Come!' Yara stumbled after him trying to keep up, as the two wove their way in and out of the houses, along alleyways full of potholes and over patches of uneven waste ground. At last they stopped. By now the moon had gone behind a bank of clouds and it was very dark but she could just discern the indistinct shape of a house directly ahead of them. 'In here,' grunted the man quietly and Yara stumbled hesitatingly up a couple of steps onto what she supposed must be the porch. She stood still wondering what was going to happen next. 'Sleep here,' he whispered. 'I'll bring you something to lie on.' Returning a few moments later he spread an old sack on the floor. Gratefully, Yara sank down on her uncomfortable bed and immediately fell fast asleep again. 'Mmm, I wonder what I've caught?'

muttered the man thoughtfully, and turning, went quietly inside.

Yara awoke the next morning as the first strong rays of sunshine spilled over the eastern horizon. Blearily she opened her eyes and sat up.

'Oh-oo! I ache all over,' she groaned, stretching and rubbing her shoulders. 'I must be getting soft. That's what comes of living in a brothel for so long!' Looking round she discovered that she was indeed sitting on the porch of a decrepit two-roomed shack. Framed in the doorway was the man who had brought her there the night before. He was about thirty years old, stocky but very untidy with a shock of ill-kempt black hair and a three-day growth of stubble. They eyed each other warily. Silence hung between them.

'Why are you wearing an overall?' said the man at last. 'Are you some sort of mechanic?' and he laughed unpleasantly at his attempt at humour.

'Mind your own business,' retorted Yara crossly.

'What are you going to do now?' he questioned.

'I don't know,' snapped Yara. 'I told you last night I've no money left. I'm stranded,' she added miserably.

'You could stay and help me for a while,' said the man looking at her searchingly. 'My wife's sick and I've three children. I'll feed you, but that's all I can afford. My name is Guilherme,' he added. Yara was astonished at his suggestion but it seemed like a temporary solution to her problems.

'What's the matter with her?' she enquired.

'Come and see,' replied Guilherme and beckoned her inside the house. The first room, which was the family's living room, was sparsely furnished with a table, four old wooden chairs and a stove. It was also very dirty. Pulling aside a dividing curtain, he motioned Yara into the inner room where she saw three boys of varying sizes lying on a mattress on the floor. Their ages seemed to range from about two to ten years old and they were all fast asleep in a jumbled heap, their arms and legs flung out this way and that. On a narrow bed lay their mother. Yara could see immediately that something was badly wrong with the woman from the way in which her limbs were arranged under the thin cover. She too was asleep, but whereas the boys slept the peaceful, relaxed sleep of childhood the mother moved restlessly on her bed making little moaning sounds. Guilherme let the curtain drop into place and motioned Yara back onto the porch.

'What's the matter with her?' repeated Yara.

'Until two months ago,' replied Guilherme, 'all of us, except my youngest son, worked on the plantation. Then my wife, Sancha, had an accident. She fell off the back of the lorry that was taking us to work. She seems to have done something bad to her hip and leg and is in constant pain, but we have no money to pay for the medicine the hospital says she needs. She's been lying here ever since with no one to care for her or Pedro. If you can help I can feed you as I said, but nothing more. What d'you say?' and he looked questioningly at his unexpected guest.

'I'll help,' answered Yara slowly, thinking that she

really had no choice. 'Show me what to do.' As they were returning to the outer room, Guilherme asked rudely,

'Do you have to wear that dirty overall? I'm not going outside with you looking like that.'

'No,' replied Yara shortly, tugging it off and hanging it over one of the chairs.

'Come then. I'll show you the tap and where the food is kept,' he said first taking her to the food cupboard and then to the nearest tap at the end of the street.

'What do I do about your wife?' Yara demanded as they carried a bucket of water between them back to the house.

'There's nothing you can do except give her a drink,' he replied shortly. 'She moans all day long. Drives me mad,' and he shook his head as if to get rid of a bad dream. By the time Guilherme and his two older sons had set off for work Yara had to agree with him, as Sancha groaned and complained constantly. Since there was nothing she could do to help the invalid her only option was to try and ignore the whining voice, which continually buzzed round her head like an irritating fly.

'I'll scream if I can't get away from this noise,' she said to herself at last. 'I can't stand it any longer. I know, I'll take Pedro to the tap and give him a wash. He needs it.' Taking the small boy firmly by the hand, the two walked together to the end of the street where Yara squatted down in the dust, thankful to have some peace and quiet at last. For the first time for many hours she began to relax as she watched the toddler excitedly holding his hands under the running water and then throwing it up into the air where it sparkled in the sunlight. His squeals of delight were the nicest sound she'd heard for a long time. 'And my face is back to normal and the pain is nearly gone,' she thought happily, gingerly giving her jaw an experimental poke.

Two days passed, but Yara was no nearer her home than she had been when the bus had deposited her at the filling station on the highway. Desperately she cudgelled her brain as she went about her chores, trying to think of ways of getting money for the rest of her journey, but no inspiration came to her.

'Well, at least things can't get much worse,' she thought wryly as she scoured the cooking pot one evening. However, little did she know that events were about to take a definite downward turn.

One night, as Yara lay asleep on her sack, now in the outer room, she awoke to feel hot breath on her cheek and turning saw, by the moon's light, that Guilherme was kneeling over her looking like a dog who has scented a bitch.

'What are you doing here?' she hissed. 'Get back to bed.'

'Not so fast little lady,' came Guilherme's answering whisper. 'You cost a lot to feed. I need some repayment.' Before Yara could move he had grabbed her with one hand and forced her onto her back. She knew it was pointless to resist. Anyway, all rebellion had been beaten out of her by Alexio, long ago.

'This is like being back at the brothel,' she reflected drearily as Guilherme roughly abused her body.

'I thought I'd left that behind,' and she longed for the comfort of a mattress beneath her to cushion her back as it was repeatedly thrust against the hard floor. At last, with one final animal grunt, he lay still beside her, licking his lips.

'I'll be back,' he hissed scrambling to his feet and tiptoeing into the bedroom.

'Yes, I bet you will be,' she thought desperately. 'I must get away. I must! I must! But how?' However Yara was right in her surmise and repeatedly in the nights that followed, she woke to find her loathsome benefactor pawing at her breasts.

One evening, after their meal, Guilherme took Yara by the arm and led her out onto the porch.

'Now what!' Yara muttered under her breath. 'What's he up to?' The man, obviously embarrassed, cleared his throat several times, looked down at his feet and mumbled,

'I've got a friend coming this evening. Be kind to him Yara.' Yara's heart sank. She knew very well what this meant. Guilherme had suddenly realized that he could make money selling her body to the men of the village. She also knew that she was powerless to resist. So began further weeks of misery. In the day she cooked, cleaned and looked after Pedro while trying to ignore Sancha's constant wailing, and for much of the evening she serviced the men of the village who crept into the outer room one by one to abuse her.

She awoke one morning, after a particularly busy night, feeling that life was unendurable. She was no nearer getting help for Tis and, if anything, her own situation had become worse than it had been in the brothel. She felt that she was fast sliding into a black pit of despair and that soon she would not care what was done to her, or by whom. Life stretched out in front of her to be measured by a constant stream of men demanding her body standing one behind the other in a never-ending queue.

'God help me!' she cried out loud but there was no one there to listen to her pleading. After completing the morning chores she left Pedro asleep and Sancha still moaning, and walked out into the street desperate to get away from the house for a while. Wandering about the village in a dull stupor she found herself outside the shop in the square where she stood drearily observing the constant stream of people coming and going. As she watched, a bus pulled up outside. Several folk got out including the driver who went into the shop. Other passengers followed to buy things they found they needed for their journey. One by one they came out again eating and chattering happily to each other and the bus drew away in a cloud of dust. Yara stared after it wishing with all her heart that she could be part of the cheerful crowd being whisked away to their homes and families.

'Come on Yara!' she muttered giving herself a reproving shake, 'there has to be something you can do to get the money to buy your ticket. Think girl, think.' Then she turned and walked resolutely back to Guilherme's house.

That evening Yara took one of the family's old chairs out onto the porch and sat down to agonize over her problem again. It was a moonlit night and she could see the neighbouring shacks quite clearly. She could also hear sounds of laughter and the clink of metal on metal as someone scraped the last vestiges of rice out of a communal supper bowl. All was mercifully quiet from inside the house as the boys and Sancha were asleep. Yara had noticed that the invalid had been sleeping a lot lately and that the constant moaning had almost ceased. On one occasion, when she'd come into the inner room and seen Guilherme giving his wife some tablets, she'd correctly concluded that he'd begun to buy powerful pain killers for her.

'At least some of the money I earn for that pig is being put to good use,' she said to herself. That night, Guilherme went drinking with his friends. 'You were too poor to do that when I first came here,' she muttered crossly to herself. 'Now you go out each Tuesday with your pals. What about me? I earn the money not you,' and she clenched her fists in anger. Then a thought popped into her head. 'I wonder,' she mused, 'if I could use your weekly outing to solve my problem? Maybe I can invite some of your customers to come here on Tuesdays after you've left, and pocket the money myself! You would never know!' A little frisson of excitement ran through her as she rapidly worked out the details of her plan. Her first concern was that Sancha would hear what was happening even if she entertained the men on the porch. 'But no, Sancha is sleeping a lot at the moment. She won't hear anything,' she concluded.

So the next night, when she had finished with her second client and before the man got up off the floor, she whispered seductively in his ear.

'Come next Tuesday, when he's at his club, I'll charge you half the amount you give him. The mean bastard never gives me anything. Don't tell him and be very quiet.'

'That sounds like a good deal. See you next Tuesday then,' he whispered in her ear, as he got up from the floor to go and pay Guilherme, who was sitting on the porch.

Over the next few days Yara spoke to another four customers, ones she thought she could trust, telling them what time to arrive. When the following Tuesday came, her plan worked well. All five men arrived and all duly paid up. At the end of the evening Yara looked gleefully at the money in her hand her heart singing.

'If things go on like this I can escape in a month,' she murmured joyfully to herself. Then she folded the money up into a tight roll and hid it carefully behind the doorjamb in the outer room. Two more weeks passed and on the fourth Tuesday night, after Guilherme had left the house, Yara sat waiting on the porch steps hugging herself with delight. By tomorrow she would have enough money to go home. For the first time in her life she found she was almost looking forward to her night's work. Then a shape loomed out of the darkness. Yara thought it was her first customer, but no, it was Guilherme!

'My God, why has he come back!' Panic flooded over her like a cold wave.

'Waiting for someone Yara?' he enquired in a sarcastic voice giving her a nasty smile. 'I think I'll just keep you company for a while,' and he promptly sat down on the step beside her. Yara's heart sank.

'Oh!' she gasped in anguish, 'you know!' and she clenched her fists in a fever of desperation. With black despair in her heart she went through the nightly ritual with her five handpicked men and watched in torment as the money, that should have been hers, was put into the outstretched hand of her pimp. After the last man had gone Guilherme turned to her and said coldly,

'If you try and double cross me again Yara you'll get the beating of your life.' Yara knew he meant it. She cowered down on her mat desperately angry and dismayed as she listened to her tormentor settling down to sleep in the inner room. Lying back on her sack she stared into the darkness for a long while. At last her panic began to subside and she was able to think clearly. Once again her innate bravery crept out from beneath her fear like a mouse easing itself from under the claws of a sleeping cat, and she determined that she would take the money she had already and get back on the bus in the morning.

'Perhaps this time I'll have a dozy driver and I'll get home at last,' she murmured hopefully to herself as she tried to find a comfortable place on the floor, 'If not I'll walk the rest of the way even if I die on the road.' Feeling a bit happier she eventually fell asleep.

The sound of someone moving quietly around the room woke her early the next morning and lifting herself on one elbow she saw that Guilherme was poking about in the room obviously looking for something.

'My God!' thought Yara. 'He's looking for my money. Please, please don't find it.' She watched in despair, knowing that she was helpless to stop him. Inexorably he got closer and closer to her hiding place until at last his questing fingers found the roll of grubby notes tucked in the door jamb and with a satisfied grunt he put it into his pocket. Quickly Yara lay back and closed her eyes again pretending to be asleep. She certainly wasn't going to give him the satisfaction of letting him know she'd seen her precious money stolen. Tears of anger and despair crept out of the corners of her tightly shut eyes and rolled slowly down her cheeks but she dared not brush them away in case he noticed.

When the family had gone to work, Yara began the day's chores, first washing little Pedro and then fetching the water from the tap for the family's needs. She went about these tasks automatically for deep inside her something had changed. She felt like a desiccated husk, or an empty cup that has been drained and thrown away; used up, abandoned and dead, too weary to try anymore. Then she heard Sancha calling to her.

'Yara, Yara,' cried the desperate, demanding voice over and over again. When she could stand it no longer, the girl crossed over to the inner room, pushed the curtain aside, and went in. There she found the woman tossing and turning on her bed pawing in agitation at her cotton cover. Her eyes were bright and staring and her face beaded with sweat. She was indeed more frantic than she'd been for many days.

'What's the matter Sancha?' demanded Yara dully. 'Keep quiet. I'm busy.'

'Guilherme forgot to give me my tablets,' whined the invalid in a desperate voice. 'Please get them for me

Yara. I can't live without them now. Please, please,' and she held up her shaking hands to Yara in frantic appeal.

'Where are they?' snapped Yara shortly, not wanting to be bothered with anyone connected to the loathsome Guilherme, but at the same time realising that none of this was Sancha's fault.

'Look on top of that beam above my bed,' gasped the distraught woman. 'There's a box up there. The key's under my mattress.' Yara walked crossly over to the beam and stood on tiptoe to feel on top. Yes, there was a small box just as Sancha had said. Then her heart missed a beat.

'If this is the place Guilherme keeps his valuables maybe my money's there too,' she thought excitedly. With trembling hands she lifted the box down, took the key from under the mattress and opened the lid. There inside was a packet of pills, and next to it two rolls of notes. One she recognised as her own and the other she realised must belong to Guilherme. Thinking quickly she removed two tablets and fetched a cup of water for Sancha to drink. She then turned her back on the woman, and deftly abstracted both bundles of notes, slipping them inside her shirt. Replacing the box she tucked the key back under the mattress on Sancha's bed and went out onto the porch. Relief and excitement washed over her and it only took a second to decide what to do next. Checking that Pedro was asleep on his mat she quietly tiptoed down the steps and then flew through the village like a homing pigeon, straight for the filling station on the highway to wait for the next bus.

'I'd better hide somewhere,' she decided when she arrived there panting. 'Someone might see me and take me back,' so she hunted anxiously around until she found a quiet place behind an old oil drum where she could keep an eye on the road. There she squatted down in the dust, her heart thumping nervously in her chest. As soon as she was sure nobody could see into her hidey-hole, she retrieved the bundles of notes from her shirt to see how much money Guilherme had. She already knew what was in her own roll, but when her shaking fingers had counted the second she was overjoyed to see how much she now had. 'But,' she whispered, 'I earned it so why shouldn't I have it?' Quickly she thrust the money back inside her shirt and curled herself into a small ball. Keeping one eye on the road, which she could just glimpse round the edge of the barrel, she listened anxiously to every sound that drifted into her hiding place from the filling station. Feet pattered past and voices floated over to her from groups of travellers who began to assemble to wait for the bus. Slowly the minutes ticked by. When it came an hour later she crept out from behind the oil drum, paid her fare to the stop nearest her home and climbing excitedly aboard, took her seat. Shrinking down below the window level she did her best to remain invisible but when the wheels slowly began to turn at last and the bus made its way out of the filling station onto the highway, her heart began to sing. 'With this money,' she crowed triumphantly, 'not only am I going home, but there will be enough to take Carlos back to Beleza. Hang on little Tis. Help is on the way!'

Chapter 16

Aidan was in the shower. The early morning sun was streaming in through the bathroom window of the small flat where he and Kirsty had been living now for over two years. He however, had no eyes for the beauty of the morning as he was watching a small, black speck of dirt swirl round and round the plughole, caught in a seemingly endless vortex of eddying water. As he watched the fragment detached itself from its endless dance and slid smoothly down the drain. Aidan breathed a sigh.

'You've escaped,' he said to himself. 'It's not so easy for me though. What, what, what am I going to do?'

His thoughts went back, for the umpteenth time, to the previous day when he'd been looking idly at the notice board in the corridor outside one of the lecture rooms, and his eye had lighted on a small notice tucked away at the bottom. This had said that there was funding from a named charity for an eight week elective in general medicine in Brazil. The position, the notice said, was on the team of Dr Miguel Romerez who, it appeared, had worked at Aidan's hospital some years previously. Since all students were given the chance in their fourth year to study a particular area of interest within medicine, either at home or abroad for a short period, Aidan had been wondering where he would go. This was intended to be both a challenge and an opportunity to gain an insight into a different medical specialism. However, until now, he hadn't felt particularly drawn to any of the possible openings either overseas or at home. Neither had he spoken to Kirsty about his search, as he didn't want to worry her until he'd made up his mind. However, what had made Aidan's heart lurch physically in his chest when he read the notice was that the placement was in Beleza, where his uncle Rhys had taken him when he'd been waiting for his A level results.

Ever since yesterday his mind had been churning with a complex mixture of thoughts and emotions. Should he go? Could he even bring himself to go back to a place which held so many dreadful memories? There was no doubt, that in some strange way he couldn't quite understand, he felt drawn towards the post but would Kirsty like the idea? She was bound to ask him why he wanted to go to that particular city and he would obviously have to tell her what had happened there. What would she think of him then? She might also dislike the idea of leaving the UK. He'd never even spoken to her about the possibility of going abroad, and what about his mum and Kirsty's dad who would hate it if they were so far away. All these thoughts and many more like them, whirled round his head clamouring for his attention and worse still for an immediate decision.

He got out of the shower and dried himself. He then began to brush his teeth as he had done thousands of times before, looking in the mirror to check that he was doing it correctly. His anxious reflection gazed back at him but he was so preoccupied that he failed to notice that his dark hair was standing up on end and his mouth now sported a rakish, white, toothpaste moustache. The door opened and Kirsty, dressed in jeans and t-shirt, came in.

'I've just put the coffee on Aidan,' she said. 'Are you nearly ready for breakfast?' Then she moved behind him and wound her arms round his neck, snuggling close to him so that her unruffled image was now next to his own tousled one. In an instant he was transported back to that moment in the cathedral when her face, like a glowing, life giving sun, had so warmed his heart in the huge horizontal viewing mirror. Then, softly, as a dim echo from another age, he heard again the words, "comfort my world." Maybe, just maybe, this was his opportunity to do that.

As he quickly dragged on his clothes Aidan thought frantically how he might broach the subject to Kirsty. He'd never, at any time, even hinted at his dreadful experiences with Rhys. The memories were still appallingly painful and indeed the only person to hear his confession had been Father James.

'What on earth is she going to think about me?' he agonised, running a comb briefly through his hair. 'I've just got to tell her now. Will she stop loving me?' The idea was so dreadful that it made him feel quite dizzy. 'At least I'm not going into the hospital today,' he thought with relief. 'I'm sure I couldn't concentrate on anything.' Fortunately both he and Kirsty had one of their rare days off together and had planned to go out for a day's walking.

As the car threaded its way out of the town, towards the countryside Aidan drove on autopilot paying no attention to either Kirsty or the passing scenery. They'd decided to follow a track high up on the South Downs, and it wasn't until they were chugging up the steep winding road to the parking area that he suddenly noticed that they were nearly at their destination. He realised then that he'd been completely absorbed with the tempestuous thoughts that were racing about in his head.

Kirsty too had her problems on the journey, since they'd borrowed their neighbour's little Westie, Joshi, to take with them. The dog was young and not used to car travel so he'd spent the first part of the journey jumping about and barking. At last, in desperation, she held him firmly on her knee so that he could look out of the window. From this vantage point he avidly watched the passing countryside looking like a small, imperious field marshal inspecting his troops. Aidan was so absorbed in his own thoughts however, that he barely noticed the commotion in the car and only dimly registered the fact that he was glad the dog had stopped making a noise.

Eventually they pulled into a car park on top of the Downs, facing a stunning view over miles of countryside spread out in a scenic panorama far below them; a patchwork of fields, woodlands, and old churches snuggled close to huddled villages. Collecting their rucksacks from the boot, and Joshi's lead and bottle of water, they set off hand in hand along the path that led along the top of the escarpment.

The little dog was entranced by all the new, exciting smells and scampered about excitedly like a small, white, furry investigating agent at the end of his retractable lead. He at least was sublimely happy. As they walked along, Kirsty tried to talk to Aidan but he was still totally absorbed in working out what he should say to her. Indeed he'd now convinced himself that when she heard his confession she would want to leave him at once. This thought filled him with despair so that he answered his wife's questions either with a grunt or silence. Usually he ambled contentedly along beside her while she chattered to him about the view, the flowers or the cloud formations, listening with half his attention and letting her observations wash over him, but today her constant commentary began to irritate him. At length, both walked along in complete silence while Joshi chased flies, ate rabbits' droppings like a gourmet sampling the best truffles, and greeted every passing dog with the enthusiasm usually reserved for celebrities.

By lunchtime they were several miles along the ridge and well ahead of any less energetic walkers.

'I'm starving. Let's have lunch now Aidan,' Kirsty said firmly. 'It's one o'clock and we've come miles. My feet are aching and I've got to sit down and rest.' Aidan visibly started, turned and looked back the way they'd come.

'How did we get here?' he muttered.

'We walked,' replied Kirsty sharply. 'For goodness sake Aidan, if you don't tell me what the matter is soon I shall walk back on my own! Hiking with a cabbage would be more exciting.'

'Let's eat our lunch first,' replied Aidan miserably, 'then I'll tell you.'

Kirsty looked round for a good place to sit and spotted a sheltered hollow a little way down the hill. She then spread out their picnic on a small waterproof groundsheet they'd brought with them, for it was October and the ground was damp. While she did this, Aidan gave Joshi some water and a couple of biscuits and the dog then curled himself up into a little ball on a corner of the ground sheet and fell fast asleep.

'It's all right for you little guy,' thought Aidan. 'You haven't a care in the world. I'd gladly change places with you right now.'

Lunch was a gloomy, silent meal. Aidan sat hunched beside Kirsty, trying to fix his attention on a distant church spire which poked up out of a small grove of trees, but the nearer he got to the end of his sandwiches, the slower he ate, until he stopped eating altogether and just gazed, with unseeing eyes at the view. He was dimly aware that Kirsty was fuming with exasperation but just couldn't face the moment when he had to tell her what was on his mind. Finally she gave up waiting for him to finish and after she had drunk the last dregs of coffee she banged the mug down onto the groundsheet and she said firmly,

'Whatever is the matter with you Aidan?'

'It's something that happened yesterday, and something that happened a long time ago,' he replied slowly not looking at her. He then told her about the advert for the elective. 'I would like to go and work with Dr Romerez for a couple of months Kirsty,' he said quietly, fixing his gaze on the church spire once more. 'How would you feel about it?' There was a long pause while Kirsty digested this information.

'I'd love to go,' she said at length. 'What an adventure! My parents never went abroad for holidays so it would be exciting to go and live in an exotic place,' and she squeezed his hand and laid her head against his shoulder. But Aidan was still totally unresponsive, and the hand lay in hers, still and impassive, the hand of a stranger. Kirsty sat up and looked closely at him.

'What else is troubling you?' she asked gently. The question hung between them like a drop of water trembling on a cobweb. 'You said something that happened long ago. Is that the real problem?'

'Yes,' replied Aidan, falling silent, totally unable to think of a way to begin. At last, taking a deep breath, he told her the whole tale, haltingly and with many pauses while the dog snored contentedly and the beautiful view lay unheeded below them.

When he'd finished, Kirsty sat very still.

'Oh no!' he thought despairingly. 'What is she thinking? What have I done?' and he lent forward, put his head in his hands and groaned aloud. Silence. At last he glanced at her and saw that she was looking very angry. Aidan had never seen Kirsty so cross before and was appalled at the effect of his confession.

'Kirsty, I'm so, so, sorry,' he said quietly, twisting his fingers together in an agony of remorse. 'Can you ever forgive me? Do you still want to go on living with me? I can see you're very angry and I don't blame you. But, oh! I can't live without you now,' and he stared fixedly at his hands in despair unable to meet her eyes.

'Silly man,' replied Kirsty gently, putting her arm lovingly round his shoulders. 'I'm not angry with you. I'm livid with your foul uncle Rhys. It wasn't your fault. He must have put something really powerful in your drink. No wonder you didn't want him to come to our wedding,' she added. 'What a dreadful experience.' Then putting her other arm round him she held him to her in a long hug that said more about her commitment to him than a thousand words could have done, and Aidan, wrapped up in that embrace, felt her love dissolve all the anxiety of the last twenty four hours.

Kirsty stopped hugging him at last, and he opened his eyes. Down below him the little towns and hamlets on the plain stretched out as far as the eye could see, glowing in the autumn sunshine. Indeed their tranquillity seemed to mirror the deep peace that had descended on his heart the moment his wife had folded him in her arms.

'Kirsty, I love you so much,' he said twinkling at her. 'Will you marry me?' She chuckled.

'No I can't,' she replied with mock seriousness. 'I don't think my husband would like that!' Aidan lay back on the ground sheet laughing at their private joke and pulled her down into his arms. This caused an elderly hiker on the ridge path above them to shake her head disapprovingly and to think gloomy thoughts about the younger generation as she continued on her way. Oblivious to the consternation they had caused, they soon sat up again and gazed at the view, the perfect panorama below now mirroring their oneness. Eventually Aidan said regretfully,

'I think we'd best be getting back to the car soon. We came a long way and the afternoon's half over.'

'Not yet Aidan,' replied Kirsty, 'I've got some news for you too,' and she eased him down once more onto the ground sheet looking like a person who is about to offer a precious gift.

'What is it Kirsty. Is something the matter?' he said suddenly concerned.

'Relax sweetheart,' replied Kirsty. 'It's nothing awful, quite the reverse. You're going to be a father.' Aidan rolled over onto his stomach and propping himself up on his elbow, gazed down at her in amazement.

'Darling how wonderful,' he breathed placing his hand gently on her stomach as if he could already feel the baby. 'When did you find out?' Kirsty told him and then said with a twinkle in her eye,

'And before you ask, it won't stop us going to Brazil. This obliging baby may not have been exactly planned but will be here before we go.'

The walk back to the car in the early afternoon sunshine couldn't have been more of a contrast to the morning. They laughed and joked, speculating on Aidan's chances of getting the post, and what it would involve.

'Do you know any more details?' Kirsty questioned as they went hand in hand together along the path.

'Well, I do know that the hospital is an old one,' he replied. 'Their website said that it used to be run by nuns in the early days and is built in the grounds of their convent. They don't run it now,' he added. 'It's been taken over by the government, but I think they still have a pastoral and an administrative role in its day to day work.'

'Nuns,' mused Kirsty thoughtfully. 'I've never even spoken to one. I always think they look so odd in their funny clothes. I know my naughty dad calls them 'penguins',' she added chuckling. As they chatted happily together the miles sped by, but this time Aidan knew it was because he was enjoying himself so much. He felt supremely happy. The air was invigorating, the view incomparable, and the dog, now rejuvenated by his rest, sniffed and scampered about, tangling his lead round their legs in unrelenting excitement. Aidan also felt as if he was seeing Kirsty for the first time, and his love for her reached a deeper level than he would have thought possible. Transformed from being a frothy exciting thing that made his heart race and his body thrill, this emotion was profound, solid, and immensely satisfying.

That night, when they lay contentedly in each other's arms, Aidan reflected that the term, 'making love' was the wrong one. It ought to be 'expressing love' or, 'showing love' or, 'making love visible' as their very love-making seemed to have a depth and fulfilment to it that neither had before experienced. No longer did it seem just the coming together of two bodies in passing ecstasy, but the melding of two beings into one new, unified whole, body, mind and spirit.

Chapter 17

Aidan and Kirsty sat waiting for their plane to Sao Paulo to take off, with Joy in a tiny bulkhead cot in front of them. The day, so far, had been an exhausting one with an early start for the long drive to Heathrow. Both Stephen and Emily had come to see them off, so there had been much hugging, kissing and surreptitious brushing away of rogue tears before they'd finally got to the departure lounge. Looking sideways at her husband Kirsty saw that he was preoccupied and unhappy.

'I know what he's thinking,' she thought. 'He's remembering the last time he set off on this journey.' As if divining her thoughts, Aidan turned to her, a worried expression on his face and said miserably,

'I'm so glad it's you darling, and not Rhys sitting beside me.'

'I guessed that's what you were thinking,' replied Kirsty. 'Don't worry,' she continued with a reassuring smile, 'you've got me now, and whatever's waiting for us in Brazil we'll face together.' Aidan took her hand and squeezed it in his own.

'Thank you darling,' he said simply.

Very soon the plane took off. Joy cried as the cabin pressure changed but quickly stopped once her ears had adjusted. She soon settled down for a nap in Kirsty's arms, who, overcome with tiredness, leant her head against Aidan's shoulder and closed her eyes.

'We must look a bit like the Holy Family sculpture

in the cathedral,' she thought sleepily with Aidan
protecting us both like Joseph. 'If only we had a manger
though. Joy would have more room in one of those.'
With that she drifted off to sleep and so missed the
hostess's sympathetic smile as she passed the little family,
returning a little while later with a blanket to tuck round
the three of them.

Eleven weary hours later they touched down in
Sao Paulo and had to scramble to catch the plane for the
next leg of their journey to the north of the country. This
time it was Aidan who went to sleep, whilst Kirsty tried to
comfort a fretful baby for the next four long, hours.
Eventually the plane touched down at Beleza, and the
tedious process of disembarkation and baggage retrieval
began. Waiting for their last case to come round the
carousel, Kirsty, who was exhausted, began to feel that she
was part of an unpleasant dream. The illusion was
intensified by the babble of hundreds of voices all talking a
foreign language, which seemed to overwhelm her mind in
a welter of alien sounds. The signs, too, were nearly all in
Portuguese so she couldn't understand them, and
everything and everyone looked so different. To regain
control of herself she focused her attention on Aidan who
was inspecting each case as it came past him. Somehow
just the sight of his long thin figure, unruly black hair and
serious face, calmed her panic and she began to feel a
sense of reality return once more. Finally, the last of their
bags began its slow trundle round the circle and putting it
on the trolley with the others they began their walk to the
arrival point.

'I do hope the Convent hasn't forgotten we're
coming today,' remarked Kirsty fretfully. 'What shall we

do if there's nobody there? They did promise to send a car didn't they?'

'Calm down,' replied Aidan giving her a reassuring smile, 'I'm sure they haven't forgotten.' At that moment he spotted a short stocky man holding up a sign, which read, 'Mr Vickers'. 'I guess that's us Kirsty,' he said in a relieved tone, shepherding the three of them through the throng of arrivals to where the man was standing. 'My name is Vickers,' said Aidan, pointing to himself, 'and this is my wife and baby.'

'I drive you to Convent,' said the man simply, and led the way out of the airport building. At once the heat hit Kirsty and she felt like running back inside into the cool of the air conditioning. Then she looked down at Joy asleep in the baby carrier on her chest.

'I hope this journey is a short one, sweetheart,' she whispered to the top of the downy head, 'or you're going to get so hot.' Her next thought was, 'I wish I had my sunglasses,' as the light was so bright it blinded her eyes after the comparative dimness of the airport buildings. However, these were in one of the cases so she was forced to squint to stop her eyes from watering.

'Stay here,' ordered the driver. 'I get car.' They stood and waited obediently with their bulwark of cases round them; a lonely little island in a sea of swirling people.

'I hope he's not going to be long,' muttered Kirsty trying to shade the baby with her hand. 'It's too hot for you. And me too,' she added feelingly. The man soon returned however, and they climbed gratefully into the back of his dilapidated old Volkswagen. The traffic was dense around the airport and they made slow progress at first, but when they reached the main highway the driver sped up until they were rattling along at a breakneck pace. In desperation Kirsty hung onto the baby with one arm and to Aidan with the other.

'I think he's practicing for the next Grand Prix,' said Aidan smiling at her. 'Don't worry darling. They all drive like this here. You'll get used to it.' Once they reached the outskirts of Beleza the car had to slow down again and they progressed at a honking crawl along busy residential streets to the city centre, which was thronged with people crowding the pavements and even the roads. Hot, stifling exhaust fumes swirled round them through the open windows of the car and the noise of the enveloping traffic began to make Kirsty's head ache. Loud music played everywhere and strong smells wafted in including the mouth-watering odour of roasting meat and garlic. This made her realise that she hadn't eaten a proper meal for hours and she began to feel very hungry.

'In fact,' she thought to herself, 'I don't even know what time my body thinks it is.' She tried to close her eyes, but found them irresistibly opening of their own accord. 'I do wish they would stay shut,' she thought crossly, 'I should be so much happier if I couldn't see this mad traffic and these huge lorries bearing down on us. I'm sure we'll be crushed before we get there.'

But at last the car turned into the gates of the Convent and slowly chugged its way along the drive amidst a throng of pedestrians and traffic. Kirsty could see a modern hospital block through the trees, but the Convent itself, when they eventually arrived, seemed to be an old Colonial style building built of white washed brick, and single storied.

'I carry,' ordered the driver cheerfully, getting out and manhandling all the cases up the steps, through an imposing, carved wooden door and into a long, empty hallway. He then abandoned them, muttering something incomprehensible in Portuguese. The big door closed behind him with a bang, leaving them completely alone. There they stood, like a bedraggled group of refugees, feeling tired and miserable. Nobody seemed to be about and it was blessedly quiet and cool. The hall was dark, but looking down its length in the dim light Kirsty could see bars of sunlight shining across the floor at intervals where doors had been left open on either side. Silence descended and several minutes slowly ticked past.

'What do we do now?' whispered Kirsty in a small voice. 'We can't stand here all day.' As she spoke they heard a door click open at the far end of the hall and a small ghostly apparition began to make its way purposefully towards them out of the gloom, passing in and out of the sunlight and shadows. 'It's a nun, but she's in white,' thought Kirsty, surprised, as a patch of sunshine briefly illuminated the figure. As she got closer, Kirsty also saw that the sister was both elderly and slightly built. 'She looks just like a little robin,' she thought amused, for the ankles and calves above the heavy leather sandals were small and skinny, but the eyes were bright, beady and dark brown. Reaching them the nun held out her hand and smiled. This seemed to light up her whole face and give it a warmth and luminosity that was immediately attractive. Her gestures too, were birdlike and quick, and when she spoke to them in perfect English, her voice had a gentle, high, fluting quality that was like nothing Kirsty had ever heard before.

'I'm Sister Maria,' she said. 'Welcome. You must be exhausted.'

'I'm Aidan Vickers,' replied Aidan, 'and this is my wife Kirsty and daughter Joy.'

'Please follow me,' ordered the nun. 'You can leave your cases. They can be fetched later,' and she led them into a bright and airy side room furnished with large comfortable chairs. 'Sit down and rest while I get you some refreshments,' she commanded and whisked out of the door again before either of them had time to say anything.

Soon she was back with a tray and setting it down on a low table proceeded to serve them with fresh fruit juice and then small cups of strong, sweet, black coffee.

'This is cafezinho,' she said, as she gracefully handed them each a cup. 'You will get a lot of this in Brazil. We Brazilians are very proud of our coffee.' As soon as they'd finished their drinks and after Sister Maria had cuddled Joy, she announced that she would take them to their house.

'I will send a man with your cases,' she chirruped. 'Follow me,' and led them out of the front door and along a pathway which wound its way through the trees. As they followed, Aidan whispered to Kirsty,

'Do you remember I told you about Father James?'

'Yes,' replied Kirsty, 'but what made you think about him now?'

'Just this,' replied Aidan. 'Father James was insubstantial like water in a cupped hand, but this 'religious' is as real as hot buttered toast!' Kirsty laughed, in spite of her tiredness, and felt her heart lift a little at the prospect of getting to know Sister Maria better, for she too had instinctively felt drawn to the small birdlike nun.

Looking round her, Kirsty realised that the grounds of the convent were spacious and beautiful. There were many mature shade trees dotted about. Some had huge feathery fern-like leaves unlike anything she'd ever seen before. But she could also see smaller trees, a few of which appeared to be sprinkled with pink or yellow blossoms. One particularly caught her eye. It was set back from the path in an open space, and its sturdy branches were covered in brilliant scarlet flowers like fat red candles. A tiny iridescent blue bird was hovering close to one of the blossoms and it looked so beautiful that she lingered for a moment to watch it, all tiredness for the time being forgotten. Sister Maria and Aidan, who were a little way ahead with Joy, turned at her exclamation of pleasure and came back to see what she was looking at.

'We have many stately and beautiful trees in this garden,' remarked the nun. 'This one's a candelabrum tree and is one of my favourites, and that's a humming bird,' she added as an afterthought. 'But come, I'm sure you want to rest and settle yourselves.'

There were several small, single storied houses dotted among the trees, and Sister Maria stopped at one of them, took a key out of her habit and let them in.

'This is our guest house,' she said, turning to Aidan. 'I'll leave you to settle in, then please come back to the Convent and we'll give you a meal. Don't forget to lock the door before you return,' she added, and trotted quickly away. Aidan looked after her retreating back and said admiringly,

'There goes a remarkable woman Kirsty. What do you think?'

'Yes, perhaps,' replied Kirsty thoughtfully. Indeed, as the days went past and she got to know Sister Maria better, she found that their first impressions were correct. She never stopped being amazed, for example, at how somebody, as thin and old as the little nun, could be so energetic. It was as if all the food she ate went into fuelling her love for people rather than nourishing her body. Kirsty also came to realize that one of the reasons the elderly sister was so vigorous was because her energy was always focused and never allowed to dissipate on useless talk and gestures. It reminded her of the power present in a steam engine, which is immense, but always rigidly channelled and under complete control.

They spent what was left of the day settling into their new home. Kirsty was amazed at the security bars on the windows, and the fact that there was metal gauze in the frames instead of glass.

'I wonder if I shall ever get used to these bars?' she wondered. 'It feels a bit like being in prison.' She was also surprised that there were no carpets on the floors, only tiles and no curtains at the windows either. The furniture was large, and looked as if it was made of mahogany, and the bed, when she sat down on it, appeared to be solid concrete. 'Fine for backs, but do you think we shall ever be able to sleep on it?' she asked Aidan in consternation, trying vainly to bounce up and down on its unyielding surface. However, after they'd put Joy to rest in her cot under her mosquito net, they climbed gratefully into the bed, tucked themselves under their own net and despite the hard mattress, soon fell into an exhausted slumber.

Apart from waking to feed Joy, they slept well and were woken the next morning by a loud banging on the front door.

'Whatever's going on?' exclaimed Aidan as he made his way blearily to open it. There on the doorstep stood a portly, smiling woman of about forty, with a mop and bucket, who shyly held out a letter to him. Without waiting for an invitation she followed him into the house and began to wash the kitchen floor with remarkable gusto, slopping a great deal of water everywhere. Taken aback, Aidan returned to the bedroom and opened the letter. It was from Sister Maria asking them to come to the Convent for breakfast. Afterwards, Dr Romerez would personally call to fetch Aidan for a tour of the hospital, and she herself would escort Kirsty to the market to buy food. The woman with the bucket, the letter informed them, was Luan, and she was their cleaner who would come every day to wash the floors. 'I don't know about washing floors,' remarked Aidan dryly to Kirsty, who hadn't yet seen what Luan was doing, 'I think she's trying to turn the kitchen into a swimming pool. Let's hurry up and get through the bathroom in case she wants to scrub that too and it floats away.'

After breakfast, where Joy had been the centre of attention for the sisters, they found that Luan had finished the floors and had now turned her attention to the wide apron of concrete that surrounded the outside of the house. Mystified Aidan asked,

'Why are you doing that?' Putting down her mop Luan stood up and smiling broadly at him put a finger to her lips and shook her head to show that she didn't understand English. Aidan then pointed to the bucket and then to the concrete, holding out his hands and opening his eyes wide. Luan soon realized what he wanted to know, and went to the edge of the path where the grass began, bent down and pointed to a group of large ants who were hurrying about among the grass stems. She then made a crawling motion with her fingers on the surface of the concrete going in the direction of the house, and they realised that the cleaning was to try to keep the ants from going inside. Kirsty shuddered. She was nervous of meeting both insects and snakes, and had already made the acquaintance of several oversized cockroaches, which she had surprised in the kitchen in the middle of the night when she had been feeding Joy. To her great relief they'd scampered away immediately she'd put the electric light on.

'In fact,' she thought shivering, 'everything here seems to be extra big. The lorries are huge, the insects are enormous and even the birds in the trees seem larger than those at home.'

'Oh Aidan,' she said turning to him, 'I hope I don't meet any really nasty bugs when you aren't here.' Aidan smiled.

'And there was I thinking you were going kill

them all for me,' he said gently.

At that moment, Dr Romerez appeared, coming along the path through the trees and after polite introductions Aidan was whisked away to inspect the hospital.

'Mmm,' thought Kirsty, looking after their retreating backs. 'I'm not sure I envy you Aidan working with him. Too portly and pompous!'

Not long afterwards, birdlike Sister Maria arrived to find Kirsty sitting on one of the large easy chairs rocking Joy and watching entranced as a humming bird hovered just outside the window feeding on the nectar from a pink flowering shrub. The little nun perched herself on the edge of a nearby chair, hands resting serenely in her lap, and smiled.

'Do you feel rested enough to come to the market with me?' she enquired. 'I thought that I could give you some idea of what food to buy, and how our money works.'

'That would be lovely Sister,' replied Kirsty enthusiastically, 'but first tell me, how is it you speak such perfect English?' Nodding her head up and down like a little bird the Sister replied,

'Everyone says that, but really I can't take any credit for it. You see my mother was English so I grew up knowing both languages well.'

'That explains it,' said Kirsty smiling. 'You had the best of both worlds then,' and she busied herself putting Joy in the baby carrier and collecting the few things she would need for their outing. Soon all was ready, and with the baby on her chest and her small pack on her back, they left the house, locking the door behind them.

The day was hot, but because it was still very early in the morning, the heat was bearable. Sister Maria took the lead along a narrow path in the opposite direction from the Convent. They had only been walking for about a minute when they came to a dense thicket of very large green plants topped with vivid scarlet leaves.

'They're poinsettias!' gasped Kirsty in astonishment. 'But they're gigantic. The one I had at home last Christmas was only about thirty centimetres high. Just look at them!' Sister Maria smiled saying,

'But you see these are where they belong, and that makes all the difference.' Rounding the astonishing red clump another surprise awaited Kirsty for there, spread out in front of her, was a spectacular vista. She realised then that the Convent had been built in a superb position, which commanded a breathtaking view over a wide river estuary just where it joined the sea. Both women stopped and marvelled at the panorama of river and sea, hills and distant forests as little Joy, seeming to sense her mother's delight, gurgled and smiled up at them.

'Yes, it's lovely isn't it?' remarked Sister Maria. 'But you're going to find it a stark contrast to what lies outside,' and a look of intense sadness flitted briefly across her serene face. In that instant Kirsty realised that Sister Maria was one of those rare souls who can retain their capacity for compassion, even after years of being exposed to the horrors of poverty and sickness. Most people, she knew, need to develop a hard shell to cope with the suffering they have to face each day, but not so Maria. Somehow she had performed that miracle of being able to cope with other people's anguish and pain while still retaining a soft heart of love.

The three of them continued on down the path and out of a side gate in the high wall. As they were turning out of the grounds Kirsty noticed that Maria was carrying a cotton satchel across her shoulders, which seemed to be full of something knobbly.

'I wonder what she's got in her bag?' she murmured to Joy bending her head low so that the Sister didn't hear what she said.

Walking along the busy road, she was glad that the nun had put her on the inside of the pavement as she felt intimidated by the roaring traffic and the throngs of hurrying pedestrians. Soon they reached the end of the high Convent wall where another road intersected theirs at right angles. Here the wall bent round to the left to enclose the top-side of the Convent-hospital complex, and Kirsty, glancing in that direction stopped, transfixed with horror.

'What's he doing here? Why isn't he in hospital?' she cried in anguish. Sister Maria came and stood beside her, a steadying hand on her arm. Together they both looked down at the man propped up against the wall. He had only one leg, and his head was done up in a filthy, blood soaked bandage. Sitting in the dust beside him was a small child who held out his cupped hands to the two women, repeating something in Portuguese over and over again.

'He's a beggar Kirsty,' sighed Sister Maria sadly, and so saying, opened her satchel taking out four of the leftover bread rolls from breakfast, which Kirsty remembered the nuns had called pãezinhos. She put these gently into the child's hands. Immediately the man snatched two and began to eat hungrily. The lad however, looked up at them dully, mumbling something incomprehensible over and over again as he stuffed the bread into his mouth.

'What did he say when you gave him the pãezinhos?' questioned Kirsty deeply shaken by the sight of such naked suffering.

'God bless you. God bless you. God bless you,' replied Maria sadly. 'Poor desperate child,' and taking Kirsty's arm she led her across the busy road. 'You'll see many beggars I'm afraid my dear,' she remarked gravely once they'd reached the safety of the opposite pavement. 'Please don't give them money, but food like I did. That's why I told you that there's much sadness outside the walls of the Convent,' she added. 'If you visit the favelas, which are our shantytowns, you would see much worse sights than that I'm afraid, but you must never go there on your own,' she added firmly.

On reaching the market, Kirsty stopped and sighed with relief, glad to get away from the road with its huge brightly painted lorries, flocks of buses, ubiquitous cars and noisy motorbikes. The busy shoppers seemed far less intimidating by comparison, and the heavily laden stalls, covered by brightly patterned awnings and holding a bewildering variety of exotic fruits and vegetables, fascinated her. Mounds of unripe bananas, green-gold pineapples, brown hairy coconuts, oranges and knobbly custard fruits were stacked everywhere, along with strange, large, green prickly objects that Sister Maria said were called jackfruits. There were some unfamiliar vegetables as well to choose from, and the little nun had a hard time trying to get her bewildered companion to decide what she should buy. Kirsty wandered from stall to stall asking innumerable questions and touching some of the more outlandish fruit with amazement. At last her pack was full and she thought how lovely it would be to get back to her shady house, as the sun was now getting really hot, and the noise of the market crowds was beginning to make her feel quite dizzy. However just at that moment Sister Maria said,

'Just wait here my dear, I'll be back in a minute or two,' and darted off into the crowd.

Kirsty stood under the shade of one of the awnings next to a heap of bright green limes. Suddenly she felt tired and drained. So much had happened in the last few hours; the journey, the convent, meeting Sister Maria and Luan, settling into the new house, coping with the heat, and the horrid insects, and worrying about Joy's health. She felt as if life was rushing along with her far too fast. Everything was so new and alien and she was aware that, for the first time in her life, she was in a place that felt hostile and intimidating. Not only was the language incomprehensible, which in itself was unsettling, but nor did she know what was dangerous in her environment and what was harmless. She felt both frightened and vulnerable, and wished that Sister Maria, her guide and protector, would come back. She was also aware that both she and Joy were very hot and sweating profusely.

'This won't do!' she said to herself. 'Take some deep breaths and think of something calming.' With that she closed her eyes and tried to focus on a place in the past that would steady her. Her mind suddenly switched to the previous autumn when she and Aidan had been visiting a National Trust property near their flat. It had been a golden October day. The leaves on the oak trees had begun to turn to russet and the air had been warm and soothing. They'd sat down on a seat near a small mill-stream and Kirsty had closed her eyes just as she had them closed now. She concentrated hard, trying to conjure up the feel of the air in the quiet, beautiful garden. Yes, it had been warm, as this foreign air was warm, but there was a gentleness about it, and a deep undercurrent of delicious coolness, like the sharp notes in an otherwise heavy perfume. Gradually, the unfamiliar noise of the foreign market began to recede and in her mind she could hear again the sound of the wind fondling the oak leaves in the trees overhead and the quiet murmur of the stream at their feet. She imagined too that she could feel the comforting shape of Aidan's arm through his fleece. 'Yes, that's where I belong,' she sighed to herself, 'not here.' However the memory had anchored her, and when she opened her eyes again it was to see Sister Maria making her way back through the throng of shoppers towards the fruit stall with a now empty bag slung across her chest and her white veil bobbing up and down among the crowd like a little cork on a choppy sea.

The rest of the day passed in haze of fresh experiences as Kirsty began to get to grips with her new environment. Enumerable small decisions had to be made, ranging from where it would be safe to store the market produce, to how Joy's routine could be arranged in their new home. Later that evening, as she and Aidan were eating their first tasty meal of rice, beans and chicken which she had somehow managed to cook in the unfamiliar kitchen, she related the details of her morning trip with Sister Maria. Aidan listened quietly.

'Poor Kirsty,' he said when she'd finished. 'You've met the real Brazil much quicker than I did on my first visit. I didn't get to see it until my very last day.'

'Shall I ever get used to it do you think?' enquired Kirsty who could still see in her mind's eye the grim sight of the beggar and the small child.

'I don't know,' replied Aidan shaking his head sadly. 'In one way, I hope not. If you're right about Sister Maria, she never has, but somehow it hasn't destroyed her in the same way it nearly destroyed me. I wonder why? She seems so small and frail. But,' he went on quizzically, spearing a chunk of fibrous yellow jackfruit, 'to come to more mundane matters, do I really have to eat this chewy stuff? It tastes peculiar and smells like a dustbin!' He looked so funny, sitting at the table waving the fruit on his upturned fork that Kirsty found herself laughing.

'I'm so glad you don't like it Aidan. I don't either and you're right about the smell. Unfortunately there's a great mound of it in the fridge. Perhaps Luan would like to take it home in the morning. I expect you have to eat it as a child to get used to it. You know the flavour isn't that bad. It's the experience of eating it that's so awful. Give me a Cox's apple any day!'

Chapter 18

The workers in the Sparkling Delight brothel were having their midday food. The Turtle, who presided over the meal in person, always insisted that everyone sat round the table to eat so that she could supervise exactly what they were consuming. This was not because she cared about the prostitutes, but because she wanted to make sure they looked attractive with none of them becoming either too fat or too thin. Each day she cast an expert eye over them, in much the same way that a farmer constantly monitors his herd of pigs to make sure they will fetch a good price at market.

Tis, who hated the communal trough, was sitting very still in between Yaritza and Magdalena, trying to make herself as small as possible. The Turtle, who was still trying to fatten her up, dumped a large bowl of beans and rice in front of her. Tis looked at it with dismay. She'd never had a huge appetite, but over the last few weeks it had been getting smaller and smaller so that now she felt she couldn't manage anything at all, not even one mouthful. Looking at the mountain of food on her plate she despaired, like a weak old man who has just been told he must climb Everest or die. To add to her misery, every time she breathed she felt a sharp pain in her chest and back. This had begun on the previous day and was getting worse as each hour passed. Desperately she shrank even further down in her chair frantically hugging herself because she knew what was going to happen next.

'Eat Little Flower,' rasped the Turtle glaring at the girl, her voice rising in a frustrated crescendo. 'Eat, eat,

eat!' Reluctantly, Tis picked up her spoon and poked it in the gooey mass on her plate. She pushed it this way and that hoping that the Turtle would find someone else to torment but she knew, without looking up, that the cruel, implacable eyes were staring straight at her. All chatter stopped and the room fell completely silent. The old woman got up from her place and walked round the table. Tis's heart contracted with fear as she heard the menacing footsteps approaching. Then the wizened old face thrust itself into hers. She shrank back in her seat gazing in terror at the circle of glowing red lips so close to her nose. 'If you don't eat, now, this minute,' snarled the harsh voice, 'I'll give you to Alexio!' Whimpering with terror, Tis lifted the spoon and with the Turtle's sour breath wafting round her face, put the food into her mouth and swallowed. Somehow, she managed to force down several mouthfuls under the old woman's watchful gaze. Satisfied, the Turtle went into the kitchen to fetch a clean plate.

'Quick,' hissed Yaritza, 'give some to me and Magdalena.' Tis rapidly transferred as much food as she dared, so that when the old woman returned she gave a triumphant smile when she looked at Tis's now almost empty plate.

At the end of the meal, Tis walked slowly upstairs to the bedroom and climbed painfully onto the top bunk, which had once been Yara's but was now hers. She sat there for a long time, very still, clutching her chest and willing the pain to go away. To console herself she pulled out from under the mattress her shell and the two handkerchiefs. Wrapping the shell up in the hankies so that it looked a little like a doll, she cradled it in her arms and peered drearily out of the tiny barred window next to the bunk. This gave a view down the steep hillside and miraculously she could glimpse, in between the jumble of the nearer roofs, the estuary and distant docks. There were the trading vessels unloading their cargoes, looking small and far away, and out on the waters of the bay yet more ships were coming and going. There were pleasure craft too. A yacht, white sails set, was tacking out towards the sea and several speed boats wrote their messages of freedom across the water, in winding, frothy white wakes. It was a beautiful sight.

After a few moments Tis turned away from the window and looked down at the shell, wrapped in its covering of hankies that lay cradled in the crook of her arm. She hugged it to her.

'Oh, shell, shell, please help me,' she murmured. 'I'm so tired.' Slowly she slumped down on her dirty mattress and put her head onto the pillow. With one hand she held the shell to her ear and listened again to the faraway sound of the sea, reliving the feel of the warm waves on her body as they'd gently rocked her back and forth. Presently she fell into an exhausted sleep.

Somehow, when work began, she managed to climb down off her bunk, put on her gaudy wrap, and slowly creep down the stairs clinging onto the banister for support. Her head swam and the pain in her chest was like a constricting red-hot band so that she felt she could hardly breathe. Once downstairs in the waiting hall she slumped down on the velvet couch, hunched over with pain and waited with the other girls to be looked over by the punters. Somehow nothing seemed to matter anymore. Customers came and went, but she was hardly aware of them, or of the foetid atmosphere of stale smoke and unwashed bodies. At last she heard the dreaded, rasping voice,

'Little Flower, go to room one at once!' Making a super human effort, Tis struggled up from the couch and walked very slowly into the bedroom.

Chinn was sitting in bedroom one of the Sparkling Delight, waiting for Tis. He hadn't been to the brothel for a few weeks because in the immediate aftermath of Yara's escape he'd been given the task of setting up a new bicycle repair shop in another suburb of the city. He'd taken Luiz and Bruno with him and together they'd worked hard developing the business so that the shop was now thriving. He was aware that he'd promised Yara that he would make sure Tis was all right, so as soon as it was humanly possible he'd made the journey back to see how she was. He'd missed her more than he could explain and during the hectic weeks of the shop's opening she'd been continually at the back of his mind like a nagging toothache. As he'd wrestled with tricky repairs, talked to new customers, and chivvied Bruno and Luiz he'd worried about her constantly.

'I hope she's all right,' he'd said to himself for the umpteenth time as he'd turned into the entrance to the brothel. Then, when he'd scanned the girls on the couch and had spotted Tis, he hadn't known whether to be happy or sad. He'd hoped that by now her father would have taken her away but there she sat, looking somehow smaller than he remembered, and here he was, sitting on the bed waiting for her.

The door was slightly ajar and he was suddenly aware of the sound of hesitant footsteps approaching across the waiting area outside. He was immediately transported back to his childhood, remembering a time when he'd sat in the living room at home listening to an identical sound. In his mind's eye he saw the living room door slowly open to reveal his old grandmother leaning on two sticks, her grey hair straggling round her vacant face, her back bent and her chin moist with spittle. His eyes widened in alarm. Who was coming? The footsteps came closer, the door was pushed slowly open and there was Tis framed in the entrance. For an awful moment Chinn thought that he was looking at his grandmother once again. The bent posture was the same and also the vacant expression, but no, it was Tis. Whatever had happened to her since his last visit? This girl was thin beyond belief. Her form, from being elfin, was now gaunt and skeletal. Her skin was a strange grey colour, and her hair dull and lifeless. But it was her face that appalled him the most. All her interior energy seemed to have died. There was only the smallest glow of life still to be seen in her eyes and this appeared to be fading while he watched. She stood there breathing in an odd, laboured fashion, one hand holding onto the doorframe for support and the other clutching her chest.

Chinn leapt to his feet and hurried over to the door. Gently he took her by the hand and sat her down on the bed.

'Tis, oh Tis, what have they done to you!' he cried sitting down beside her. In a tiny croaking voice, she replied,

'It's my chest Chinn. It hurts. I can't breathe.'

'Lie down,' he commanded, and gently arranged the soiled pillow under her head, pulled up the room's only chair and sat down beside her. Tis seemed unable to say anything else and lay like a corpse on the bed. Chinn sat frozen with alarm as he listened to her erratic, rasping breathing. 'She's dying!' said a voice in his head. 'Do something!' But what could he do? Suddenly, like an epiphany from on high the answer came to him: he had to get her away from here and take her to hospital. He sat very still, running his hand agitatedly through his hair trying to think. Gradually as his hairstyle became more and more dishevelled, a plan formed in his mind. He would come next morning, with Luiz and Bruno, and together they would snatch Tis away from the brothel and take her to hospital. Gently he bent over the recumbent form on the bed and spoke urgently into Tis's ear.

'Tis, where's your room? I'm coming to get you tomorrow to take you to hospital.'

'Up the stairs. First room. On the, right,' came the gasping reply. 'Top bunk under the window.'

'Be waiting for me,' commanded Chin and then sat down again, trying to plan exactly what he would do. He thought dismally of the immense Alexio, and the indomitable Turtle. What would happen if they tried to stop him? But try as he might he couldn't work out an easy way to get the terrible duo out of the way, so giving his hair one last absent minded ruffle, he stood up and walked swiftly towards the door knowing that whatever happened he was going to rescue Tis before she died.

On his way out, he drifted across the hall looking for the staircase Tis had told him about, trying hard to look unobtrusive. As he reached the far side of the waiting area, the Turtle spotted him and assumed he wanted another girl.

'Which one do you want now?' she called in her hard cracked voice. Pretending to inspect the prostitutes, Chinn suddenly spotted Magdalena sitting at the end of the couch. Bending over her he whispered hurriedly in her ear,

'Where's the door to the staircase? I'm coming to rescue Tis early tomorrow to take her to hospital. Make sure she's ready for me.' Magdalena looked up startled but quickly understood what he was asking.

'The door's there,' she whispered pointing. 'I'll get her ready. She's really ill.'

'Make up your mind. Who do you want?' The Turtle's voice crackled across the hall. Chin straightened up, looked round mumbling something about not being sure, and ambled out of the brothel as casually as he could.

The next morning, when his two assistants came to work, Chinn called them into the little room that served as his office. Thinking they had done something wrong they stood in the doorway gazing at him apprehensively. Chinn wasn't sure whether he ought to ask for their help but at last he looked up from his desk and said quietly,

'Amigos, I have a favour to ask you. I want to rescue my favourite prostitute from the Sparkling Delight. She's very ill and if she stays there she'll die. I'm going to get her this morning and take her to hospital. Will you help me? There might be a fight. I don't know, and I need a bit of support. We can shut the shop for a couple of hours and just hope the owner doesn't come along to check on us.'

'You can count on me Boss,' replied Bruno, his eyes dancing. 'It'll be like the cinema,' and crouching down he whipped two imaginary guns from their holsters and fired a quick round out of the office door. Tucking the guns back into place he looked at Chinn, eyes wide with excitement and a big grin on his large, amiable face.

'Me too,' said Luiz. 'I owe you one for bringing me here. When do we go?'

'We'll go now,' replied Chinn looking at his watch. 'We'll stay in our overalls, and we can each carry a large spanner then no one will think there's anything strange going on.' So armed with a spanner apiece they set out across the city like a small, determined, industrial posse.

The first thing Chinn did when they arrived at the Sparkling Delight was to get a taxi and instruct the driver to park outside the brothel with his engine running.

'We'll look after that creep Alexio,' Luiz volunteered gleefully as they stood opposite the brothel. 'You go and find Tis.'

'Don't touch him unless you have to,' ordered Chinn. 'We don't want to go to prison.'

'OK Boss,' responded Bruno cheerfully. 'Just leave him to us. We'll do fine, we promise.'

The three walked across the road and pushed open the street door leading into the passage where Alexio usually sat on guard. To their satisfaction they found him lounging on his chair fast asleep and snoring loudly.

'Keep guard over him,' ordered Chinn quietly and swiftly made his way past the Turtle's blessedly empty desk and into the hallway where the prostitutes usually sat. This too was empty. A shaft of light from the open street door illuminated the tawdry scene - the faded glamour of the couches, the dirty floor and the pervasive stench of sour cigarette smoke and unwashed bodies.

Quickly he scurried across to the staircase and up to the first floor. He hesitatingly opened the door Tis had told him about and was confronted by the small dormitory where the prostitutes slept. Since this was early in the morning, all of them were still in bed asleep after their night's work. Going to the bunk by the window, he found that Tis too was asleep. She was lying facing him clutching something wrapped in dirty bits of rag. Her face was pale and her breath whistled through her teeth in shallow gasps.

'Tis, Tis, wake up,' he whispered urgently but she seemed not to hear him. Desperately he gazed at her wondering how he was going to get her down from the top bunk. His voice however, had woken Magdalena asleep on the bunk below.

'What are you doing here?' she questioned sleepily. 'Oh, it's you Chinn. Wait a moment and I'll help you.'

'You'll have to,' replied Chinn urgently. 'She can't hear me.'

'Right,' said Magdalena scrambling out of bed. Between the two of them they managed to lift Tis off the bunk and onto the floor. She stood swaying unsteadily, still clutching the small bundle tightly in her hand, but even though she was so desperately ill she refused to let go of it. At last, after a few frantic attempts the two gave up.

'We'll just have to take it with us whatever it is,' said Chinn in desperation. It was clear however, that Tis was incapable of walking, so Chinn took her in his arms. Magdalena opened the door for him and he managed to struggle down the stairs and across the hall. Just as they got level with Alexio the snoring stopped and the fat man opened his eyes.

'Hey, what's happening? Where are you taking her? You can't do that!' he grunted and tried to get to his feet. It was then he became aware that his shoulders were being firmly held down by two strong men who seemed to be brandishing large spanners.

'Sit still old fool!' commanded Luiz in his best film star voice. 'If you don't it will be the worst for you!' and he waved his spanner menacingly in front of Alexio's face. Quickly Chinn hurried down the passage and out to the waiting taxi. He laid Tis on the back seat and ran back inside.

'Get going,' he shouted. Bruno gave Alexio a quick shove, which half toppled him off his chair and the two of them ran swiftly out of the door, round the corner and into the maze of alleys that surrounded the brothel.

Chinn hopped into the taxi beside the driver saying,

'Quick! To the nearest hospital!' By the time the doorman had regained his balance, lifted his vast bulk off the chair and lumbered down the passage, the taxi was well out of sight. He gazed up and down the road rubbing his eyes but there was nothing to be seen but the everlasting traffic and the bustling crowds.

'I must have had a nightmare,' he said to himself. 'I could have sworn I saw a young man in an overall carrying Little Flower out of the door. How odd. There's nothing there though,' and he sat back down on his chair and lit a cigarette.

So it was that until the mid-day meal, when Tis's absence was discovered, nobody except Magdalena knew that she'd escaped, by which time she'd completely disappeared.

As the taxi made its slow way along the roads near the brothel Chinn leant his head back on the headrest and let out a sigh.

'Phew, that was a near thing!' he said to the taxi driver.

'What are you up to amigo?' the man queried. 'Is she your girlfriend or what?' Chinn laughed wryly.

'No. She's not my girlfriend, she's a prostitute I know, and she's very ill. What hospital do you think I should take her to? I don't think she's any money. In fact I'm sure she hasn't.' The taxi driver thought for a few seconds.

'I think the Sacred Heart would be your best bet amigo. It used to be run by the convent, but it's a government hospital now although the nuns still do a lot. It's a kinder place than most. My wife went there last year and they treated her really well.'

'Take us there then,' ordered Chinn.

The taxi threaded its way slowly through the city traffic and eventually drove through an imposing gateway and up a tree lined drive. Hospital buildings could be seen in among the trees and eventually the car came to rest outside the outpatients department. Chinn paid the driver and thanked him for his kindness. Together they lifted Tis out and set her down on a nearby bench. Many people were sitting on seats under the trees or on the grass while members of their family queued at the out patients' door. The taxi driver looked at them shrewdly, and then turned to Chinn who was standing irresolutely behind the seat supporting Tis and not knowing what to do next.

'Looks to be a fair sized queue amigo,' he said 'but I've seen worse. I come here quite often and I've known days when people were nearly dead by the time they were seen. You go through that door and get a ticket from the desk,' he added pointing to the entrance to the department. 'I'll stay with your friend until you get back. The sooner you book your place in the queue the better. When your turn comes your number will come up in that window over there.' Chinn looked at the window and saw a large number forty. As he watched, it changed to forty-one. A woman near the head of the queue then waved and a man got up from his seat under a nearby tree and made slowly for the doorway. Chinn followed him into a noisy crowded waiting area and was given ticket number one hundred and one by a disinterested clerk behind a desk.

Returning, he sat down beside Tis who was slumped on the seat barely breathing and put his arm around her holding her up.

'We must sit in the shade,' he thought desperately as the sweat began to trickle down his back, so lifting her in his arms he stumbled over to the space on the bench under a nearby tree that number forty had just vacated. There were already two people sitting on it, a mother and her young daughter who had her arm in plaster, but when they saw how ill Tis was they moved close together and Chinn was able to put Tis onto the bench and sit beside her with his arm around her for support. She sat with her head on his shoulder, breathing with great difficulty through clenched teeth and parted lips.

'What's the matter with your friend?' questioned the mother. 'She looks very ill.'

'I don't know,' replied Chinn. 'I wish I did. Tell me,' he added, 'do I have to go and queue as well as look in the window for my number?'

'No,' replied the woman. 'But sometimes if you don't the people in the line won't let you through when your turn comes.'

'Oh no!' said Chinn anxiously. 'What am I going to do? I can't leave her. She'll fall off the seat.'

'Look,' replied the mother kindly, 'what number are you?'

'One hundred and one,' replied Chinn.

'We're one hundred and three,' said the woman. 'My husband's in the queue. I'll go and tell him to keep your place too. He's a big man. Nobody messes with him!'

'Thank you,' he replied gratefully. 'Thank you very much.'

Chinn became very anxious as the minutes ticked by and the numbers slowly crawled up and up. He sat willing them to go faster but it made no difference. Two hours passed before 101 at last appeared in the window. He got stiffly to his feet, lifted Tis off the bench and hurried as fast as he could through the queue, past the burly husband and into the waiting room. There he stood, not sure what to do next while his arms ached and the patients and their relatives walked round him as if he wasn't there. The noise too confused him as babies were screaming, children crying and patients were chatting to each other at the tops of their voices. At last a helpful orderly took his number and leading him down a corridor showed him into a small, sparsely furnished consulting room. Chinn laid Tis on the couch and sat down on a chair, profoundly grateful, not only to have escaped from the waiting room, but to be inside the hospital at last. Abstractedly he ran his hands through his hair willing the Doctor to come soon before it was too late. Tis lay on the couch, eyes glazed, rolling restlessly from side to side and gasping in an alarming way. Magdalena had managed to find an old pair of jeans and a t-shirt for her to wear, but these were far too large for her emaciated body and made her seem even smaller and more shrunken. At last the door opened and two men in white coats came into the room. One was portly and much older than the other with an air of confidence about him, which seemed to indicate that he was the senior of the two. He was speaking in a foreign language to the younger man who was tall and thin and appeared to be in his early twenties.

'What's the matter with your wife?' said the senior doctor to Chinn in Portuguese.

'She's just a friend,' replied Chinn, 'and I don't know what the matter is. She seems to be finding it difficult to breathe. She's desperately ill. Please save her Doctor.' The Doctor made no reply but turned to the slight body lying on the bed looking grave. He spoke to her but she made no reply seeming totally unaware of anything that was going on. Indeed it took the combined efforts of all three of them to hold her in an upright position in order that the senior Doctor might sound her chest. She sat on the couch in their arms, lolling like a floppy rag doll. After he'd finished and his patient was once more lying down, he turned to Chinn and said gravely,

'Your friend has pneumonia. What did you say she did for a living?'

'She's a prostitute Doctor,' replied Chinn quietly. The Doctor pursed his lips and stood looking thoughtfully down at the slight body on the couch. At last he turned to Chinn and said sadly,

'Given her occupation, I think there's a good chance that she may have Aids related pneumonia.' Chinn looked despairingly at the Doctor.

'Is she dying?' he asked in a low voice.

'Let's hope I'm wrong,' replied the Doctor not answering the question. He then added thoughtfully, 'Whatever form of pneumonia she has, she's desperately ill, so I should stay near the phone. I'll admit her to hospital and we must hope that we can save her. I'll send a clerk to fill in the necessary forms. You do have a telephone I hope?' he added ominously. Chinn gave the number of the shop and watched numbly as both men left the room talking together in grave tones. Almost immediately two orderlies appeared with a trolley. Tis was lifted onto it where she lay with eyes closed barely moving. The trolley was wheeled out, and the door closed. She was gone. Chinn sat down on the chair feeling as if all the life had been drained out of him too. Now that he could do no more, he felt exhausted and depressed. If only he'd gone to the Sparkling Delight sooner, she would have had a better chance of surviving, but now it looked as if it was too late.

After all the admissions procedures were completed, Chinn made his way back to the shop wondering miserably if he would ever see Tis alive again. When he walked through the door Luiz and Bruno greeted him cheerfully. They'd enjoyed looking after the business on their own, and were still high on the excitement of the morning.

'How'd ya get on Boss?' questioned Bruno still playing the gangster. Then seeing the misery on Chinn's face, he fell silent, shuffling his feet in embarrassment.

'Bad news?' queried Luiz quietly.

'Tis may have Aids related pneumonia,' replied Chinn sadly. 'The Doctor doesn't think she'll make it.'

'Sorry boss,' muttered Bruno and turning away got back to work on the bicycle he was mending.

Chapter 19

Aidan and Kirsty were eating a late evening meal at the kitchen table. Although they'd been in Brazil for only five days, such a lot had happened and there had been so many adjustments to make, that it felt a great deal longer. Both had fallen in love with their small house in its beautiful surroundings. Kirsty had even discovered that from the netted front porch, with its wreaths of eye-catching cerise bougainvillea and fragrant frangipani, she could catch a glimpse of the estuary.

However dinner was not going well. Joy had woken early for her last meal of the day so Kirsty was trying to feed her while at the same time eating her own food and also catching up with Aidan's day.

'How was the hospital darling?' she enquired distractedly.

'I'm still shadowing Dr Romerez,' answered Aidan briefly without looking up from his plate.

'Joy and I went to the market on our own this morning for the first time. No Sister Maria to hold our hands,' remarked Kirsty after a pause. 'I've even managed to make friends with one of the stallholders who can speak a little English. I said "hello how are you," to him in Portuguese but that just made him laugh.' Still no response. At last she said sharply, 'What's the matter Aidan? You've hardly said two words during the whole of dinner. Has something bad happened at work?' Aidan looked up from the mango he was eating and smiled at her, seeming to see her properly for the first time since the meal began.

'How beautiful you look Kirsty!' he said lovingly. 'Being a mother really suits you.'

'Oh Aidan, how can you say that?' she replied laughing ruefully, 'I must look a fright; hair in a mess, no makeup and breast feeding a baby!'

'Darling, you make a beautiful picture just as you are, with Joy so happy and contented, cuddled in your arms. You don't know how lovely you look. Do you remember the sculpture of the Holy Family in the cathedral? Well, you look just like that, and I'm here to protect both of you.' Kirsty put down her fork, reached over the table trying hard not to disturb the baby, and gave his hand a squeeze.

'I thought of them too in the plane coming over,' she said smiling. 'You make a good Joseph, Aidan. Joy and I feel really safe and cherished. But you still haven't answered my question sweetheart! What's the matter?' Aidan looked thoughtful again.

'I'm worried,' he answered. 'We had a poor girl come in this morning to the outpatients' department suffering from pneumonia and I'm not sure she's going to last the night. She was one of the most pathetic scraps of humanity I've ever seen in my life. I just have a feeling that I ought to look in on her before we turn in for the night. I'm not sure why I want to. I only know I shall feel happier if I see she's still alive. I know which ward she was sent to. Would you mind? I won't be long.'

'No, of course not,' replied Kirsty. 'I know you. You won't settle until you've checked. Try not to be too long though. Joy might even let us have four or five hours now she's been fed.' Bending down she gently kissed the golden halo of down on top of the baby's tiny head and then smiled lovingly across the table at her husband, glad that he really cared about his patients.

Taking his torch, Aidan set out along the small path that led from the house to the long single storey wards built among the trees. The scent of frangipani filled the air, and the moon, which was nearly full, illuminated the night with her silvery magic. Aidan could see the twinkling lights of ships on the estuary and the far distant hills silhouetted against the moonlit sky. For a brief moment he stood looking out over the tranquil scene.

'Not so tranquil as it looks,' he thought to himself suddenly noticing some black storm clouds massing over the sea. 'I'd better hurry.'

On entering the women's medical ward by a door at the far end he found a nurse in a small office sitting at a desk, busily filling in forms. The ward itself was in semi darkness, but the small room was brilliantly lit, the light spilling out to illuminate the nearer beds. She looked up enquiringly as he came into the room and said something to him in Portuguese. Hoping she spoke English Aidan said slowly,

'We had a patient in Dr Romerez's clinic this morning with acute pneumonia. I have come to check her if I may. Where is she?'

'She is in the little room at the end of the ward,' said the nurse in halting English. 'She is very ill. Poor girl. Very ill. Perhaps she dies?' and she raised her shoulders and held out both hands looking sadly at him.

'I hope you're wrong,' he thought gloomily as he began to walk down the length of the ward between the two parallel rows of beds. Glancing around, he noticed that some of the patients were still awake. These stared at him curiously as he quietly passed by, but most were asleep, snatching a few brief hours of relief from their troubles.

He opened the door to the small room where the girl lay, and sat down for a moment on the wooden chair beside the bed scanning her face with concern. It was a stifling, airless night so she lay spread-eagled on top of the sheets, her breath coming in quick, harsh gasps. A single, low powered electric light bulb, hanging from the centre of the ceiling shed enough light for him to see that one of her small hands was tightly clutching some unidentifiable object. Rising from his seat he bent down, gently released her hold and extricated a beautiful shell, which appeared to be loosely wrapped in two bits of grubby cloth. He placed it quietly on the bedside locker and was about to throw the wrappings in the bin by the bed, when a flash of colour caught his eye and he found himself looking at a couple of letters, an 'A' and a 'V' intertwined with two beautifully embroidered little fish. He sat back down heavily on the chair. What could this mean? 'A V' - those were his father's initials, Andrew Vickers. There was no doubt that these were two of his grandmother's hankies. Frantically he searched in his pocket and drew out a handkerchief embroidered with an identical monogram. He looked at it in disbelief and then at the grubby bits of rag in his other hand. As far as he knew, he'd never lost any of the handkerchiefs his grandmother had embroidered for his father, certainly not here in this hospital. And then a memory from long ago began to surface. He saw in his mind's eye the sun setting over the ocean and outlined black against the gold, a small child's silhouette, arms upraised. Then a boat and a small sleeping girl, with a beautiful heart shaped face, lying in its lea. He seemed to feel again the heat of the sun as he bent to cover the bare limbs with sand and the elfin features with one of these now dirty hankies. But, what of the other? How did she get that one? Suddenly fear and horror gripped his heart as another more unwelcome memory resurfaced, of a cheap brothel and a terrified, young prostitute. Drawing a long shuddering breath he heard a voice scream in his head,

'It's her. You covered her face with it, you coward! You couldn't even bear to look at her after what you did. It's her, it must be her! And now she's dying.' Dropping the three handkerchiefs Aidan sat down heavily on the chair. His mind seemed to be on fire and he couldn't think. His breath came in short gasps and he felt as if a huge weight was being pressed down on his chest. At last, he managed to lift his eyes and take another look at the figure on the bed. This time he took in every part of her. Her face, yes that could well be the grown up face of the child who nestled beside the boat all those years ago. But she was so appallingly thin! Suddenly he noticed that the moon, shining through the window frame had formed a black cross over the body on the bed. Her motionless, bare, emaciated legs and matchstick arms stuck out on either side of the shadow symbol, making it look as if she'd been crucified. His mind immediately sprang back to the picture in Father James' cell of Christ contorted and mangled on his cross.

'And you too,' Aidan whispered to himself, his words barely audible. 'Why did it have to be you they crucified? Can't anyone escape?'

In deep despair he rose from his seat and made his way past the rows of sleeping patients and back up the path to his house. There he found Kirsty already in bed waiting for him. Aidan slipped off his clothes and joined her. Joy was asleep in her crib by the window and they could hear her quick quiet breathing. Aidan took Kirsty in his arms. He held her tightly feeling her comfortable reassuring covering of flesh. Raising himself on one elbow, he looked at her beautiful face, lying trustingly beside him on the pillow with its frame of auburn curls, mellowed now to a silvery gold by the transforming moonlight. With one finger he traced the outline of her eyes, nose and full mouth, the curve where neck met shoulder and the bountiful shape of her breasts, now the palest most delicate alabaster in the lambent light from the window. But as he gazed down at her the oncoming rain clouds slid across the moon and they were plunged into darkness. For a long moment he sat staring into the blackness listening to the first heavy raindrops spattering the window screens. Then the storm struck the little house in all its frenzy. Rain thrummed a deafening rhythm on the roof, and the wind harried and tormented the trees outside. Continuous sheet lightening, awful in its violet beauty, lit up the room and thunder crashed and reverberated out over the sea.

'Hold me tight,' said a small voice from the bed beside him after a particularly loud, rolling clap. 'I do hope Joy doesn't wake.' But she did, so all three of them lay wrapped up in bed together waiting for the storm to pass. At length the last distant roll of thunder died away and Aidan returned the baby to her crib. Wide-awake now, and with a mind no longer distracted by the noise, he got back into bed and drew Kirsty roughly to him.

That night his lovemaking had a desperate frenzy about it. It was almost as if a frantic attempt at exorcism was taking place deep within his body. When it was over, he sat up in bed, wrapped his arms round his long legs and drew some deep shuddering breaths.

'What's the matter Aidan?' enquired Kirsty anxiously out of the darkness. 'I don't know the man who's just made love to me. Please tell me. What's gone wrong?'

'It's her, Kirsty. It's her,' he replied in a low desperate voice.

'Who?' replied Kirsty, perplexed. 'Who Aidan? Whoever are you talking about?' Like a dying sigh came the reply,

'The girl I've just been to see is same girl I raped in the brothel.'

'How could you know that?' exclaimed Kirsty in astonishment. 'She'd be different now even if you thought you recognised her. It can't be her. There must be hundreds of girls in this city who look just like her.'

'Oh but it is, it is! She has my two hankies. The ones I gave her. You know, the ones with the AV and the fishes that my grandma embroidered for my dad. She's dying Kirsty. What can I do?'

'How on earth did she get two of your Grandma's hankies?' asked Kirsty in amazement. So Aidan then told her the story of how the two came to be in Tis's possession. 'It must be her then,' said his wife thoughtfully. 'It can't be anyone else can it?'

'What's she ever done that she should end up like this?' groaned Aidan. 'And there are thousands more like her I know; poor, forgotten women, dying from sexual abuse and Aids. It seems to me sometimes,' he went on bitterly, 'that life is no more than a soulless machine. In at one end go the small, innocent girl children, and out at the other, like a river of sewerage, come their dead battered bodies. The rubbish of the world, to be swept up into the dustbin without anyone noticing they've gone. And I don't even know her name!' he added. 'But then why should I?' he muttered miserably. 'She's only a prostitute!'

Kirsty was silent for a long moment, trying to come to terms with this bleak picture of life. At last she spoke.

'No Aidan, it's not quite like that,' she said slowly. 'Yes, life may seem to be one vast machine to most of us, but if you think carefully you can see that there is, amazingly, a joke hiding in it.'

'Joke,' replied Aidan surprised. 'Whatever do you mean? I don't see anything funny.'

'Just this,' replied Kirsty. 'We are the joke in the machine, you and I. We care. We love. We've come here to learn how to do something to give meaning to lives like these. Surely every act of love and compassion means that the machine ceases to be merely a machine for an instant. Everything you will do as a doctor Aidan, beginning with your care for this girl now, means that they become real human beings, not just forgotten refuse crushed by some relentless cosmic juggernaut.'

Silence fell for a long moment as Aidan thought about this. The moonlit room was quiet and still now, the only sounds coming from the rhythmic breathing of the baby in her cot and the distant sounds of traffic outside the convent walls. At last he spoke.

'I hope you're right,' he said quietly. 'And if she lives until tomorrow, I'm going to do everything I can to save her.'

'I'll help you Aidan,' said Kirsty sitting up in bed beside him and putting her arm round his shoulder. She was silent for a moment and then said slowly, 'There's another thing that troubles me though.'

'What's that?' queried Aidan.

'It's just that life is so unfair,' she replied slowly. 'Here I am. A fairly average western woman with a wonderful marriage, a home, a family, a career and I feel I have a right to all those things. But these girls have no status, no rights, no future even. Somehow it seems so unjust. They can't help where they're born can they?'

'No, they can't,' replied Aidan grimly. 'That's why I'm going to do my damnedest to save this one.' Then he paused and added almost under his breath, 'If she lives.'

But live she did, and when the sun rose in the sky,

inexorably waking the world to another day, it was to find
Tis still miraculously clinging on to life.

Chapter 20

Carlos, Ana and Davi were sitting eating their evening meal in Tis's old home in the village. On Ana's lap sat an eighteen-month-old baby girl. Night had fallen, and the room was lit by a weak electric light bulb suspended low over a container of rice and beans placed in the centre of the table. Its feeble beam illuminated the heads and faces of the eaters in a pale amber glow, while wisps of steam, rising from the hot food, formed a ghostly aura round the bowl. The rest of the room was in shadow.

'I'm so glad you get one day off a month in this new job Carlos,' said Ana reaching out and covering her husband's large hand with her small, work worn one. 'It goes so quickly though,' she added sadly. 'As soon as you're gone we want you back again. Isn't that right Davi?'

'Yes,' replied Davi plaintively, 'but I want Tis too. Where is she? Why doesn't she come home?'

'Oh Davi, please don't say that anymore,' pleaded his mother, distressed. 'You know we've done all we can to find her. Manolo calls the number we were given constantly on his mobile, and he asks around for her each time he goes to Beleza. He told me he'd rung again only yesterday when he brought your dad home. There's never any answer. You know that.'

'Make your friend write another letter,' said Davi flatly, turning to his father. 'Perhaps the first one didn't get there.'

'Davi,' replied Carlos gravely, 'I've sent three. If the address is genuine at least one of them would have got there by now. I can't think of anything else to do,' he added despairingly.

'Our Tis seems to have disappeared off the face of the earth doesn't she,' said Ana dismally. 'Every day I long to see her come running in at the door like she used to. Whatever can have happened to her? I've a feeling deep inside me that I'll never see her again. I pray I'm wrong.'

While they were eating, the wind began to rise and gust noisily round the dilapidated shack finding chinks and gaps through which it squeezed to join the small family. Ana wrapped an old blanket round the baby, holding her tightly to try and keep out the draughts. She shivered, thinking how sad life had become now Tis had disappeared.

Meanwhile, Yara was out on the road battling against the same wind. The bus had finally set her down about three kilometres from the village. It had meandered its way there via innumerable drop off points at filling stations on the highway. Many people had got on and off and the driver had examined tickets, stowed luggage and shouted at passengers, until Yara's head had begun to ache. It was almost dark when she alighted at the start of the dusty track that led to her home and the road was deserted. It was never busy at the best of times since very few people visited the village, and hardly any ever left it. She was still trudging wearily along when the first playful zephyrs tugged at her ragged shirt, and by the time she got to the last grove of trees nearly half an hour later, the wind was whipping her face and trying to pull the clothes off her back. She was hungry and tired, but inside her, glowing like a warm fire, was the knowledge that she would soon be back at home with her mother.

'Mamãe will be so surprised to see me,' she said to herself for the twentieth time as she struggled to keep her hair from blowing across her face.

Eventually, she reached the village and made her way along the familiar street. Nobody was about as all the inhabitants were relaxing indoors after the day's work. As her shack came into view however, Yara slowed her excited pace. Something was wrong. No light was coming from the windows. Quickly she ran the last few paces, up the decrepit steps and in through the door which was wide open and swinging to and fro in the wind. By the weak light of a gibbous moon, which sailed out from behind the tattered clouds for a few seconds, she could see that the room was completely empty. Rubbish had collected in ruffled heaps in the corners and it was plain that nobody had lived there for a very long time. With a loud bang the door blew shut behind her and Yara was left alone in the dark, in a state of horror and despair.

'This is a nightmare,' she muttered under her breath. 'It's not really happening. In a little while I shall wake up and find myself in bed at the brothel.' After a long bewildered moment she turned and went slowly to the top of the steps. It was then she became aware of the house next door, Tis's house. A faint light was shining from its windows. 'Ana's there,' she said to herself, dashing across the intervening space and bursting in. Carlos, who was sitting by the door, leapt to his feet as it was flung open. His chair went flying backwards as he made a grab for her, catching her by the arm.

'Hey, who are you?' he shouted. It was Ana who recognised her first.

'Yara!' she exclaimed struggling to her feet and giving the baby to Davi to hold, 'is it really you?'

'Yes it's me,' shouted Yara, 'but where's my mother?'

'Oh Yara,' replied Ana, standing very still, 'I'm so sorry. Your mother died from a heart attack soon after you left.' At this devastating news, all the courage and determination, which had sustained Yara throughout her perilous flight from the brothel, disappeared, and as the rabbit gripped in the eagle's talons abandons its hopeless struggle, she gave way to despair.

'No! No!' she groaned, and putting her head in her hands began to cry as if her heart would break. Ana took her in her arms, rocking her back and forth as she would rock a baby, and gradually Yara's tears began to hush and the torment of her grief to ease a little.

'You must eat, Yara,' she said at last, helping her to a bowl of beans and rice and filling a mug with water. Yara ate slowly, pausing now and then to wipe the tears from her eyes. When she'd finished her food, Carlos put the question all of them had been longing to ask.

'Where have you been Yara?' he said quietly. So Yara told them. When she began explaining about the Sparkling Delight, Ana became very agitated.

'But Yara,' she interrupted, 'it was the same man who took Tis. He said she was going to be a maid.'

'Tis,' said Yara slowly, 'is still there now. She's a

prostitute too. I escaped so that I could take you back with me Carlos, to come and rescue her. She's very sick.'

Both parents gazed at each other in horror, and Davi, who didn't understand the full significance of the disaster, but realised that something terrible had happened to his sister, buried his head in the baby's neck and began to cry.

'You will come with me won't you Carlos?' said Yara looking at him beseechingly. 'I've enough money for the journey there and back,' and she told them of her own experience in Guilherme's village and how she'd obtained the bus fare.

'Yes,' said Carlos grimly. 'I'll come. I'll have to go back to work tomorrow and ask for a couple of days leave. Then we'll go and get her.'

After the meal ended, Yara took out the two rolls of notes and laid them on the table. Ana looked at them warily as if they were contaminated.

'That's like blood money,' she said thoughtfully. 'They nearly killed you for it Yara. Thank God you escaped in time,' she added. 'Poor, poor child,' she thought looking at the girl with tears in her eyes. 'She endured so much to earn this. So many hours of suffering and torture are here in this money.' Reaching out she hesitatingly touched one of the bundles with her finger and it rolled across the table towards Carlos who looked enquiringly at Yara.

'What are you going to do with this Yara?' he queried. 'There's a lot of money here. You earned it. Are you sure about spending it all on bus fares?'

'Yes. I am,' replied the girl. 'I added it up roughly when I was waiting for the bus, but let's see exactly how much we've got,' and she set about sorting the notes into piles. When at last it was counted and checked she sat back in her chair and looked at him. 'There's enough here to get us both to Beleza and return with Tis. There'll be some over as well,' she announced with satisfaction.

'I'm coming too,' announced a voice from the other side of the table. It was Davi. 'Tis needs me,' he said loudly, standing up straight. 'I know she does. You shan't leave me behind. If you do, I'll lie down in front of the bus.' All three of them looked at the small boy. Even the baby gazed at him with interest. Somehow they all knew that he meant what he said. There was silence in the room, broken eventually by Yara who said uncertainly,

'There's enough for a ticket for him too, Ana. Perhaps he'd better come. I know Tis will be glad to see him.' Davi ran round the table and threw his arms around her squeezing her so hard that she cried out in protest.

'You must pay for it Davi,' Ana said smiling at her son. 'Yara must have your bed tonight and you'll have to sleep on the floor.'

'She can have it forever,' he replied simply, 'if it means I can go to Tis.'

Two days later Ana watched the three of them walk down the village street on the first part of their journey back to the pickup point on the main highway.

'What if something dreadful happens to them?' she said fearfully to herself. 'Then I'd be on my own just like Yara's mother was.' Slowly she made her way back inside the house, put the baby to sleep on the bed and sat at the table to thread beads. One by one they clicked into place on the string. The sun was already shining brightly and some of the beads seemed to sparkle as her deft fingers formed the gaudy pattern of the necklace. However it wasn't the sunlight that caused the beads to glisten, but the tears that trickled down Ana's face and spilled over them as she thought of her beloved daughter in a brothel.

Meanwhile with every hour that passed, the bus was getting nearer to Beleza. It was a noisy place with music blaring out of the speakers and Carlos had to put up with being jostled and pushed every time it stopped to let passengers on and off. He didn't care however, as he was glad of the time to plan what he would do when they arrived at the brothel.

'I wonder how Davi is coping with this?' he thought after they'd been travelling for some time. 'He's never been on a bus before.' He looked down at his son, who was sitting quietly beside him gazing out of the window, and wondered what he was thinking. 'How are you doing Davi? Are you enjoying yourself?' he questioned at last. The boy turned, looked at his father and said slowly,

'Not really, dad. It's so noisy and I don't know any of these people. But it's ok,' he added managing a small grin. 'We're going to get Tis and that's all that matters.' Carlos looked back at him encouragingly and then turned to see how Yara, who was sitting across the gangway, was getting on. As soon as he glanced at her face he could see something was wrong.

'What's the matter?' he enquired raising his voice above the level of the music and the chatter of the other passengers. Yara looked at him frowning.

'We'll soon be at Guilherme's village,' she replied. 'What if he gets on?' Carlos smiled a grim smile, and lifted his fist, waving it near his face.

'It would be a pleasure to meet that rat. I hope he does,' he said fiercely. Seeing that his words had put her mind at rest he sat back in his seat and went to sleep, only waking when they drew into the bus station in Beleza.

An hour later the three arrived at the top of the road in sight of the brothel. Yara stopped. 'It's no good,' she said in some agitation. 'I can't go back there. Alexio will see me and grab me. You'll have to go on your own Carlos. I'll wait here.'

'You look after Davi then,' he ordered. 'I'll be back with Tis in a little while. I'm looking forward to meeting this Alexio,' he added grimly and strode off.

When he arrived outside the Sparkling Delight, he stood for a while on the other side of the street and took a long look at the outside of the brothel. He'd not, in fact, got any idea in his mind of what he was going to do, but he knew the layout of the building and where Alexio usually sat, since Yara had described it to him during the journey. The road was a busy one and traffic was passing up and down it as fast as the steepness of the hill would allow. The entrance door was half open and Carlos watched it carefully for some time, but nobody came either in or out. He could dimly see Alexio however, sitting in the shadows keeping guard on the front window where a semi naked young girl sat. She'd adopted what was supposed to be a suggestive pose, but it was obvious to Carlos that she was feeling both bored and wretched.

No matter how he wracked his brain for a clever way of rescuing Tis no inspiration came to him, so in desperation he decided to march straight into the brothel and see what would happen next. Accordingly, he strode across the road and into the lobby. Alexio thought he was a customer and since the brothel was closed for a while, shouted after him as he burst into the inner waiting room. This was empty so he made for the door into the dining room where Yara had told him the prostitutes sometimes gathered round the table to play cards in the afternoon. However, when he rushed in, there were no girls there, only the Turtle, sitting at the far end of the table giving her vermillion nails another coat of varnish. With her head bent over one outstretched hand and her scarlet mouth pursed in concentration, she looked like a shrivelled vampire crouching over its kill.

'Where's Little Flower?' demanded Carlos, striding down the length of the table and coming to a halt inches from the old woman. The Turtle looked up. She was used to dealing with difficult people, as the men who came to the Sparkling Delight were often drunk and truculent.

'Who wants to know?' she enquired in a disinterested voice, looking up from the little brush poised over her index figure.

'I do,' rapped Carlos. 'I'm her father. I've come to take her home.'

'Oh really,' replied the Turtle disdainfully. 'I don't know where she is. She disappeared a while ago so you're too late,' and bending her head she stroked another brush full of crimson varnish over her nail.

At this, the gorge rose in Carlos' throat and his anger became uncontrollable. He leaned forward, grabbed the Turtle by the shoulders shaking her so violently that the polish bottle flew out of her hand. It shot across the table and smashed against the wall causing a tiny stream of blood red varnish to trickle down the dingy white paint.

'Where is she, you old witch? Where's Little Flower?' he raged, and shook the Turtle again so hard, that her head bent backwards and forwards on her scrawny neck and her teeth made an irritating clacking noise in her head.

Hearing the commotion, Alexio hurried in. He was just in time to hear Carlos's last question, so as he lumbered towards them he yelled,

'She's telling you the truth. The girl's gone!' Suddenly Carlos noticed the glint of a knife in the fat man's hand. Releasing the old woman he ran round to the other side of the table. The Turtle blinked and stared at Carlos so viciously that he felt his blood run cold.

'If you ever come in here again,' she hissed in a hard, venomous voice, 'I'll have you killed.' Carlos knew she meant it so he raced for the door, catching one last glimpse of the Turtle's face grinning coldly at him, scarlet lips drawn back and head thrust forward.

Quickly, heart pounding, he sprinted back to Yara and Davi his breath coming in great gasps. Haltingly he explained what had happened. Davi let out a wail that startled several passers-by.

'Tis, oh Tis what have they done with you!' he cried in dismay. Yara's face fell in despair, but suddenly a thought struck her.

'Was there a girl in the window?' she asked urgently.

'Yes, there was,' replied Carlos. 'Do you think she might know something?'

'She might,' said Yara slowly. 'It's worth a try.'

'I daren't go back again,' said Carlos in a troubled voice. 'Alexio will be watching for me now, and he has that knife.' Yara stood for a long moment, twisting her hands in perplexity.

'There's only one thing for it,' she said in a small, frightened voice. 'I'll have to go.'

'I'll go too,' piped Davi. 'I'll look after you Yara.'

'You're a brave girl Yara,' said Carlos. 'I'll keep watch from this end of the street. Surely nobody will connect you with the brothel if you're holding a child's hand. I know, why don't we buy a cheap hat for you to wear as a disguise?'

'Quick, then,' said Yara. 'The girl might be going in soon.' Hurriedly they bought a broad brimmed sun hat from a nearby pavement vendor and taking Davi by the hand Yara set off down the street towards the brothel, her heart beating fast.

The street seemed endless, but when they at last

drew near the Sparkling Delight she saw with relief that the girl on show was Magdalena. Cautiously she sidled up to a small open window on the side of the shop front furthest away from Alexio, who was now sitting on guard in the half open doorway and hissed,

'Magdalena, it's me, Yara.' Magdalena turned and said in a frighteningly loud voice,

'Yara, where have you been? Is it really you?'

'Yes! Quick,' whispered Yara urgently. 'Tell me what's happened to Tis.'

'Chinn came and took her to the hospital. That's all I know,' replied Magdalena.

At that moment Alexio came out to see who was talking. Yara took one look at him, turned and fled up the street dragging Davi behind her. They rounded the corner at speed, dodging in and out of the people crowding the pavements. As soon as they got to Carlos, Yara grabbed him.

'Quick!' she cried, 'Alexio's seen me! Tis is in hospital. Run!' All three of them dashed rapidly away, turning into the maze of small alleys that wound their way along the hillside. After a short while Davi began to lag behind. He had a stitch in his side, and his legs felt as if they were going to collapse.

'Stop!' he gasped at last, 'I can't run anymore.' All three came to a breathless halt while Carlos listened to see if he could detect sounds of pursuit, but all he could hear was the noise of the traffic and the hum of voices from the folk hurrying up and down the main thoroughfare. 'It's ok,' he gasped. 'I don't think we're being followed. Let's sit for a moment.' All three squatted down on a convenient doorstep. When they'd recovered their breath, Carlos said,

'Yara, do you know where the hospital is?'

'No,' replied Yara wearily. 'We'll have to ask someone. I hope it's not too far. My legs are aching and I'm very hungry.'

'Come on then,' said Davi who had now recovered from his stitch and was longing to find Tis. 'Let's go.'

Chapter 21

Full of foreboding at what he might find, Aidan quietly opened the door of the little room the following morning and looked inside. But no, she was still there. Moving across to the bed he stood looking down at the slight form, which lay so still under the coverlet.

'Still fighting,' he said quietly, 'but for how much longer?' As he watched, the girl groaned and rolled over on her side. Closing his eyes he willed her to live with all the energy he had. Eventually he tiptoed out of the ward wondering if this was the last time he would ever see her alive. 'She has to die soon,' he said to himself despondently as he made his way across the grounds to his house among the trees. Questions swirled round in his head to which there seemed to be no answer. How had she got here to Beleza when the first time he'd seen her she'd been miles away? How could her parents have let her come to work in a brothel? What would happen to her if she survived?

On the third day, too restless to stay in bed, he got up early just as the first light of dawn was fingering the horizon, and made his way once more down the path from his house to Tis's bedside. The air was blessedly cool from an early morning shower, and raindrops sparkled on the bushes and trees; but he noticed none of these things as he was dreading what he would find when he got to the ward. She'd looked so desperately ill the previous evening that he couldn't bring himself to believe that she hadn't died in the night. However, on entering he saw a sight that astonished him, for there she was, propped up in bed, eyes open, looking very much better.

'She looks,' thought Aidan, 'like a precious, china vase that has been smashed and stuck back together again, very, very carefully.' Tis glanced up as the door opened with a look of helpless bewilderment on her face.

'You look better. How do you feel?' he asked, forgetting in his delight that it was unlikely she could understand English.

'Where am I?' she whispered, automatically answering his question in the same language she had used to reply to her mother when they'd been threading beads and practicing their English conversation.

'In hospital,' replied Aidan, surprised that she'd understood him. 'You've been very sick, and you're here for us to make you better.'

He sat down on the chair, and his glance fell on his two handkerchiefs that now lay neatly folded on the bedside locker. Taking a deep breath he drew from his pocket one of his grandmother's neatly folded, clean hankies with its fish monogram plainly showing, and held it out to her.

'Take it,' he said gently. Tis took the handkerchief, looked at the monogram then glanced at her two hankies.

'Why have you got - a handkerchief - like mine?' she asked haltingly, taking several shallow breaths between the words.

'Because,' replied Aidan quietly, 'your handkerchiefs once belonged to me. Those are my father's initials, 'A.V.', Andrew Vickers. The fishes were embroidered by my grandmother. These hankies are unique. You and I are the only people in the world who have them.'

For a while there was silence in the room as Tis lay back on her pillows, pondering what she'd just heard. Aidan sat very still. In through the window drifted the 'good to see you' cry of a bem-te-vi bird sitting in a nearby tree, and the distant sound of early morning traffic passing by on the road, but Aidan was oblivious to these. In the ward nothing moved. It was indeed, as if time was holding its breath. At last she spoke, the words coming like pebbles being dropped slowly, one by one into a deep pool.

'Then - it was you - who covered my face - as I - slept on the beach,' she gasped, struggling to breathe and looking straight at him. Aidan stared down at his hands, too ashamed to look directly at her. Again, silence descended. This time it was he who eventually broke it.

'It was also me,' he said very slowly and quietly, still unable to meet her gaze, 'who gave you the other one that dreadful night in the brothel. I didn't want to be there. My uncle drugged me, and I bitterly regret it. Can you ever forgive me for what I did to you?' Tis looked at him steadily. Even in her weakened state she could see how sad and desperate he was. Then she turned her face away, and gazed out of the window. The first sunbeams of the day were stealing in through the branches of the tree outside making a moving pattern of light and shade on her bed cover. Abstractedly she glanced down at them, her fingers slowly tracing the trembling golden shapes.

Without looking up she said gently,

'Yes, I forgive you. You're the first man - ever to say – sorry - to me.' Looking at him once more she saw to her surprise that two tears were trickling slowly down his cheeks.

'Please - don't cry,' she said quietly. Aidan reached out and captured the small fluttering hand in his. It lay in his large one like a helpless baby bird.

'Listen,' he said, with all the firmness he could put into his voice, 'I'll look after you now, and I'll never, never let you go back to that life, I promise. I'll do all I can to make you better. Do you understand?'

For a long moment they both sat perfectly still gazing at each other. Somehow, it seemed to Aidan that she could see into his soul and knew that she could trust him. Then all the tension in her small body appeared to melt away and she relaxed onto the pillows. Very quietly, like the sighing of the dawn wind in the trees outside came a single word,

'Obrigada - thank you.' Then, exhausted, she closed her eyes and slept.

Aidan rose from the chair and crept quietly out of the room. As he retraced his steps his feet felt as light as air, and his heart full of joy. Looking round, he thought that he'd never seen the world look so beautiful. It was almost as if it had been newly created just for him. A crimson liveried macaw startled him as it flew low across his path, and he realised with a shock that he'd been too preoccupied to notice anything around him for the last few days.

'Were these raindrops really glistening on the grass when I walked down the path half an hour ago?' he asked himself in wonder. 'I suppose they must have been, but I didn't even see them.'

Back at home, he found Kirsty sitting on the veranda, feeding Joy.

'What's happened?' she asked as he came up the last step. Aidan drew up a chair and sat down.

'How do you know something's happened?' he said laughing.

'Because,' replied Kirsty, 'we've been married long enough for me to know something's happened without you having to tell me. You didn't have that sparkle in your eyes when you went out.'

'She's forgiven me,' said Aidan simply. 'I told her who I was, and she's forgiven me! I don't know how she could, but she has and it's made me want to sing. It seems as if something heavy I've been carrying around deep inside has suddenly been taken away. You can't imagine how light I feel. If I go outside now, I might just float off into the sunshine,' and taking Joy from his wife's lap he held her high in the air until the baby began to chuckle in delight. Kirsty laughed too.

'Please don't float off anywhere,' she said. 'Joy and I need you here. When Tis is a bit stronger,' she added, 'may I meet her please? There might be something I could do for her too.'

'Darling, that would be wonderful,' Aidan replied. 'Do you know what she told me though?' he said, suddenly sad. 'She said no man had ever asked her forgiveness before.' Kirsty looked thoughtful.

'I suppose,' she said, 'that men like that see prostitutes as some sort of lower life form, and just as you wouldn't apologise to your dog if you beat it, so they feel they have a perfect right to use women's bodies in any way they wish. Besides, they pay money don't they, so they feel they can do whatever they want.'

'I guess that must be it,' said Aidan. 'Wow, it's been quite a morning! The next few days are going to seem dull after this.'

But in that he was wrong. The next afternoon, when he visited Tis once more, he found a stocky young man with untidy clothes and unruly hair, seated by her bedside.

'I recognise your face,' he thought 'but I can't quite place where I've seen you before.' Tis was asleep when he entered the room but woke when she heard the door open. Aidan held out his hand to the visitor and said firmly,

'I'm Aidan Vickers, a trainee doctor. I've a special interest in this young girl's welfare and I have to say to you very firmly that there's no way she's ever going back to the brothel.' Chinn looked helplessly at Tis, not understanding what was being said so she translated Aidan's speech into Portuguese.

'I will translate for you,' she said looking first at Aidan and then at Chinn. 'My breathing feels a bit better today. I think I can manage it,' she added.

'My name is Chinn,' the young man said. 'I agree with you. Tis is never going back to the brothel.' Aidan relaxed a little and sat down on the edge of the bed.

'Have you got a few moments to talk?' Aidan enquired. 'I should be interested to know who you are and how you know my patient?' For a long moment Chinn was silent wondering how much he dared tell this doctor. He looked enquiringly at Tis who nodded encouragingly at him saying simply,

'You can trust him Chinn. He's a good man.' There was silence for a few moments but at last Chinn asked anxiously,

'If I tell you the truth, you won't tell anyone will you?'

'No,' responded Aidan gravely, 'I won't.'

'I'm in charge of a bicycle repair shop, and I'm gay,' he began slowly. 'My assistants suspected this and started to tease me so I decided to deceive them by going to a brothel. There I met Tis. We talked together and are best friends now. She helps me and I help her.'

'But why,' interrupted Aidan at this point, 'if she's such a friend of yours, did you let her get so sick?'

'I was sent to a better shop on the other side of Beleza,' he replied. 'It was very busy and I couldn't return for six or seven weeks but as soon as I saw Tis like this,' he added, 'Luiz, Bruno and I came and rescued her, and brought her here. It was very exciting,' he said his face lighting up as he thought back to their raid on the Sparkling Delight. 'We took large spanners with us, and the boys pinned down the fat doorman while I found Tis.'

'Well done,' laughed Aidan, 'well done. I wish I could have been there.' He then sat thoughtfully beside the bed, turning over in his mind what he should say next. Nobody spoke, and Tis lay back looking exhausted. At last Aidan broke the silence.

'I too,' he said 'have a connection with Tis. Two, in fact. If I tell you, will you also promise not to tell anyone?'

'Yes,' replied Chinn. 'You keep my secret, I'll keep yours.' Quietly, Aidan told Chinn of his meetings with Tis.

'That's amazing,' said Chinn, when the story was finished. A thought then occurred to Aidan,

'Tis' he said, for he now knew her name, 'I know hardly anything about you. I've heard about Chinn, but tell me about your life before you came to the brothel.'

'I was on the beach the day you first saw me,' she began, 'because my uncle had brought me there from my home where I live with my mother, father and younger brother Davi. I wanted to see the sea. Later, when my brother got TB and we had no money to make him better, Thiago came and said he would take me to be a maid in the city. He gave my parents cash. I love Davi with all my heart,' she added, 'but I don't know whether he's alive or dead. If he's alive,' she concluded simply, 'I'm glad I came.' Aidan was deeply moved by the heroic choice Tis had made, and the simple way in which she spoke about it.

'Could I do that?' he wondered looking at the

gaunt face resting against the white pillows. 'I don't know if I could.' Then another thought occurred to him. 'Tis,' he said. A couple of days before I saw you on the beach, our car broke down on the road and my mother gave some chocolate to two little girls who were peeping at us from behind a tree. Was that you too? Tis's eyes opened wide in astonishment.

'Yes, that was me and my friend Yara. So we've met three times already Doctor,' she exclaimed in amazement, 'not twice.' Before Aidan could comment further Chinn interrupted saying,

'I helped Yara after she escaped, Tis. She hid in my workshop. It must have been about seven or eight weeks ago. I hope nothing bad happened to her on the way home,' he added looking worried. 'She was supposed to be fetching your father to take you away wasn't she?'

'Was it only seven weeks?' asked Tis amazed. 'It feels as if it was months ago. I miss her,' she added simply. 'She's my best friend.'

'Oh Tis,' Chinn said looking even more anxious than ever, 'she won't know you're here. What if she goes back to the Sparkling Delight with your father to find you?' All three looked at each other in dismay.

'There's not much we can do about that is there?' said Aidan. 'We can hardly leave a message for her at the brothel.'

'No,' said Chinn, 'we can't. We'll just have to hope that somehow they find out you're here if they come.' Aidan looked at his watch.

'I must be going now,' he said, 'I have to get back to work. Shall I see you again?'

'Yes,' said Chinn, 'I shall get here as often as I can. Now I'm in charge of this new shop, I can leave it with Bruno every few days and come for an hour in the afternoon to see how Tis is doing. I'm very pleased to have met you Doctor,' he said quietly, as both men stood, 'I'm glad we shall meet again.'

Two days later when Aidan popped into Tis's room to see how she was, he found Chinn sitting beside her bed once more. The two were sharing a packet of sweets, which lay open on the coverlet.

'You're looking better,' he said to his patient in delight. Tis, who was sitting up in bed, smiled at him.

'I feel it,' she said. Aidan looked out of the window at the warm, sunlit grounds and a good idea occurred to him.

'Would you like to go for a ride in a wheelchair?' he asked. 'It would get you out of this stuffy room for half an hour. There's a fresh breeze coming in off the sea and it would do you good.' Tis's face lit up.

'Can Chinn come too?' she enquired.

'Of course,' replied Aidan. 'We'll all go together, and then he can bring you back to the ward.' So the two men gently lifted Tis into a wheelchair and together the three of them set off. Tis gazed round her at the beautiful grounds. She'd been too ill when she'd arrived at the hospital to pay any attention to her surroundings, But now the sight of the tall shady trees, the brilliant displays of poinsettias, and the pink and white of the bougainvillea and frangipani caused a little spark of interest to glow in her face for an instant. When the path eventually wound its way up a short incline and she had her first view of the estuary however, she caught her breath.

'Please, please can we stay here and look at the sea?' she pleaded, so Chinn parked the wheelchair by a bench, under a large jacaranda, and sat down beside it. Aidan however remained standing.

'Tis,' he enquired looking down at her. 'Would you mind if I went and fetched my wife and baby daughter? My house is close by, and I know Kirsty would very much like to meet you.'

'I'd like that,' she replied quietly.

When Aidan arrived home he found Kirsty in the kitchen doing battle with a large pineapple. She had just decapitated it and her knife was poised to attack its knobbly skin when he appeared in the doorway.

'Is something the matter?' she asked, looking up in surprise and lowering the knife. 'You're home early.'

'Tis is in a wheelchair just down the path,' he replied. 'Will you come with Joy and meet her for a few moments? Can the pineapple wait?' he added smiling.

'Of course,' replied Kirsty, putting the fruit back in the fridge, and collecting the baby from her crib in the bedroom. When they neared the bench and could see the two figures gazing out at the view she whispered to him. 'Oh Aidan, they look so forlorn. I do hope she'll get better.'

'Me too,' he responded quietly. 'That's Chinn with her. He cares about her almost as much as I do.' When they reached the seat, Kirsty bent over Tis and taking both of her thin shoulders gently in her hands said softly,

'I'm glad to meet you Tis. Aidan has told me so much about you. Can we be friends?' Tis looked up at her solemnly.

'Yes,' she said simply. 'We can.' Chinn moved along the bench so that Kirsty could sit down, but Aidan, still standing, bent down and showed Tis the baby who was asleep in his arms. The girl gazed at Joy for a long moment then a look of indescribable pain passed across her face.

'Tis, what is it?' asked Kirsty very gently. 'What's the matter?'

'I remember my brother when he was a baby,' she replied sadly. 'He looked a bit like Joy. I miss him so much and I don't even know if he's alive. I do wish too that I knew where Yara is. She promised to come back and I was sure she would. Perhaps something dreadful happened to her on the way home,' she added fearfully.

At that precise moment something truly remarkable happened, for glancing up, Aidan noticed three figures stumbling towards them along the path from the hospital. As they drew nearer he could see that the group consisted of a tall, stooping man, a young woman and a boy of about nine or ten years old. All three walked like people who were tired to the point of utter exhaustion.

'Tis,' said Aidan sharply, 'look down the path. Do you know them?'

Tis turned her head and cried out,

'Papai, Davi, Yara!' At the sound of her voice the three began to run, but it was the little boy who outran them all. Arriving breathless and panting, he hurled himself onto Tis's lap and flung his arms round her neck.

'Tis, my Tis,' he cried, 'I've found you at last. I'm never, never going to leave you again!'

Aidan and Chinn stepped forward to meet Carlos and Yara.

'You must be Tis's father,' said Aidan holding out his hands in welcome. 'And you must be Yara. You made it then!' They turned to look at Tis who had her thin arms wrapped tightly round her brother as if she would never let him go. As they watched, she raised her head and a brilliant smile lit up her face. It was like watching the sun come out after days of cloud and rain; unexpected and radiant. Carlos gave a sigh of pleasure at the sight and collapsed exhausted onto the bench, but Yara remained standing, almost too weary to make the effort to sit. Aidan and Kirsty looked at each other.

'Darling,' said Kirsty, 'I think this is all a bit too much for Tis, and these three are obviously hungry and exhausted. Let Chinn take her back to her ward for an hour's rest, while I feed the three of them and then I'll bring them down to see her.'

It took a lot of persuasion to get Davi to agree, but eventually, after Tis had explained to him what was going to happen, he reluctantly released his hold on the wheelchair and consented to go to the house, while Chinn wheeled the patient back to the quietness of the ward.

Taking Davi by the hand, Kirsty led the way back up the path. Once she'd settled them in the sitting room with Aidan and the baby, she went quickly into the kitchen to expand the evening meal to feed three more mouths.

'I don't think I've ever seen people so hungry and tired before,' she thought as she bustled about laying places and willing the rice to cook extra quickly so that they could be fed as soon as possible. A few moments later Yara came into the kitchen.

'Where will you stay?' enquired the ever-practical Kirsty.

'I don't know,' replied Yara in broken English. 'Carlos must go home tomorrow to keep his job. Davi and I will go as well. We have no money to stay in Beleza,' she added sadly.

'You could all sleep on the porch if that would help,' suggested Kirsty. 'Then you'd be near Tis for the rest of your time.'

'That would be good,' said Yara gratefully and went to tell Carlos and Davi the news.

Early next day Kirsty made a big breakfast for her three guests, and then she, Aidan and Joy accompanied the others back to the ward. They made their way down the path, a sad little group facing the pain of a parting that might be forever.

Tis was awake and greeted them with a smile of welcome.

'Tis,' said Carlos, trying to keep the anguish out of his voice, 'we have to go now, or I shall lose my job. As soon as you're better I'll send you money to come home.'

'I understand Papai,' replied Tis miserably. 'I wish I was coming too. I miss Mamãe so much.' Suddenly Davi spoke in a loud, clear voice,

'I'm not coming. I'm staying here with Tis,' and marching to the metal rail which formed the head of the bed he grasped it with both hands. 'I'm not going to leave ever,' he announced fiercely, and burst into tears. Nobody moved. They all gazed at the determined, small boy clinging like a suffragette to the railing as if his life depended on it. Aidan and Kirsty didn't even need Davi's speech translated. It was obvious what he'd said.

'Why don't Yara and Davi stay with us for a while? We could probably get Yara a job at the hospital, and Davi could help me,' Kirsty said impulsively. She looked at her husband for confirmation, surprised by her own reaction.

'That's a good idea,' he replied smiling. Tis translated what Kirsty had said and the next instant the lad hurled himself across the room and hugged her ecstatically.

'Obrigado, obrigado!' he cried over and over again. Then returning to the head of the bed he stood up very straight, looked at his sister and announced firmly to them all. 'I'm here now Tis. I'll care for you and I won't let anything bad happen to you ever again.'

'Come with me now Davi, and you too Yara,' said

Kirsty smiling at his ferocity. 'We'll let Carlos say goodbye to Tis by himself.' Quietly they went out and father and daughter were left on their own together.

Gently Carlos bent over the emaciated body of his beloved child. He dared not trust himself to speak. One word, he knew would bring his searing misery to the surface in a torrent of weeping. He took Tis in his arms and gave her a long fierce hug then turned, quickly making for the door. There he stopped and looked back at her one last time. She lay there, large eyes fixed pleadingly on his face, a small scrap of rubbish washed up on the shore of a hostile world. Turning he stumbled down the path and through the hospital gates, his eyes blinded by tears. Outside on the road, people and traffic surged round him in a relentless cataract filling the air with noise and petrol fumes, but deep inside him his heart was breaking, for somehow he knew he'd never see his beloved daughter alive again.

Chapter 22

Kirsty and Sister Maria were sharing a cup of cafezinho together on the porch. Joy, cradled on the nun's lap, was waving her arms and gurgling as she gazed into Maria's face. The sister was whispering to her in Portuguese and the baby seemed to understand every word. At last Maria looked up and with a grave face remarked,

'I'm sorry Tis is so ill Kirsty. It must have been a hard blow for Aidan when she was officially diagnosed with Aids related pneumonia.'

'Yes it was,' agreed Kirsty sighing. 'Dr Romerez is doing all he can but she seems to be deteriorating despite their best efforts. She improved a bit at first but she's fading now I'm afraid.'

'Does Davi know?' the nun inquired.

'We've told him that there's a chance that she won't recover,' replied Kirsty sadly, but I don't think he wanted to believe us. He's a remarkable little boy,' she added. 'He's a real help to me with Joy and the house and I'm teaching him English too.' She smiled to herself thinking of the child's loyalty and determination. 'He's brilliant in the market too,' she added, 'sniffing out bargains and carrying my shopping for me.'

'Yara's also doing well in her cleaning job at the hospital,' remarked the Sister. 'She's good with the patients and cheerful. If she wants to stay, I'm sure she could.'

'That would be wonderful for her,' replied Kirsty sincerely. 'She could make a fresh start and put the horror of the past few years behind her couldn't she.'

'It's not as easy as that,' said Maria sadly. 'Now she's been sexually ill used for so long, even though she's escaped, it will live with her for the rest of her life and affect everything she tries to do. But,' she added smiling, 'Yara is strong both mentally and physically, so maybe she'll make something of herself. Lots of prostitutes are like Tis though,' she said gravely. 'I'm afraid we see many young women in the hospital who have been abused in exactly the same way and even if their bodies recover, their minds don't.' As she said these words the nun's normally serene face looked deeply troubled. Silence fell between them and Kirsty, distressed by what she had just heard, gazed out of the veranda at a nearby Magnolia. It had only just stopped raining and the shiny wet surface of each dark green leaf was glistening in the sunlight as if it had just been polished.

'So much beauty but so much pain,' she said to herself and the thought made her feel helpless and angry. 'Sister,' she said at last. 'How do you cope with the misery of life? You see so much of it and yet it doesn't seem to crush you like it does me. I'm only helping one girl but sometimes I lie in bed and think about all the others. Then I just want to run away and hide.'

'That's a question I get asked a lot,' replied Maria, smiling. 'Over the years I've come to realise that there are two things that keep me loving and energised. The first will encourage you to keep going. It's this: I concentrate on what I can do. Not, what I can't. The second concerns my personal faith, so won't help you much, but I'll share it anyway. You see I have a God who suffers with the helpless. He's not outside their pain just observing. He shares it and that makes all the difference to me.' She looked gravely at Kirsty and added. 'Each time I look at Tis, it's Him I see.'

Later on that morning, Kirsty, Joy and Tis were sitting under a tree looking at the view. The air was oppressively hot and Kirsty thought longingly of walks on the downs on April days, of the refreshing feel of a cold wet wind on her face, and the sight of wispy white clouds scudding across the sky. She turned and looked at Tis who was half asleep in her wheel chair beside the bench.

'How ill she looks,' thought Kirsty sadly. 'We've all tried so hard but she's failing fast.' Then thinking back to what Sister Maria had told her earlier, she gave herself a good mental shake. 'I'm doing what I can,' she said to herself, 'and even if Tis's body is dying her spirit is reviving with all our love and care. She seems to be coming alive again while we watch.'

Sensing Kirsty's gaze, Tis turned and looked at her.

'What are you thinking Senhora Kirsty?' she inquired. 'You look sad.'

'Tis,' replied Kirsty, 'is there anything you want to do that I could arrange for you?' There was a pause whilst Tis thought this over. At last she replied.

'Yes, there's one thing I long to do every day and that's to go back to the sea. I've only been once. That was when I met Senhor Aidan for the second time, and it was the most wonderful experience of my life. I want to go again so badly. It hurts me deep down inside every time I look at it from up here on this seat.' As she said this she gazed wistfully at Kirsty and clasped her hands tightly together.

'I'll see what I can do,' said Kirsty firmly. 'I'm sure we can work out a way of getting you to the beach. I'll talk to Aidan about it.'

'Obrigada Senhora Kirsty,' said Tis, her eyes shining. 'That would mean so much to me.'

'Aidan,' said Kirsty as she lay in her husband's arms that night, 'Tis would like to go to the sea. It's her dearest wish. She told me this morning. Do you think we could take her?' There was a pause as Aidan thought through this request. At last he said hesitatingly,

'I suppose so. It'll be a strain on her. But I don't think she has long left,' he added sadly 'so it would be good for her to do something she really wants.' Kirsty let out her breath in a sigh of relief, as she'd been afraid that the Doctor in Aidan would say it was too dangerous. A thought then occurred to her.

'Do you think we could take Davi and perhaps Chinn too? Yara will be working though.'

'I suppose so,' he replied. 'I don't expect it makes much difference how big the party is, and I'm sure it would do Davi good to go to the beach. Take his mind off Tis for a few hours. I'll borrow the hospital mini bus,' he added. 'Then we'll have room for all the gear Joy will need as well. Let's go the day after tomorrow shall we?'

The bus nosed its way out of the hospital gates two days later and Kirsty settled back in her seat to enjoy the journey. Tis sat beside her gazing out of the window, and Kirsty realised that, even though she was very ill, Tis was enjoying herself. Davi was talking excitedly to Chinn behind her and although the latter said nothing in reply the little boy didn't seem to notice and went on chattering away in Portuguese. Joy was also awake, sitting contentedly in her baby seat beside him.

'Perhaps,' she thought, wishing she could understand what he said, 'Davi is talking to the baby and not to Chinn at all.' As the bus threaded its way along the busy city streets Kirsty noticed that the pavements were thronged with young couples. Many of the girls were in their best clothes and looked so happy that the little party in the minibus began to feel that the whole city was sharing in the joy of their outing.

'Why is everybody dressed up?' Kirsty asked at last.

'Because,' replied Tis, 'it's 'O dia dos Namorados' meaning the day for young lovers and courting couples, when all the young men must give their girls a present if they love them. See, they've bought them flowers to put in their hair,' she said pointing to a group of young men and women laughing and joking on the pavement. Kirsty could see indeed that the men were in their best clothes, and that all the girls had many coloured blossoms in their dark hair, which made them look like an excited flock of exotic tropical birds. Soon however, the city was left behind and the bus began to wind its way along a quiet road, which ran beside the edge of the estuary.

The journey was not a long one as the confluence of river and sea was not too far from the city.

When they arrived at the quiet beach, which Doctor Romerez had suggested to Aidan, they could see that the white sands were deserted save for a few brightly coloured fishing boats drawn up above the high water mark.

'Why don't we go and sit on the shady side of that blue boat?' suggested Aidan pointing. 'We can't stay in the full sun, that's for sure.' So he and Chinn carried Tis's wheelchair between them and put it beside the boat, then Chinn fetched Tis and carefully arranged her chair so that the vessel's peeling sides shaded her from the sun. All the others sat on blankets on the sand, with baby Joy asleep close to Kirsty. The air was fresh and invigorating after the heat of the city, and the sea was so calm that it appeared almost motionless. Only the tiny wavelets gently breaking on the shore reminded them that a few miles beyond the headland at the bay's entrance, the real ocean began. Overhead the seagulls wheeled and called as they swept to and fro across an azure sky.

Presently Joy woke up and Aidan carried her down to the water's edge to dabble her feet. The baby was immediately captivated with both water and sand and laughed and gurgled in delight. He then brought her back up the beach to Kirsty who dried her legs and fed her. Instead of sitting back down on the blanket however, Aidan turned to Davi saying,

'Come on Davi, let's make a sand castle.' Davi looked at him questioningly, not knowing what Aidan wanted him to do. 'Come on,' urged Aidan again. 'It's what we mad English do whenever we get on a beach,' and he proceeded to dig with his hands, moulding the sand into the beginnings of a central keep. Curiosity got the better of Davi at last, and Kirsty and Tis watched with interest as an impressive sand castle took shape in front of them. Chinn however, took no part in this activity but sat quietly by the wheel chair watching impassively.

'I wonder what he's thinking?' Kirsty asked herself.

As soon as they had finished eating their midday meal Kirsty began to repack the picnic bag.

'I think we ought to be getting you and Tis back soon,' she said to Joy. 'It's so hot,' and shading her eyes she looked across the sand to the nearby headland where a dead tree had begun to shimmer in the heat. Before she had time to speak to Aidan however, she saw Tis bend her head and murmur something to Chinn. He immediately got up and went over to where Aidan and Davi were putting some finishing touches to the sandcastle with small shells Davi had found at the water's edge. Chinn bent down and spoke to Aidan but it was obvious that he didn't understand. Then both Davi and Chinn pointed out to the sea and back at Tis. Eventually Aidan got to his feet and came over to Kirsty with a troubled look on his face.

'Kirsty,' he said quietly so that Tis couldn't overhear, 'Tis has asked if she can go into the water. Do you think that's safe? I'm not sure it's a good idea in her weak state.' Kirsty knew that he was right and that it would be a foolish thing to do, but she also realised that this might be Tis's last chance to go into the sea so she looked at Aidan, and whispered sadly,

'I don't much think it matters too much now does it?' Aidan looked at her gravely nodding his head.

'You may go,' he said turning to Tis whose face immediately lit up with a radiant smile.

'Obrigada Doutor Aidan,' she said simply.

Without more ado, Chinn picked Tis up in his arms and carried her down the beach. Slowly he began to wade out into the shallow water of the bay. On and on they went until it seemed to the watchers on the shore that they were never going to stop. At last, when the sea was nearly up to his waist, he halted.

'Put me in the water please,' said Tis, and Chinn lowered her gently into the sea so that it covered her small body. She then laid her head back and her long dark hair flowed all around her like strands of living seaweed, gently rising and falling with the pulsing rhythm of the ocean. Closing her eyes in ecstasy, she abandoned herself to its tender embrace, sensing that the water was somehow washing away the abuse of the years with its gentle caresses. She floated like this for a long time and Kirsty, straining her eyes to watch from the shore, felt that she was seeing a Greek myth come alive and that Tis, like a Botticelli Venus, would rise up out of the water, radiantly beautiful, innocent and whole again.

At last Chinn bent down, and whispered softly,

'Tis, I think I'd better take you back now.' Tis opened her eyes and looked at him almost as if she were seeing him for the first time.

'I love you Chinn,' she said simply. 'I feel clean

again now. Thank you for looking after me.' Chinn
smiled down at her, then tenderly lifted her out of the
water and waded slowly shoreward. All around them the
sea swirled and sparkled and up above the sun shone in
fierce strength but neither noticed as they were wrapped
up in a timeless moment of deep intimacy.

All was quiet in the bus as it made its way back to
the hospital. Tis, Joy and Davi slept the whole way home,
and Kirsty spent the journey pondering on what had
happened in the water. Just where Tis had been, when her
body had been floating on the sea, she didn't know.

'She looked so serene when Chinn laid her on the
blanket,' she mused. 'I've never seen a face look so
peaceful before. What happened out there in the bay I
wonder?'

By the time the minibus turned into the hospital
gates all the party were awake again. Aidan parked as near
to Tis's small room as he could, and Chinn carried her the
rest of the way in his arms. As they got nearer he bent his
head and whispered to her,

'Yara and I have a surprise for you Tis.' Two
more steps and they were at the door, and there were Yara
and Sister Maria, both smiling broadly. Chinn carried her
inside, and what a sight met their eyes! Every conceivable
space in the tiny room had been filled with flowers. There
were flowers on the floor, on the window-sill, and on the
locker. Flowers had been wreathed round the metal bars
of the bedstead and yet more laid on the coverlet. Yara
had even placed four long stemmed red roses on the
pillow. The room indeed was ablaze with a kaleidoscope
of colour and a beautiful aroma wreathed itself around the

four of them like the smell of rare incense.

'Its 'O dia dos Namorados' remember?' said Yara with a catch in her voice, 'and Chinn and I want you to know that we love you. Now you just have to get better.' Tis said nothing, but her face shone with happiness as Chinn laid her gently on the bed.

But it was not to be, for that night Tis lost her battle with Aids. And so it was that by the time the morning sunlight crept through the tiny window, one small withered Little Flower lay dead in a bower of beautiful blossom.

Chapter 23

Aidan was at home sitting at his desk. He'd turned the smallest bedroom in the house into a temporary office and was busily trying to compose a report for Dr Romerez. However, he was finding it almost impossible to focus on hospital matters for his mind kept returning to the events of the last forty-eight hours. He'd tried hard not to dwell on them but they were forever fixed in his brain and kept tumbling round and round inside his head tormenting him. Eventually he gave up trying to work and sat back in his chair, letting his mind wander at will over the grim memories.

Immediately he recalled the dreadful moment when he'd gone into Tis's room early on the morning after their outing and found her dead among the flowers. In that instant he'd experienced a sense of failure so intense that he'd thought his spirit would break under the weight. Clasping his hand to his forehead he tried to dislodge, not only that memory, but also the sound of Kirsty's gratingly cheerful voice saying to him as she too gazed at Tis,

'But darling, during her stay in hospital her life was happier than it had ever been before.' He recalled with shame that he'd snapped back at her,

'Not much comfort in that when she's dead is there! Why couldn't we save this one patient above all others?' he thought despairingly. 'God knows Dr Romerez tried. We all did our best but we failed.'

His next memory was of Sister Maria coming into the small hospital room and saying matter-of-factly,

'Our funeral customs here are different to yours. Here the body has to be buried within twenty-four hours. Can you, Chinn and Yara find enough money for a cheap funeral, do you think? Why not ask them. Then come and see me and I'll explain what else you have to do.' The next problem had been presented to him when he'd gone to her office to say that the funeral could go ahead. He could see her now in his memory, sitting behind her large desk; so small, so old, but so alive.

'It's the custom in this country,' she'd announced after he'd sat down, 'to have the body lying in its coffin in the home so that relatives can come to pay their last respects. However,' she went on, 'since Tis has no home here, Mother Superior has given permission for her to rest in our small oratory in the grounds. It's also our custom,' she explained, 'not to leave the body alone, and since Davi is the only available relative and is so young, we must take it in turns to keep vigil with Tis. I'll help, and so will some of the other sisters.' She'd then taken from a drawer in the desk a plain white dress and given it to Aidan. 'This is a postulant's habit,' she informed him getting up. 'I'm afraid it's the best we can do to provide Tis with a suitable shroud.'

And so it was that Kirsty and Sister Maria laid Tis out, dressed in a borrowed nun's habit. Kirsty had taken one of the red roses, which Yara had placed on the pillow to welcome Tis home the previous night, and put it on her breast in an attempt to relieve the severe whiteness of the dress. The bitter irony of the habit was not lost on Aidan, who had thought how tragic it was that one, who had been so sexually abused, should be dressed in the clothes of a celibate in death. She was then put in the cheapest coffin available which was all they could afford. Aidan vividly recalled how he'd gazed down at the slight body dressed in white, so pale and still.

There she lay in her shroud, in the same position on her back as he'd seen her first in the brothel. Then she'd been helpless in the face of his male strength, now death had brutally prostrated her for the last time and she would never experience what true love and happiness were. At that moment he'd been completely overwhelmed by black despair.

His next painful memory was of Davi, who was allowed into the side ward once the coffin had been removed, in order to collect the flowers. He would never forget how the small boy had stumbled round the room with tears streaming down his face as he tried to gather them into bunches. Aidan had helped him and together they'd walked slowly across the Convent grounds to the oratory. This turned out to be a simple building, consisting of a single room illuminated by a coloured window at one end. The open coffin had been placed in front of this and the light coming in through the glass had softened the white of Tis's shroud to a gentle pink. The only other objects in the room were two benches, one prayer desk, and to the left of the window, a statue of the Virgin Mary. Sister Maria had been kneeling at the prayer desk when they arrived, but she'd stood up immediately, taken the flowers and arranged them on the floor round the coffin. Although most of them had begun to wilt they were still beautiful and Aidan had thought they looked like coloured rushes, strewn on the flagstones of a medieval castle.

Later that evening, after work, he'd fetched Davi and Yara from the oratory leaving Chinn to keep vigil, and had taken them back to the house for a meal. Then the three of them had walked quietly across the dark gardens to resume their watch. When they entered they'd discovered Sister Maria and two other nuns sitting in perfect stillness on the benches, their faces dimly lit by the light of several candles now burning round the coffin. One had also been lit in front of the statue, illuminating the serene face of the Virgin Mary who seemed to be looking down at Tis with sadness and compassion. Soon after their arrival the two sisters had left leaving the five of them alone together. There they'd sat in silence, as the leaden hours had slowly crept past, for there had seemed nothing they could say to each other that would ease their grief. When midnight came Aidan had felt he ought to take Davi back home to get some sleep. The small boy had refused to come however, saying something to him in Portuguese that Aidan hadn't understood. He'd looked enquiringly at Sister Maria who explained,

'He says that tomorrow he's going to lose Tis forever, so he must stay with her until the end.'

In the early hours of the morning Aidan had finally decided to go back home. At the doorway to the oratory he'd turned and taken one last look at the coffin and the four watchers on the bench. There in the dim flickering light was Sister Maria, an invincible rock, with Yara and Davi either side of her, their heads resting on her shoulders. Chinn, head bowed, was sitting a little way apart from the other three. It was a poignant tableau he would never forget. Quietly he'd crept away back to Kirsty and Joy.

The next day had been even worse for, when their small party had reached the burial ground, Aidan had been appalled at the sight that had met his eyes. He'd expected the cemetery to be something like the graveyards in England, but this one was merely a huge excavation in the ground, about the size of a swimming pool. Coffins were being stacked into it; close together like containers on a ship. Sister Maria, on seeing his horrified expression, had explained that the hole would be covered in once it was full and this was all the poor could afford. When he'd recovered a little from the initial shock, he'd looked at Davi and had seen that the scene profoundly affected him too. He vividly recalled the small boy's eyes growing round with horror as his sister's coffin was placed among the others. At that point he'd put his arm round him and they'd both stood, forcing their eyes to watch, until her coffin finally disappeared from view buried, not in soil, but by the dead themselves in their wooden shrouds.

'What an ignominious and subhuman way to be remembered,' he thought bitterly. 'Is this really going to be my last memory of Tis?'

The harsh screech of a macaw outside the window broke his reverie and he glanced up at the filing cabinet next to his desk. On top of this was the shell that had been Tis's dearest possession. Aidan wasn't yet sure who should have it, but the very fact that it was there seemed to give him a palpable connexion with her and to ease the ache in his heart.

'What is she now?' he murmured sadly to the shell, 'but just a decomposing body in a coffin! And she didn't even have any children - at least that would have been a kind of immortality. It seems ironic,' he mused thoughtfully, 'that she was raped and abused so many times and yet not one child was conceived.' He thought again of his last view of Tis before the coffin lid had been fitted. 'She looked so very small and shrunken,' he murmured still half addressing the shell. 'You didn't see her then. Mind you, even when she was alive and healthy her body was so slender it only filled a small space didn't it? And when she crumbles into dust she'll take up an even smaller space won't she? Eventually of course, she'll become part of the carbon cycle in the world,' he reflected, remembering with a shiver that all living things are made from recycled stars. 'Then at that point she'll enter into the stream of life again I suppose, but as what I wonder?' Inexplicably he began to find a little bit of comfort in the fact that the raw materials of Tis's body would be reused to make other new life. Toying with the idea in his head he eventually gave up trying to compose his report altogether and instead, took a clean sheet of paper and began marshalling his thoughts into a poem.

After a while he sat back in his chair looking at the words he'd written. It was only a short poem but it had taken some time to write and the paper was covered with crossings out. Quietly he read began to read.

The space that's full of me
Sits here beside the desk.
When I move on,
The space fills up
And I take up a space next door.

Deborah Varen

In death, my space will gently fade
Into a small heap of dusty particles.

Then one day,
Earth's revolutions hence,
I may become your space.

The question hangs,
'How many spaces am I?'

'Well that didn't cheer me up much,' he said to himself when he'd finished. 'The thought of her becoming a tree, or even another person, isn't very consoling, it's too remote. And philosophising aside, I still have the problem of what to do with this shell and it's bothering me!' It suddenly occurred to him that perhaps Sister Maria could help him decide how to dispose of it. 'Maybe she'll think that Davi should have it, or perhaps Tis' mum,' he thought. 'Whoever I give it to the others are going to be upset. I wonder if she's in her office? When I've finished this report I'll go and see.' He sighed, and turned once more to his work.

Later that morning Aidan made his way to Sister Maria's small office in the hospital. The nun was working at her desk, an unaccustomed frown on her face as she added up a column of figures with a calculator. She looked up at him enquiringly as he entered.

'Sister,' he said as he stood in front of the desk, 'I was wondering what we ought to do with this? It was Tis's most treasured possession,' and he held the shell out to her. Sister Maria took it and turned it over and over in her hands looking thoughtful.

'I wonder,' she mused, 'who should have it? You know you have as much right to it as anyone Aidan. You and Tis go back a long way together.'

'No, Sister. I don't feel I ought to keep it, but whether it should go to Davi, her mother or Yara, I can't decide. What's the right answer?' Sister Maria bowed her head a moment. 'I do believe she's praying!' thought Aidan amazed. 'She can't really be expecting God to tell her what to do with a shell!' A few seconds later, the wise old eyes opened again and regarded him thoughtfully.

'You know Aidan,' she said slowly, 'I don't believe anybody should have it. I'm sure we should give something to Tis's mother, but I think we should send her one of the handkerchiefs. Davi must have the other one. With regard to the shell I know that you and Davi, and I'm sure Yara too, although she didn't say much, found Tis's burial very upsetting. If you would like to do something beautiful to remember her by why don't you take the shell to the sea, go out in a fishing boat and drop it in the water. This would be a fitting way to mark her death don't you think, and it's something you could all do together?'

'That's a wonderful idea Sister,' Aidan replied enthusiastically. 'We'll go to the same bay we visited the day before she died. Thank you so much. I agree that Tis's mother ought to have a handkerchief,' he added. 'She must have seen one by her bed many times and know the story of the trip to the seaside mustn't she.'

At lunch-time, Aidan returned to the house, and went into the kitchen for a quick snack before going back to the hospital for the afternoon. There he found Kirsty and Yara busily preparing vegetables for the evening meal. Davi was sitting on a chair holding the baby who lay asleep in his arms. Aidan hesitated for a moment on the doorstep knowing that once he showed them the shell this veneer of tranquillity would be wrenched aside and their desolate grief would take possession of them again. They looked up as he came in and Kirsty said enquiringly,

'What's that darling?'

'It's Tis' shell,' he replied, holding it out.

'Oh,' said Kirsty. Nobody spoke and the four of them remained in photographic stillness gazing at the shell. At last Kirsty got up, gently took it from him and laid it on the table. There it sat, silent and beautiful. They all stared at it again until Davi said at last,

'Who's going to have it Senhor?' The question hung in the air.

'I asked Sister Maria that this morning,' replied Aidan, 'and she made a good suggestion.' He explained what it was.

'I like that,' said Davi simply. 'Tis loved that shell and she loved the sea. The two must be together again.'

'I think that's a good idea too,' said Yara. 'I can't forget all those coffins. It was horrible, horrible,' and she covered her face with her hands and groaned.

'Why don't I go with Yara to the market this

afternoon and get a beautiful box to put it in?' said Kirsty. 'Would that help Yara?'

'Yes,' replied Yara in a voice heavy with grief, 'yes it would. Tis would like us to do that.'

The market, when they arrived later that afternoon, was as vibrant as ever. Merchants stood behind their stalls shouting their wares, their vegetables and fruit tumbling over the tables in a kaleidoscope of colours. Wherever she looked there were people moving about like an ever-flowing river, and everywhere boys and girls were running around looking busy, as only children and dogs can look when they're not actually doing anything. Kirsty usually felt overwhelmed by all this noise and exuberance but that afternoon she was glad of all the frantic activity, for somehow its very intensity assured her that death had been put temporarily on hold.

They began to walk round the stalls looking for the right box but the task they had set themselves began to look increasingly difficult, for although there were several different boxes for sale, none were really suitable; they were either too large or too small, and many were very expensive. At last however, they came to a small stall which seemed to be selling vases and storage jars, and there at the back of the table Kirsty spotted a white china jar that had a mouth wide enough to accommodate the shell. It also had a pretty gilded stopper made of wood and cork.

'Look Yara, look at that jar at the back of the stall. That would do wouldn't it?' enquired Kirsty hopefully. Yara looked at it doubtfully.

'It's very plain,' she said sadly.

'Don't worry about that,' replied Kirsty. 'We can easily decorate it with flowers from the garden, and it'll look lovely then.'

'Yes, I suppose so,' conceded Yara brightening. 'You're right. We could make it look beautiful.' And so they bought it and took it back to the house.

When they got home Kirsty carefully removed the golden lid, lined the bottom with a blue silk scarf, and gently put the shell inside, finally replacing the golden stopper. She then cut a long strand of pink bougainvillea from the garden and deftly fixed it around the outside. It twined round the jar, its pink flowers and green leaves standing out against the white porcelain.

'That looks very attractive,' said Kirsty with satisfaction when she'd finished. 'Are you pleased Yara?'

'Yes,' said Yara simply, 'I am.'

That evening Kirsty and Joy went to the hospital gates to wave goodbye as Tis's shell started on its journey back to the sea. At the last moment she stepped up to the open car window and handed the baby to Aidan.

'Hold Joy for a minute will you darling,' she requested. 'I need to fetch something for you.' In a few minutes she was back again with another spray of bougainvillea. 'This is just in case the frond on the jar gets damaged on the journey,' she said smiling, laying it on the back seat beside Davi, who sat cradling the flower covered receptacle in his arms as if it were Tis herself. Then taking the baby back from Aidan she watched until the car turned out into the main road and joined the dense stream of passing traffic.

After picking Chinn up from his shop, Aidan drove along the same route they'd taken on the day of Tis's last trip to the beach. Nobody said much on the journey as each of them were busy with their own sad thoughts. Aidan found himself thinking of Chinn and Davi as he drove along.

'All of us had a very special relationship with Tis,' he said to himself amazed that he hadn't realised this before. 'She saved Davi's life, and probably mine too because, had she not been a virgin, I might have caught Aids as well.' The thought then crossed his mind that it was a wonder Rhys hadn't yet been infected. 'Give it time,' he thought grimly, 'and that old goat will surely get what's coming to him. Then there's Chinn too,' he mused. 'Tis gave him safety and friendship. She gave the three of us so much,' he thought sadly. 'Her life for ours, but what did she get in return? Nothing!'

When they got to the bay, Aidan parked the car near the beach. Chinn found a fisherman who was prepared to hire them his boat and row for them. The four splashed through the warm shallows and climbed aboard. Chinn and Aidan sat in the stern and Yara and Davi, who was carrying the jar, in the prow. When they were settled the fisherman took his place on the central thwart and began to row slowly out into the bay. It was evening time and the sun was beginning to set in the west. A shining golden path stretched ahead of them and all was still and quiet. The only noise came from the rhythmic splash, splash of the oars as they moved up and down shedding droplets of shining water, which fell in glistening showers back onto the surface of the sea.

'This reminds me of when I met Tis on the beach so many years ago,' mused Aidan as the boat glided along. He recalled again the sight of her standing at the water's edge silhouetted against the sunset, hands upraised.

Time drifted dreamily by as the fisherman rowed slowly on, but at last Aidan said quietly, 'I think this is far enough. Put the jar in Davi.' The fisherman shipped his oars and Davi, lifting the jar from his knees, leaned over the side and placed it gently in the water. Just at that moment, the tide in the estuary was at that magic point of stillness, neither coming in nor yet going out, and the jar bobbed gently up and down beside the boat, hardly moving. Soon however, it began to turn and drift slowly towards the mouth of the bay. Suddenly Aidan noticed with astonishment that he could see small pink flowers moving serenely after it, like a bride's retinue, and he realised that Davi had taken the spare frond of bougainvillea which Kirsty had given him, and was putting the flowers into the water one by one. All four of them watched mesmerised as the jar floated slowly just ahead of the blossoms, its golden stopper sparkling and glinting in the rays of the setting sun.

'It looks,' thought Aidan wistfully, 'like a tiny golden coracle sailing back to its home.'

The moment was so perfect that he longed for it to go on forever, but at last the time came for the fisherman to dip his oars into the water once more, turn the boat, and begin rowing back to shore. Aidan, who was now facing away from the bay's mouth, turned in his seat to watch the burnished stopper as long as his aching eyes could see it, until at last it seemed to him that the golden jar had become one with the setting sun.

Back on land, none of them felt that they wanted to return to the city, so they made their way round to one of the bay's headlands. There they sat down and Aidan put his arm around Davi holding him close. He could feel the child's small body trembling and sensed that he was struggling with intense grief. As they sat watching, the sun finally set behind the far hills, the moon rose and stars gleamed in the pale, translucent sky. Ships made their unhurried way out of the estuary on the tide and all was peace and beauty. It seemed to Aidan, that in such a perfect place it would be possible to grasp the very edge of eternity.

'Is Tis's soul somewhere out there?' he wondered. He knew that Father James' God had a reputation for mercy, but would that mercy embrace one who'd been so insignificant? 'I don't believe in souls anyway,' he said mentally shaking himself. 'No! I must get back to the sweat of daily life; the patients dying of Aids, the young girls sold into slavery, and do something about them. That's a battle I shall enjoy fighting and I'll do it for you Tis. I'll do it for you.' Suddenly he felt his heart lighten as if some cosmic power had approved of his resolve to be the 'joke in the machine.'

Still they sat, and as night descended, a solitary white dove came and perched in the branches of the dead tree on the headland, and sang and sang as if its heart would break.

Back in the village, Ana was threading clear glass beads.

They made a tiny clicking noise as each dropped into its appointed place on the string, where they glowed in the light of the setting sun, like teardrops caught on gossamer. Beside her on the table lay a carefully folded handkerchief monogrammed with the initials 'A.V' and two intertwining fish. The wind was rising, and under Tis's old bed a dead ant lay buried under a pile of dust.

Epilogue

Several years ago, I attended a lecture given by an organisation called ECPAT which campaigns on behalf of children trafficked into prostitution. Up to that point I had been unaware that this was a problem. I came away that day blazingly angry that such things should happen to 27 million women, girls and boys worldwide. But what could I do since if I had met any traffickers or exploiters in person or sat next to them on bus or train, would I recognise them as such? So I sat down and began to write this story in the hopes that you will join me in my rage. It may be too that someone will read this book who has real influence in this world and can get something positive done on an international level. Meanwhile if you would like to do something to help, please get in touch with one of the following organisations.

All the proceeds from this book are going to the organisations listed on the next page. If you do get in touch with one of these agencies to offer your help or to give, please mention that you have read this book.

PLEASE RECOMMEND THIS BOOK TO ALL YOUR FRIENDS.

Thank you.

Deborah Varen

debvaren.blogspot.co.uk

ECPAT UK

(End Child Pornography and Trafficking) is active in the United Kingdom in research, campaigning and lobbying government to prevent child exploitation and to protect children in tourism and child victims of trafficking.

www.ecpat.org.uk

Meninadança

An international charity committed to fighting child prostitution along the remote highways in Brazil. They also provide a place of safety where rescued girls can go and be rehabilitated.

www.meninadanca.org

the A21 Campaign

A global NGO that fights to abolish injustice in the 21st Century. A21 focus is on those affected by human trafficking, with prevention and protection schemes throughout Europe, Australia and the United States.

www.thea21campaign.org

Stop The Traffik

A global movement of individuals, communities and organizations fighting to prevent human trafficking around the world.

www.stopthetraffik.org

Printed in Great Britain
by Amazon.co.uk, Ltd.,
Marston Gate.